The Path of A Star

MRS. EVERARD COTES
(SARA JEANNETTE DUNCAN)

1st WORLD
LIBRARY
Literary Society

The Path of A Star

Mrs. Everard Cotes

© 1st World Library – Literary Society, 2004
PO Box 2211
Fairfield, IA 52556
www.1stworldlibrary.org
First Edition

LCCN: 2004091184

Softcover ISBN: 1-59540-630-1
eBook ISBN: 1-59540-730-8

Purchase *"The Path of A Star"*
as a traditional bound book at:
www.1stWorldLibrary.org/purchase.asp?ISBN=1-59540-630-1

1st World Library Literary Society is a nonprofit
organization dedicated to promoting literacy by:

- Creating a free internet library accessible from any computer worldwide.
- Hosting writing competitions and offering book publishing scholarships.

Readers interested in supporting literacy
through sponsorship, donations or
membership please contact:
literacy@1stworldlibrary.org
Check us out at: www.1stworldlibrary.org

The Path of A Star
contributed by the Mahaney Family
in support of
1st World Library Literary Society

CHAPTER I

She pushed the portiere aside with a curved hand and gracefully separated fingers; it was a staccato movement and her body followed it after an instant's poise of hesitation, head thrust a little forward, eyes inquiring and a tentative smile, although she knew precisely who was there. You would have been aware at once that she was an actress. She entered the room with a little stride and then crossed it quickly, the train of her morning gown - it cried out of luxury with the cheapest voice - taking folds of great audacity as she bent her face in its loose mass of hair over Laura Filbert, sitting on the edge of a bamboo sofa, and said -

"You poor thing! Oh, you POOR thing!"

She took Laura's hand as she spoke, and tried to keep it; but the hand was neutral, and she let it go. "It is a hand," she said to herself, in one of those quick reflections that so often visited her ready-made, "that turns the merely inquiring mind away. Nothing but feeling could hold it."

Miss Filbert made the conventional effort to rise, but it came to nothing, or to a mere embarrassed accent of their greeting. Then her voice showed this feeling to be superficial, made nothing of it, pushed it to one side.

"I suppose you cannot see the foolishness of your pity," she said. "Oh Miss Howe, I am happier than you are - much happier." Her bare feet, as she spoke, nestled into the coarse Mirzapore rug on the floor, and her eye lingered approvingly upon an Owari vase three feet high, and thick with the gilded landscape of Japan, which stood near it, in the cheap magnificence of the room.

Hilda smiled. Her smile acquiesced in the world she had found, acquiesced, with the gladness of an explorer, in Laura Filbert as a feature of it.

"Don't be too sure," she cried; "I am very happy. It is such a pleasure to see you."

Her gaze embraced Miss Filbert as a person, and Miss Filbert as a pictorial fact, but that was because she could not help it. Her eyes were really engaged only with the latter Miss Filbert.

"Much happier than you are," Laura repeated, slowly moving her head from side to side as if to negative contradiction in advance. She smiled too; it was as if she had remembered a former habit, from politeness.

"Of course you are - of course!" Miss Howe acknowledged. The words were mellow and vibrant; her voice seemed to dwell upon them with a kind of rich affection. Her face covered itself with serious sweetness. "I can imagine the beatitudes you feel - by your clothes."

The girl drew her feet under her, and her hand went up to the only semi-conventional item of her attire. It was a brooch that exclaimed in silver letters "Glory to His

Name!" "It is the dress of the Army in this country," she said; "I would not change it for the wardrobe of a queen."

"That's just what I mean." Miss Howe leaned back in her chair with her head among its cushions, and sent her words fluently across the room, straight and level with the glance from between her half-closed eyelids. A fine sensuous appreciation of the indolence it was possible to enjoy in the East clung about her. "To live on a plane that lifts you up like that - so that you can defy all criticism and all convention, and go about the streets like a mark of exclamation at the selfishness of the world - there must be something very consummate in it or you couldn't go on. At least I couldn't."

"I suppose I do look odd to you." Her voice took a curious, soft, uplifted note. "I wear three garments only - the garments of my sisters who plant the young shoots in the rice-fields, and carry bricks for the building of rich men's houses, and gather the dung of the roadways to burn for fuel. If the Army is to conquer India it must march bare-footed and bare-headed all the way. All the way," Laura repeated, with a tremor of musical sadness. Her eyes were fixed in appeal upon the other woman's. "And if the sun beats down upon my uncovered head, I think, 'It struck more fiercely upon Calvary'; and if the way is sharp to my unshod feet, I say, 'At least I have no cross to bear.'" The last words seemed almost a chant, and her voice glided from them into singing -

"The blessed Saviour died for me,
On the cross! On the cross!
He bore my sins at Calvary,
On the rugged cross!"

She sang softly, her body thrust a little forward in a tender swaying -

"Behold His hands and feet and side,
The crown of thorns, the crimson tide,
'Forgive them, Father!' loud He cried,
On the rugged cross!"

"Oh, thank you!" Miss Howe exclaimed. Then she murmured again, "That's just what I mean."

A blankness came over the girl's face as a light cloud will cross the moon. She regarded Hilda from behind it, with penetrant anxiety. "Did you really enjoy that hymn?" she asked.

"Indeed I did."

"Then, dear Miss Howe, I think you cannot be very far from the Kingdom."

"I? Oh, I have my part in a kingdom." Her voice caressed the idea. "And the curious thing is that we are all aristocrats who belong to it. Not the vulgar kind, you understand - but no, you don't understand. You'll have to take my word for it." Miss Howe's eyes sought a red hibiscus flower that looked in at the window half drowned in sunlight, and the smile in them deepened.

"Is it the Kingdom of God and His righteousness?" Laura Filbert's clear glance was disturbed by a ray of curiosity, but the inflexible quality of her tone more than counterbalanced this.

"There's nothing about it in the Bible, if that's what you mean. And yet I think the men who wrote 'The time of the singing of birds has come,' and 'I will lift mine eyes unto the hills,' must have belonged to it." She paused, with an odd look of discomfiture. "But one shouldn't talk about things like that - it takes the bloom off. Don't you feel that way about your privileges now and then? Don't they look rather dusty and battered to you after a day's exposure in Bow Bazar?"

There came a light crunch of wheels on the red soorkee drive outside, and a switch past the bunch of sword-ferns that grew beside the door. The muffled crescendo of steps on the stair and the sound of an inquiry penetrated from beyond the portiere, and without further preliminary Duff Lindsay came into the room.

"Do I interrupt a rehearsal?" he asked; but there was nothing in the way he walked across the room to Hilda Howe to suggest that the idea abashed him. For her part she rose and made one short step to meet him, and then received him as it were with both hands and all her heart.

"How ridiculous you are!" she cried. "Of course not. And let me tell you it is very nice of you to come this very first day when one was dying to be welcomed. Miss Filbert came too, and we have been talking about our respective walks in life. Let me introduce you. Miss Filbert - Captain Filbert, of the Salvation Army - Mr. Duff Lindsay of Calcutta."

She watched with interest the gravity with which they bowed, and the difference in it: his the simple formality of his class, Laura's a repressed hostility to such an epitome of the world as he looked, although any Bond Street tailor would have impeached his waistcoat, and one shabby glove had manifestly never been on. Yet Miss Filbert's first words seemed to show a slight unbending. "Won't you sit there?" she said, indicating the sofa corner she had been occupying. "You get the glare from the window where you are." It was virtually a command, delivered with a complete air of dignity and authority; and Lindsay, in some confusion, found himself obeying. "Oh, thank you, thank you," he said. "One doesn't really mind in the least. Do you - do you object to it? Shall I close the shutters?"

"If you do," said Miss Howe delightedly, "we shall not be able to see."

"Neither we should," he assented; "the others are closed already. Very badly built these Calcutta houses, aren't they? Have you been long in India, Miss - Captain Filbert?"

"I served a year up-country, and then fell ill and had to go home on furlough. The native food didn't suit me. I am stationed in Calcutta now, but I have only just come."

"Pleasant time of the year to arrive," Mr. Lindsay remarked.

"Yes; but we are not particular about that. We love all the times and the seasons, since every one brings its appointed opportunity. Last year, in Mugridabad, there were more souls saved in June than in any other month."

"Really?" asked Mr. Lindsay; but he was not looking at her with those speculations. The light had come back upon her face.

"I will say good-bye now," said Captain Filbert. "I have a meeting at half-past five. Shall we have a word of prayer before I go?"

She plainly looked for immediate acquiescence; but Miss Howe said, "Another time, dear."

"Oh, why not?" exclaimed Duff Lindsay. Hilda put the semblance of a rebuke into her glance at him, and said, "Certainly not."

"Oh," Captain Filbert cried, "don't think you can escape that way! I will pray for you long and late to-night, and ask my lieutenant to do so too. Don't harden your heart, Miss Howe - the Lord is waiting to be compassionate."

The two were silent, and Laura walked toward the door. Just where the sun slanted into the room and made leaf-patterns on the floor she turned and stood for an instant in the full tide of it; and it set all the loose tendrils of her pale yellow hair in a little flame, and gave the folds of the flesh-coloured sari that fell over her shoulder the texture of draperies so often depicted as celestial. The sun sought into her face, revealing nothing but great purity of line and a clear pallor except where below the wide light blue eyes two ethereal shadows brushed themselves. Under the intentness of their gaze she made as if she would pass out without speaking; and the tender curves of her limbs, as she wavered, could not have been matched out of mediaeval stained glass. But her courage, or her conviction, came back to her at the door, and she raised her hand and pointed at Hilda.

"She's got a soul worth saving."

Then the portiere fell behind her, and nothing was said in the room until the pad of her bare feet had ceased upon the stair.

"She came out in the Bengal with us," Hilda told him - this is not a special instance of it, but she could always gratify Duff Lindsay in advance - "and she was desperately seedy, poor girl. I looked after her a little, but it was mistaken kindness, for now she's got me on her mind. And as the two hundred and eighty million benighted souls of India are her continual concern, I seem a superfluity. To think of being the two hundred and eighty millionth and first oppresses one."

Lindsay listened with a look of accustomed happiness.

"You weren't at that end of the ship?" he demanded.

"Of course I was - we all were. And some of us - little Miss Stace, for instance - thankful enough at the prospect of cold meat and sardines for tea every night for a whole month. And, after Suez, ices for dinner on Sundays. It was luxury."

Lindsay was pulling an aggrieved moustache. "I don't call it fair or friendly," he said, "when you know how easily it could have been arranged. Your own sense of the fitness of things should have told you that the second-class saloon was no place for you. For YOU!"

Plainly she did not intend to argue the point. She poised her chin in her hand and looked away over his head, and he could not help seeing, as he had seen before, that her eyes were beautiful. But this had been so long acknowledged between them that she could hardly have been conscious that she was insisting on it afresh. Then by the time he might have thought her launched upon a different meditation, her mind swept back to his protest, like a whimsical bird.

"I didn't want to extract anything from the mercantile community of Calcutta in advance," she said. "It would be most unbusinesslike. Stanhope has been equal to bringing us out; but I quite see myself, as leading lady, taking round the hat before the end of the season. Then I think," she said with defiance, "that I shall avoid you."

"And pray why?"

"Because you would put too much in. According to your last letters you are getting beastly rich. You would take all the tragedy out of the situation, and my experience would vanish in your cheque."

"I don't know why my feelings should always be cuffed out of the way of your experiences," Lindsay said. She retorted, "Oh yes, you do"; and they regarded each other through an instant's silence with visible good-fellowship.

"A reasonably strong company this time?" Lindsay asked.

"Thank you. 'Company' is gratifying. For a month we have been a 'troupe' - in the first-class end. Fairish. Bad to middling. Fifteen of us, and when we are not doing Hamlet and Ophelia we can please with light comedy, or the latest thing in rainbow chiffon done on mirrors with a thousand candlepower. Bradley and I will have to do most of the serious work. But I have improved - oh, a lot. You wouldn't know my Lady Whippleton."

It was a fervid announcement, but it carried an implication which appeared to prevent Lindsay's kindling.

"Then Bradley is here too?" he remarked.

"Oh yes," she said; and an instinct sheathed itself in her face. "But it is much better than it was, really. He is hardly ever troublesome now. He understands. And he teaches me a great deal more than I can tell you. You know," she asserted, with the effect of taking an independent view, "as an artist he has my unqualified respect."

"You have a fine disregard for the fact that artists are men when they are not women," Duff said. "I don't believe their behaviour is a bit more affected by their artistry than it would be by a knowledge of the higher mathematics."

She turned indignant eyes on him. "Fancy YOUR saying that! Fancy your having the impertinence to offer me so absurd a sophistry! At what Calcutta dinner-table did you pick it up?" she cried derisively. "Well, it shows that one can't trust one's best friend loose among the conventions!"

He had decided that it would be a trifle edged to say that such matters were not often discussed at Calcutta dinner-tables, when she added, with apparent inconsistency and real dejection, "It IS a hideous bore."

Lindsay saw his point admitted, and even in the way she brushed it aside he felt that she was generous. Yet something in him - perhaps the primitive hunting instinct, perhaps a more sophisticated Scotch impulse to explore the very roots of every matter, tempted him to say, "He gives up a good deal, doesn't he, for his present gratification?"

"He gives up everything! That is the disgusting part of it. Leander Morris offered him - But why should I tell you? It's humiliating enough in the very back of one's mind."

"He is a clever fellow, no doubt."

"Not too clever to act with me! Oh, we go beautifully - we melt, we run together. He has given me some essential things, and now I can give them back to him. I begin to think that is what keeps him now. It must be awfully satisfying to generate artistic life in - in anybody, and watch it grow."

"Doubtless," said Lindsay, with his eyes on the carpet; and her eyebrows twitched together, but she said nothing. Although she knew his very moderate power of analysis he seemed to look, with his eyes on the carpet, straight into the subject, to perceive it with a cynical clearness, and as Hilda watched him a little hardness came about her mouth. "Well," he said, visibly detaching himself from the matter, "it's a satisfaction to have you back. I have been doing nothing, literally, since you went away, but making money and playing tennis. Existence, as I look back upon it, is connoted by a varying margin of profit and a vast sward."

She looked at him with eyes in which sympathy stood remotely, considering the advisability of returning. "It's a pity you can't act," she said; "then you could come away and let it all go."

Lindsay smiled at her across the gulf he saw fixed. "How simple life is to you!" he said. "But anyway I couldn't act."

"Oh no, you couldn't, you couldn't! You are too intensely absorbent, you are too rigidly individual. The flame in you would never consent even for an instant to be the flame in anybody else - any of those people who, for the purpose of the state, are called imaginary. Never!"

It seemed a punishment, but all Lindsay said was: "I wish you would go on. You can't think how gratifying it is - after the tennis."

"If I went on I have an idea that I might be disagreeable."

"Oh then, stop. We can't quarrel yet - I've hardly seen you. Are you comfortable here? Would you like some French novels?"

"Yes, thank you. Yes, please!" She grew before him into a light and conventional person, apparently on her guard against freedom of speech. He moved a blind and ineffectual hand about to find the spring she had detached herself from, and after failing for a quarter of an hour he got up to go.

"I shan't bother you again before Saturday," he said; "I know what a week it will be at the theatre. Remember you are to give the man his orders about the brougham. I can get on perfectly with the cart. Good-bye! Calcutta is waiting for you."

"Calcutta is never impatient," said Miss Howe. "It is

waiting with yawns and much whisky and soda." She gave him a stately inclination with her hand, and he overcame the temptation to lay his own on his heart in a burlesque of it. At the door he remembered something, and turned. He stood looking back precisely where Laura Filbert had stood, but the sun was gone. "You might tell me more about your friend of the altruistic army," he said.

"You saw, you heard, you know."

"But - "

"Oh," cried she, disregardingly, "you can discover her for yourself, at the Army Headquarters in Bentinck Street - you man!"

Lindsay closed the door behind him without replying, and half-way down the stairs her voice appealed to him over the banisters.

"You might as well forget that. I didn't particularly mean it."

"I know you didn't," he returned. "You woman! But you yourself - you're not going to play with your heavenly visitant?"

Hilda leaned upon the banisters, her arms dropping over from the elbows. "I suppose I may look at her," she said; and her smile glowed down upon him.

"Do you think it really rewards attention? - the type, I mean."

"How you will talk of types! Didn't you see that she

was unique? You may come back if you like, for a quarter of an hour, and we will discuss her."

Lindsay looked at his watch. "I would come back for a quarter of an hour to discuss anything, or nothing," he replied, "but there isn't time. I am dining with the Archdeacon. I must go to church."

"Why not be original and dine with the Archdeacon without going to church? Why not say on arrival: 'My dear Archdeacon, your sermon and your mutton the same evening - c'est trop! I cannot so impose upon your generosity. I have come for the mutton!'"

Thus was Captain Laura Filbert superseded, as doubtless often before, by an orthodox consideration. Duff Lindsay drove away in his cart; and still, for an appreciable number of seconds, Miss Howe stood leaning over the banisters, her eyes fixed full of speculation on the place where he had stood. She was thinking of a scene - a dinner with an Archdeacon - and of the permanent satisfactions to be got from it; and she renounced almost with a palpable sigh the idea of the Archdeacon's asking her.

CHAPTER II

"Oh, her gift!" said Alicia Livingstone. "It is the lowest, isn't it - in the scale of human endowment? Mimicry."

Miss Livingstone handed her brother his tea as she spoke, but turned her eyes and her delicate chin up to Duff Lindsay with the protest. Lindsay's cup was at his lips, and his eyebrows went up over it as if they would answer before his voice was set at liberty.

"Mimicry isn't a fair word," he said. "The mimic doesn't interpret. He's a mere thief of expression. You can always see him behind his stolen mask. The actress takes a different rank. This one does, anyway."

"You're mixing her up with the apes and the monkeys," remarked Surgeon-Major Livingstone.

"Mere imitators!" cried Mrs. Barberry.

Alicia did not allow the argument to pursue her. She smiled upon their energy and, so to speak, disappeared. It was one of her little ways, and since it left seeming conquerors on her track nobody quarrelled with it.

"I've met them in London," she said. "Oh, I remember one hot little North Kensington flat full of them, and their cigarettes - and they were always disappointing. There seemed to be somehow no basis - nothing to go upon."

She looked from one to the other of her party with a graceful deprecating movement of her head, a head which people were unanimous in calling more than merely pretty and more than ordinarily refined. That was the cursory verdict, the superficial thing to see and say; it will do to go on with. From the way Lindsay looked at her as she spoke, he might have been suspected of other discoveries, possible only to the somewhat privileged in this blind world, where intimacy must lend a lens to find out anything at all.

"You found that they had no selves," he said, and the manner of his words was encouraging and provocative. His proposition was obscured to him for the instant by his desire to obtain the very last of her comment, and it might be seen that this was habitual with him. "But Miss Hilda Howe has one."

"Is she a lady?" asked Mrs. Barberry.

"I don't know. She's an individual. I prefer to rest my claim for her on that."

"Your claim to what?" trembled upon Miss Livingstone's lips, but she closed them instead, and turned her head again to listen to Mrs. Barberry. The turns of Alicia's head had a way of punctuating the conversations in which she was interested, imparting elegance and relief.

"I saw her in A Woman of Honour, last cold weather," Mrs. Barberry said; "I took a dinner-party of five girls and five subalterns from the Fort, and I said, 'Never again!' Fortunately the girls were just out, and not one of them understood, but those poor boys didn't know where to look! And no more did I. So disgustingly real."

Alicia's eyes veiled themselves to rest on a ring on her finger, and a little smile, which was inconsistent with the veiling, hovered about her lips.

"I was in England last year," she said; "I - I saw A Woman of Honour in London. What could possibly be done with it by an Australian scratch company in a Calcutta theatre! Imagination halts."

"Miss Howe did something with it," observed Mr. Lindsay. "That and one or two other things carried one through last cold weather. One supported even the gaieties of Christmas week with fortitude, conscious that there was something to fall back upon. I remember I went to the State ball, and cheerfully."

"That's saying a good deal, isn't it?" commented Dr. Livingstone, vaguely aware of an ironical intention. "By Jove! yes."

"Hamilton Bradley is good, too, isn't he?" Mrs. Barberry said. "Such a magnificent head. I adore him in Shakespeare."

"He knows the conventions, and uses them with security," Lindsay replied, looking at Alicia; and she, with a little courageous air, demanded -

"Is the story true?"

"The story of their relations? I suppose there are fifty. One of them is."

Mrs. Barberry frowned at Lindsay in a manner which was itself a reminiscence of amateur theatricals. "Their relations!" she murmured to Dr. Livingstone. "What awful things to talk about!"

"The story I mean," Alicia explained, "is to the effect that Mr. Bradley, who is married, but unimportantly, made a heavy bet, when he met this girl, that he would subdue her absolutely through her passion for her art - I mean, of course, her affections - "

"My dear girl, we know what you mean," cried Mrs. Barberry, entering a protest as it were, on behalf of the gentlemen.

"And precisely the reverse happened."

"One imagines it was something like that," Lindsay said.

"Oh, did she know about the bet?" cried Mrs. Barberry.

"That's as you like to believe. I fancy she knew about the man," Lindsay contributed again.

"Tables turned, eh? Daresay it served him right," remarked Dr. Livingstone. "If you really want to come to the laboratory, Mrs. Barberry, we ought to be off?"

"He is going to show me a bacillus," Mrs. Barberry announced with enthusiasm. "Plague, or cholera, or something really bad. He caught it two days ago, and put it in jelly for me - wasn't it dear of him! Good-bye, you nice thing" - Mrs. Barberry addressed Alicia - "Good-bye, Mr. Lindsay. Fancy - a live bacillus from Hong Kong! I should like it better if it came from fascinating Japan, but still - goodbye."

With the lady's departure an air of wontedness seemed to repossess the room, and the two people who were left. Things fell into their places, one could observe relative beauty, on the walls and on the floor, in Alicia's hair and in her skirt. Little meanings attached themselves - to oval portraits of ladies, evidently ancestral, whose muslin sleeves were tied with blue ribbon, to Byzantine-looking Persian paintings, to odd brass bowls and faint-coloured embroideries. The air became full of agreeable exhalations traceable to inanimate objects, or to a rose in a vase of common country glass; and if one turned to Alicia one could almost observe the process by which they were absorbed in her and given forth again with a delicacy more vague. Lindsay sometimes thought of the bee, and flowers and honey, but always abandoned the simile as a trifle gross and material. Certainly as she sat there in her grace and slenderness and pale clear tints - there was an effect of early morning about her that made the full tide of other women's sunlight vulgar - anyone would have been fastidious in the choice of a figure to present her in. With a suspicion of haughtiness she was drawn for the traditional marchioness; but she lifted her eyes and you saw that she appealed instead. There was an art in the doing of her hair, a dainty elaboration that spoke of the most approved conventions beneath, yet it was impossible to mistake the freedom of spirit that lay in the lines of her blouse. Even her gracefulness ran now and then into a downrightness of movement which suggested the assertion of a primitive sincerity in a personal world of many effects. Into her making of tea, for example, she put nothing more sophisticated than sugar, and she ordered more bread and butter in the worst possible rendering of her servants' tongue, without a thought except that the bread and butter should be brought. Lindsay liked to think that with him she was particularly simple and direct, that he was of those who freed her from the pretty consciousness, the elegant restraint that other people fixed upon her. It must be admitted that this conviction had reason in establishing itself, and it is perhaps not surprising that, in the security of it, he failed to notice occasions when it would not have held, of which this was plainly one. Alicia reflected, with her cheek against the Afghan wolf-skins on the back of the chair. It was characteristic of her eyes that one could usually see things being turned over in them. She would sometimes keep people waiting while she thought. She thought perceptibly about Hilda Howe, slanting her absent gaze between sheltering eyelids to the floor. Presently she rearranged the rose in its green glass vase, and said, "Then it's impossible not to be interested."

"I thought you would find it so."

Alicia was further occupied in bestowing small fragments of cress sandwich upon a terrier. "Fancy your being so sure," she said, "that you could present her entertainingly!" She looked past him toward the light that came in at the draped window, and he was not aware that her regard held him fast by the way.

"Anyone could," he said cheerfully. "She presents herself. One is only the humblest possible medium. And the most passive."

Alicia's eyes were still attracted by the light from the window. It silhouetted a rare fern from Assam which certainly rewarded them.

"I like to hear you talk about her. Tell me some more."

"Haven't I exhausted metaphor in describing her?"

"Yes," said Miss Livingstone, with conviction; "but I'm not a bit satisfied. A few simple facts sometimes - sometimes are better. Wasn't it a little difficult to make her acquaintance?"

"Not in the very least. I saw her in A Woman of Honour, and was charmed. Charmed in a new way. Next day I discovered her address - it's obscure - and sent up my card for permission to tell her so. I explained to her that one would have hesitated at home, but here one was protected by the custom. And she received me warmly. She gave me to understand that she was not overwhelmed with tribute of that kind from Calcutta. The truthful ring of it was pathetic, poor dear."

"That was in - "

"In February."

"In February we were at Nice," Alicia said, musingly. Then she took up her divining-rod again. "One can imagine that she was grateful. People of that kind - how snobbish I sound, but you know what I mean - are rather stranded in Calcutta, aren't they? They haven't any world here;" and, with the quick glance which deprecated her timid clevernesses, she added, "The arts conspire to be absent."

"Ah, don't misunderstand. If there was any gratitude it was all mine. But we met as kindred, if I may vaunt myself so much. A mere theory of life will go a long way, you know, toward establishing a claim of that sort. And, at all events, she is good enough to treat me as if she admitted it."

"What is her theory of life?" Alicia demanded quickly. "I should be glad of a new one."

Lindsay's communicativeness seemed to contract a little, as at the touch of a finger light, but cold.

"I don't think she has ever told me," he said. "No, I am sure she has not." His reflection was: "It is her garment - how could it fit another woman!"

"But you have divined it - she has let you do that! You can give me your impression."

He recognised her bright courage in venturing upon impalpabilities, but not without a shade of embarrassment.

"Perhaps. But having perceived, to pass on - it doesn't follow that one can. I don't seem able to lay my hand upon the signs and symbols."

The faintest look of disappointment, the lightest cloud of submission, appeared upon Miss Livingstone's face.

"Oh, I know!" she said. "You are making me feel dreadfully out of it, but I know. It surrounds her like a kind of atmosphere, an intellectual atmosphere. Though I confess that is the part I don't understand in connection with an actress."

There was a sudden indifference in this last sentence. Alicia lay back upon her wolf-skins like a long-stemmed flower cast down among them, and looked away from the subject at the teacups. Duff picked up his hat. He had the subtlest intimations with women.

"It's an intoxicating atmosphere," he said. "My continual wonder is that I'm not in love with her. A fellow in a novel, now, in my situation, would be embroiled with half his female relations by this time, and taking his third refusal with a haggard eye."

Alicia still contemplated the teacups, but with intentness. She lifted her head to look at them; one might have imagined a beauty suddenly revealed.

"Why aren't you?" she said. "I wonder, too."

"I should like it enormously," he laughed. "I've lain awake at nights trying to find out why it isn't so. Perhaps you'll be able to tell me. I think it must be because she's such a confoundedly good fellow."

Alicia turned her face toward him sweetly, and the soft grey fur made a shadow on the whiteness of her throat. Her buffeting was over; she was full of an impulse to stand again in the sun.

"Oh, you mustn't depend on me," she said. "But why are you going? Don't go. Stay and have another cup of tea."

CHAPTER III

The fact that Stephen Arnold and Duff Lindsay had spent the same terms at New College, and now found themselves again together in the social poverty of the Indian capital, would not necessarily explain their walking in company through the early dusk of a December evening in Bentinck Street. It seems desirable to supply a reason why anyone should be walking there, to begin with, anyone, at all events, not a Chinaman, or a coolie, a dealer in second-hand furniture, or an able-bodied seaman luxuriously fingering wages in both trouser pockets, and describing an erratic line of doubtful temper toward the nearest glass of country spirits. Or, to be quite comprehensive, a draggled person with a Bulgarian, a Levantine, or a Japanese smile, who no longer possessed a carriage, to whom the able-bodied seaman represented the whole port. The cramped twisting thoroughfare was full of people like this; they overflowed from the single narrow border of pavement to the left, and walked indifferently upon the road among the straw-scatterings and the dung-droppings; and when the tramcar swept through and past with prodigious whistlings and ringings, they swerved as little as possible aside. Three parts of the tide of them were neither white nor black, but many shades of brown, written down in the census as "of mixed Mood," and wearing still, through the degenerating centuries, an eyebrow, a nostril of the first Englishmen who came to conjugal ties of Hindustan. The place sent up to the stars a vast noise of argument and anger and laughter, of the rattling of hoofs and wheels; but the babel was ordered in its exaggeration, the red turban of a policeman here and there denoted little more than a unit in the crowd. There were gas-lamps, and they sent a ripple of light like a sword-thrust along the gutter beside the banquette, where a pariah dog nosed a dead rat and was silhouetted. They picked out, too, the occasional pair of Corinthian columns, built into the squalid stucco sheer with the road that made history for Bentinck Street, and explained that whatever might be the present colour of the little squat houses and the tall lean ones that loafed together into the fog round the first bend, they were once agreeably pink and yellow, with the magenta cornice, the blue capital, that fancy dictated. There where the way narrowed with an out-jutting balcony high up, and the fog thickened and the lights grew vague, the multitude of heads passed into the blur beyond with an effect of mystery, pictorial, remote; but where Arnold and Lindsay walked the squalor was warm, human, practical. A torch flamed this way and that, stuck in the wall over the head of a squatting bundle and his tray of three-cornered leaf-parcels of betel, and an oiled rag in a tin pot sent up an unsteady little flame, blue and yellow, beside a sweetmeat seller's basket, and showed his heap of cakes that they were well-browned and full of butter. From the "Cape of Good Cheer," where many bottles glistened in rows inside, came a braying upon the conch, and a flame of burnt brandy danced along the bar to the honour and propitiation of Lakshmi, that the able-bodied seaman might be thirsty when he came, for the "Cape of Good Cheer" did not owe its prosperity, as its name might suggest, to any Providence of our theology. But most of the brightness abode in the Chinamen's shoe shops, where many lamps shone on the hammering and the stitching. There were endless shoe shops, and they all belonged to Powson or Singson or Samson, while one sign-board bore the broad impertinence "Macpherson." The proprietors stood in the door, the smell came out in the street - that smell of Chinese personality steeped in fried oil and fresh leather that out-fans even the south wind in Bentinck Street. They were responsible but not anxious, the proprietors: they buried their fat hands in their wide sleeves and looked up and down, stolid and smiling. They stood in their alien petticoat trousers for the commercial stability of the locality, and the rows of patent leather slippers that glistened behind them testified to it further. Everything else shifted and drifted, with a perpetual change of complexion, a perpetual worsening of clothes. Only Powson bore a permanent yoke of prosperity. It lay round his thick brown neck with the low clean line of his blue cotton smock, and he carried it without offensive conscious-ness, looking up and down by no means in search of customers, rather in the exercise of the opaque, inscrutable philosophy tied up in his queue.

Lindsay liked Bentinck Street as an occasional relapse from the scenic standards of pillared and verandahed Calcutta, and made personal business with his Chinaman for the sake of the racial impression thrown into the transaction. Arnold, in his cassock, waited in the doorway with his arms crossed behind him, and his thin face thrust as far as it would go into the air outside. It is possible that some intelligences might have seen in this priest a caricature of his profession, a figure to be copied for the curate of burlesque, so accurately did he reproduce the common signs of the ascetic school. His face would have been womanish in its plainness but for the gravity that had grown upon it, only occasionally dispersed by a smile of scholarliness and sweetness which had the effect of being permitted, conceded. He had the long thin nose which looked as if for preference it would be forever thrust among the pages of the Fathers; and anyone might observe the width of his mouth without perhaps detecting the patience and decision of the upper lip. The indignity of spectacles he did not yet wear, but it hovered over him; it was indispensable to his personality in the long-run. In figure he was indifferently tall and thin and stooping, made to pass unobservedly along a pavement or with the directness of humble but important business among crowds. At Oxford he had interested some of his friends and worried others by wistful inclinations toward the shelter of that Mother Church which bids her children be at rest and leave to her the responsibility. Lindsay, with his robust sense of a right to exist on the old unmuddled fighting terms, to be a sane and decent animal, under civilised moral governance a miserable sinner, was among those who observed his waverings without prejudice or anything but an affectionate solicitude that, whichever way Arnold went, he should find the satisfactions he sought. The conviction that settled the matter was accidental, the work of a moment, a free instinct and a thing made with hands - the dead Shelley where the sea threw him and the sculptor fixed him, under his memorial dome in the gardens of University College. Here one leafy afternoon Arnold came so near praying that he raised his head in confusion at the thought of the profane handicraftsman who might claim the vague tribute of his spirit. Then fell the flash by which he saw deeply concealed in his bosom, and disguised with a host of spiritual wrappings, what he uncompromisingly identified as the artistic bias, the aesthetic point of view. The discovery worked upon him so that he spent three days without consummated prayer at all, occupied in the effort to find out whether he could yet indeed worship in purity of spirit, or how far the paralysis of the ideal of mere beauty had crept upon his devotions. In the end he cast the artistic bias, the aesthetic point of view, as far from him as his will would carry, and walked away in another direction, from which, if he turned his head, he could see the Church of Rome sitting with her graven temptations gathered up in her skirts, looking mournfully after him. He had been a priest of the Clarke Mission to Calcutta, a "Clarke Brother," six years when he stood in the door of Ahsing's little shop in Bentinck Street, while Lindsay explained to Ahsing his objection to patent leather toe-caps; six years which had not worn or chilled him, because, as he would have cheerfully admitted, he had recognised the facts and lowered his personal hopes of achievement - lowered them with a heroism which took account of himself as no more than a spiritual molecule rightly inspired and moving to the great future already shining behind coming aeons of the universal Kingdom. Indeed, his humility was scientific; he made his deductions from the granular nature of all change, moral and material. He never talked or thought of the Aryan souls that were to shine with peculiar Oriental brightness as stars in the crown of his reward; he saw rather the ego and the energy of him merged in a wave of blessed tendency in this world, thankful if, in that which is to come, it was counted worthy to survive at all. It should be understood that Arnold did not hope to attain the simplicity of this by means equally simple. He held vastly, on the contrary, to fast days and flagellations, to the ministry of symbols, the use of rigours. The spiritual consummation which the eye of faith enabled him to anticipate upon the horizon of Bengal should be hastened, however imperceptibly, by all that he could do to purify and intensify his infinitesimal share of the force that was to bring it about. Meanwhile he made friends with the fathers of Bengali schoolboys, who appreciated his manners, and sent him with urbanity flat baskets of mangoes and nuts and oranges, pomegranates from Persia, and little round boxes of white grapes in sawdust from Kabul. He seldom dwelt upon the converts that already testified to the success of the mission; it might be gathered that he had ideas about premature fruition.

As they stepped out together into the street, Lindsay thrust his hand within Arnold's elbow. It was an impulse, and the analysis of it would show elements like self-reproach, and a sense of value continually renewed, and a vain desire for an absolutely common ground. The physical nearness, the touch, was something, and each felt it in the remoteness of his other world with satisfaction. There was absurdly little in what they had to say to each other; they talked of the Viceroy's attack of measles and the sanitary improvements in the cloth dealers' quarter. Their bond was hardly more than a mutual decency of nature, niceness of sentiment, clearness of eye. Such as it was, it was strong enough to make both men wish it were stronger, a desire which was a vague impatience on Lindsay's part with a concentration of hostility to Arnold's soutane. It made its universal way for them, however, this garment. Where the crowd was thickest people jostled and pressed with one foot in the gutter for the convenience of the padre sahib. He, with his eyes cast down, took the tribute with humility, as meet, in a way that made Lindsay blaspheme inwardly at the persistence of ecclesiastical tradition.

Suddenly, as they passed, the irrelevant violence of tongues, the broken, half-comprehensible tumult was smitten and divided by a wave of rhythmic sound. It pushed aside the cries of the sweetmeat sellers, and mounted above the cracked bell that proclaimed the continual auction of Kristo Dass and Friend, dealers in the second-hand. In its vivid familiarity it seemed to make straight for the two Englishmen, to surround and take possession of them, and they paused. The source of it was plain - an open door under a vast white signboard dingily lettered "The Salvation Army." It loomed through the smoke and the streetlights like a discovery.

"Our peripatetic friends," said Arnold, with his rare smile; and as if the music seized and held them, they stood listening.

> "I've got a Saviour that's mighty to keep
> All day on Sunday and six days a week!
> I've got a Saviour that's mighty to keep
> Fifty-two weeks in the year."

It was immensely vigorous; the men looked at each other with fresh animation. Responding to the mere physical appeal of it, they picked their steps across the street to the door, and there hesitated, revolted in different ways. Perhaps, I have forgotten to say that Lindsay came to Calcutta out of an Aberdeenshire manse, and had had a mother before whose name, while she lived, people wrote "The Hon." Besides, the singing had stopped, and casual observation from the street was checked by a screen.

"I have wondered sometimes what their methods really are," said Arnold.

Their methods were just on the other side of the screen. A bullet-headed youth, in a red coat with gold letters on the shoulders, fingering a cap, slunk out round the end of this impediment, passing the two men beside the door, and a light, clear voice seemed to call after him -

"Ah! don't go away!"

Lindsay was visited by a flash of memory and a whimsical speculation whether now, at the week's end, the soul of Hilda Howe was still pursuing the broad road to perdition. The desire to enter sprang up in him: he was reminded of a vista of some interest which had recently revealed itself by an accident, and which he had not explored. It had almost passed out of his memory; he grasped at it again with something like excitement, and fell adroitly upon the half inclination in Arnold's voice.

"I suppose I can't expect you to go in?" he said.

"Precisely why not?" Stephen retorted. "My dear fellow, we make broad our sympathies, not our phylacteries."

At any other time Lindsay would have reflected how characteristic was the gentle neatness of that, and might have resented with amusement the pulpit tone of the little epigram. But this moment found him only aware of the consent in it. His hand on Arnold's elbow clinched the agreement; he half pushed the priest into the room, where they dropped into seats. Stephen's hand went to his breast instinctively, for the words in the air were holy by association, and stopped there, since even the breadth of his sympathies did not enable him to cross himself before General Booth. Though absent in body, the room was dominated by General Booth; he loomed so large and cadaverous, so earnest and aquiline and bushy, from a frame on the wall at the end of it. The texts on the other walls seemed emanations from him; and the man in the short loose, collarless red coat, with "Salvation Army" in crooked black letters on it, who stood talking in high, rapid tones with his hands folded, had the look of a puppet whose strings were pulled by the personality in the frame above him. It was only by degrees that they observed the other objects in the room - the big drum on the floor in the empty space where the exhorters stood, the dozen wooden benches and the possible score of people sitting on them, the dull kerosene lamps on the walls, lighting up the curtness of the texts. There were half a dozen men of the Duke's Own packed in a row like a formation, solid on their haunches; and three or four unshaven and loose-garmented, from crews in the Hooghly, who leaned well forwards their elbows on their knees, twirling battered straw hats, with a pathetic look of being for the instant off the defensive. One was a Scandinavian, another a Greek, with earrings. There was a ship's cook, too, a full-blooded negro, very respectable with a plaid tie and a silk hat; and beside, two East Indian girls of different shades, tittering at the Duke's Own in an agony of propriety; a Bengali boy, who spelled out the English on the cover of a hymn-book; and a very clean Chinaman, who appreciated his privilege, since it included a seat, a lamp, and a noise, though his perception of it possibly went no further. The other odds and ends were of the mixed country blood, like the girls, dingy, undecipherable. They made a shadow for the rest, lying along the benches, shifting unnoticeably.

Three people, two of them women, sat in the open space at the end of the room where the smoky fog from outside thickened and hung visibly in mid-air, and there was the empty seat of the man who was talking. Laura Filbert was one of the women. She might have been flung upon her chair; her head drooped over the back, buried in the curve of one arm. A tambourine hung loosely from the hand nearest her face; the other lay, palm outward in its abandonment, among the folds that covered her limbs. The folds hung from her waist, and she wore above them a short close bodice like a Bengali woman. Her head covering had slipped, and clung only to the knot of hair at the nape of her neck; she lacked, pathetically, the conscious hand to draw it forward. She was unaware even of the gaze of the Duke's Own, though it had fixity and absorption.

The man with folded hands went on talking. He seemed to have caught as a text the refrain of the hymn that had been sung. "Yes, indeed," he said. "I can tell heveryone 'ere this night, heveryone, that the Saviour is mighty to keep. I 'ave got it out of my own personal experience, I 'ave. Jesus don't only look after you on a Sunday, but six days a week, my friends, six days a week. Fix your eye on Him and He'll keep His eye on you - that's all your part of it. I don't mean to say I don't stumble an' fall into sin. There's times when the Devil will get the upper 'and, but oh, my friends, I ask you, each an' hevery one of you, is that the fault of Jesus? No, it is not 'Is fault, it is the fault of the person. The person 'as been forgetting Jesus, forgetting 'is Bible an' 'is prayers; what can you expect? And now I ask you, my friends, is Jesus a-keeping you? And if He is not, oh, my friends, ain't it foolish to put off any longer? 'Ere we are met together to-night; we may never all meet together again. You and I may never 'ear each other speaking again or see each other sitting there. Thank God," the speaker continued, as his eye rested on Arnold and Lindsay, "the vilest sinner may be saved, the respectable sinner may be saved. We've got God's word for that. Now just a little word of prayer from Ensign Sand 'ere - she's got God's ear, the Ensign 'as, and she'll plead with 'im for all unconverted souls inside these four walls to-night."

Laura lifted her head at this and dropped with the other exhorters on her knees on the floor. As she moved she bent upon the audience a preoccupied gaze, by which she seemed to observe numbers, chances, from a point remote and emotionally involved. Lindsay's impression was that she looked at him as from behind a glass door. Then her eyes closed as the other woman began, and through their lids, as it were, he could see that she was again caught up, though her body remained abased, her hands interlocked between her knees, swaying in unison with the petition. The Ensign was a little meagre freckled woman, whose wisps of colourless hair and tight drawn-down lips suggested that in the secular world she would have been bedraggled and a nagger. She gained an elevation, it was plain, from the Bengali dress; it kept her away from the temptation of cheap plush and dirty cotton lace; and her business gave her a complacency which was doubtless accepted as sanctification by her fellow-officers, especially by her husband, who had announced her influence with the Divine Being, and who was himself of an inferior commission. She prayed in a complaining way, and in a strained minor key that assumed a spiritual intimacy with all who listened, her key to hearts. She told the Lord in confidence that however appearances might be against it every soul before him was really longing to be gathered within His almighty arms, and when she said this, Laura Filbert, on the floor, threw back her head and cried "Hallelujah!" and Duff started. The mothers broke in upon the Ensign with like exclamations. They had a recurrent, perfunctory sound, and passed unnoticed; but when Laura again cried "Praise the Lord!" Lindsay found himself holding in check a hasty impulse to leave the premises. Then she rose, and he watched with the Duke's Own to see what she would do next. The others looked at her too, as she stood surprisingly fair and insistent among them, Ensign Sand with humble eyes and disapproving lips. As she began to speak the silence widened for her words, the ship's cook stopped shuffling his feet. "Oh come," she said, "Come and be saved!" Her voice seemed to travel from her without effort, and to penetrate every corner and every consciousness. There was a sudden dip in it like the fall of water, that thrilled along the nerves. "Who am I that ask you? A poor weak woman, ignorant, unknown. Never mind. It is not my voice but the voice in your heart that entreats you 'Come and be saved!' You know that voice; it speaks in the watches of the night; it began to speak when you were a little, little child, with little joys and sorrows and little prayers that you have forgotten now. Oh, it is a sweet voice, a tender voice" - her own had dropped to the cooing of doves - "it is hard to know why all the winds do not carry it, and all the leaves whisper it! Strange, strange! But the world is full of the clamour of its own foolishness, and the voice is lost in it, except in places where people come to pray, as here to-night, and in those night watches. You hear it now in the echo from my lips, 'Come and be saved.' Why must I beg of you? Why do you not come hastening, running? Are you too wise? But when did the wisdom of this world satisfy you about the next? Are you too much occupied? But in the day of judgment what will you do?" -

"When you come to Jordan's flood,
How will you do? How will you do?"

It was the voice and tambourine of Ensign Sand, quick upon her opportunity. Laura gave her no glance of surprise - perhaps she was disciplined to interruptions - but caught up her own tambourine, singing, and instantly the chorus was general, the Big drum thumping out the measure, all the tambourines shaking together.

"You who now contemn your God,
How will you do? How will you do?"

The Duke's Own sang lustily with a dogged enjoyment that made little of the words. Some of them assumed a vacuity to counteract the sentiment, but most of the sheepish countenances expressed that the tune was the thing, one or two with a smile of jovial cynicism, and kept time with their feet. Through the medley of voices - everybody sang except Arnold and Lindsay and the Chinaman - Laura's seemed to flow, separate and clear, threading the jangle upon melody, and turning the doggerel into an appeal, direct, intense. When Lindsay presently saw it addressed to him, in the unmistakable intention of her eyes, he caught his breath.

"Death will be a solemn day
When the soul is forced away,
    It will be too late to pray;

Mrs. Everard Cotes

How will you do?"

It was simple enough. All her supreme desire to convince, to turn, to make awfully plain, had centred upon the single person in the room with whom she had the advantage of acquaintance, whose face her own could seek with a kind of right to response. But the sensation Duff Lindsay tried to sit still under was not simple. It had the novelty, the shock, of a plunge into the sea; behind his decorous countenance he gasped and blinked, with unfamiliar sounds in his ears. His soul seemed shudderingly repelling Laura's, yet the buffets themselves were enthralling. In the strangeness of it he made a mechanical movement to depart, picked up his stick, but Arnold was sitting holding his chin, wrapped in quiet interest, and took no notice. The hymn stopped, and he found a few minutes' respite, during which Ensign Sand addressed the meeting, unveiling each heart to its possessor; while Laura turned over the leaves of the hymn-book, looking, Lindsay was profoundly aware, for airs and verses most likely to help the siege of the Army to his untaken, sinful citadel. There was time to bring him calmness enough to wonder whether these were the symptoms of emotional conversion, the sort of thing these people went in for, and he resolved to watch his state with interest. Then, before he knew it, they were all down on their knees again, and Laura was praying; and he was not aware of the meaning of a single word that she said, only that her voice was threading itself in and out of his consciousness burdened with a passion that made it exquisite to him. Her appeal lifted itself in the end into song, low and sweet.

"Down at the Cross where my Saviour died,
Down where for cleansing from sin I cried,

There to my heart was the blood applied,
Glory to His name!"

They let her sing it alone, even the tempting chorus,
and when it was over Lindsay was almost certain that
his were not the preliminary pangs of conversion by
the methods of the Salvation Army. Deliberately,
however, he postponed further analysis of them until
after the meeting was over. He would be compelled
then to go away, back to the club to dinner, or
something; they would put out the lights and lock the
place up: he thought of that. He glanced at the lamps
with a perception of the finality that would come when
they were extinguished - she would troop away with
the others into the darkness - and then at his watch to
see how much time there was left. More exhortation
followed and more prayer; he was only aware that she
did not speak. She sat with her hand over her eyes, and
Lindsay had an excited conviction that she was still
occupying herself with him. He looked round almost
furtively to detect whether anyone else was aware of it,
this connection that she was blazoning between them,
and then relapsed, staring at his hat, into a sense of
ungrammatical iterations beating through a room full
of stuffy smells. When Laura spoke again his eye
leaped to hers in a rapt effort to tell her that he
perceived her intention. That he should be grateful,
that he should approve, was neither here nor there; the
indispensable thing was that she should know him
conscious, receptive. She read three or four sacred
verses, a throb of tender longing from the very
Christheart, "Come unto Me." . . . The words stole
about the room like tears. Then she would ask "all
present," she said, to engage for a moment in silent
prayer. There was a wordless interval, only the vague
street noises surging past the door. A thrill ran along

the benches as Laura brought it to an end with sudden singing. She was on her feet as the others raised their heads, breaking forth clear and jubilant.

"I am so wondrously saved from sin,
Jesus so sweetly abides within;
There at the Cross where He took me in,
Glory to His name!"

She smiled as she sang. It was a happy confident smile, and it was plain that she longed to believe it the glad reflection of the last ten minutes' spiritual experience of many who heard her. Lindsay's perception of this was immediate and keen, and when her eyes rested for an instant of glad inquiry upon his in the chartered intimacy of her calling, he felt a pang of compunction. It was a formless reproach, too vague for anything like a charge, but it came nearest to defining itself in the idea that he had gone too far - he who had not left his seat. When the hymn was finished, and Ensign Sand said, "The meeting is now open for testimonies," he knew that all her hope was upon him, though she looked at the screen above his head; and he sat abashed, with a prodigal sense surging through him of what he would rejoice to do for her in compensation. In the little chilly silence that followed he surprised his own eyes moist with disappointment - it had all been so anxious and so vain - and he felt relief and gratitude when the man who beat the drum stood up and announced that he had been saved for eleven years, with details about how badly he stood in need of it when it happened.

"Hallelujah!" said Ensign Sand cheerfully, with a meretricious air of hearing it for the first time. "Any more?" and a Norwegian sailor lurched shamefacedly upon his feet. He had a couple of inches of straggling yellow beard all round his face, and fingered an old felt hat.

"I haf' to say only dis word. I goin' sdop by Jesus. Long time I subbose I sdop by Jesus. I subbose - "

"Glory be to God!" remarked Ensign Sand again, spiking the guns of the Duke's Own who were inclined to be amused. "That will do, thank you. Now, is there nobody else? Speak up, friends. It'll do you no harm, none whatever; it'll do you that much good you'll be surprised. Now, who'll be the next to say a word for Jesus?" She was nodding encouragement at the negro cook as if she knew him for a wavering soul, and he, sunk in his gleaming white collar, was aware, in silent smiling misery, that the expectations of the meeting were toward him. Laura had again hidden her eyes in her hand. The negro fingered his watch chain foolishly, and the prettiest of the East Indian half-castes tried hard to disguise her perception that an African in his best clothes under conviction of sin was the funniest thing in the world. The silence seemed to focus itself upon the cook, who fumbled at his coat collar and cleared his voice. It was a shock to all concerned when Stephen Arnold, picking up his hat, got upon his feet instead.

"I also," he said, "would offer my humble testimony to the grace of God - with all my heart."

It was as if he had repeated part of the creed in the performance of his office. Then he turned and bent gravely to Lindsay, "Shall we go now?" he whispered, and the two made their way to the door, leaving a silence behind them which Lindsay imagined, on the part of Ensign Sand at least, to be somewhat resentful. As they passed out a voice recovered itself, and cried, "Hallelujah!" It was Laura's; and all the way to the club - Arnold was dining with him there - Lindsay listened to his friend's analysis of religious appeal to the emotions, but chiefly heard that clear music above a sordid din, "Hallelujah!" "Hallelujah!"

CHAPTER IV

When Alicia Livingstone, almost believing she liked it, drove to Number Three, Lal Behari's Lane, and left cards upon Miss Hilda Howe, she was only partially rewarded. Through the plaster gate-posts, badly in want of repair, and bearing, sunk in one of them, a marble slab announcing "Residence with Board," she perceived the squalid attempt the place made at respectability, the servants in dirty livery salaaming curiously, the over-fed squirrel in a cage in the door, the pair of damaged wicker chairs in the porch, suggesting the easiest intercourse after dinner, the general discoloration. She observed with irritation that it was a down-at-heels shrine for such a divinity, in spite of its six dusty crotons in crumbling plaster urns, but the irritation was rather at her own repulsion to the place than at any inconsistency it presented. What she demanded and expected of herself was that Number Three, Lal Behari's Lane should be pleasing, interesting, acceptable on its merits as a cheap Calcutta boarding-house. She found herself so unable to perceive its merits that it was almost a relief to see nothing of Miss Howe either; Hilda had gone to rehearsal, to the "dance-house" the servant said, eyeing the unusual landau. Alicia rolled back into streets with Christian names, distressed by an uncertainty as to whether her visit had been a disappointment or an escape. By the next day, however, she was well pulled together in favour of the former conclusion - she could nearly always persuade herself of such things in time - and wrote a frank sweet little note in her picturesque hand - she never joined more than two syllables - to say how sorry she had been, and would Miss Howe come to lunch on Friday. "I should love to make it dinner," she, said to herself, as she sealed the envelope, "but before one knows how she will behave in connection with the men - I suppose one must think of the other people."

It was Friday, and Hilda was lunching. The two had met among the faint-tinted draperies of Alicia's drawing-room - there was something auroral even about the mantelpiece - a little like diplomatists using a common tongue native to neither of them. Perhaps Alicia drew the conventions round her with the greater fluency; Hilda had more to cover, but was less particular about it. The only thing she was bent upon making imperceptible was her sense of the comedy of Miss Livingstone's effort to receive her as if she had been anybody else. Alicia was hardly aware of what she wanted to conceal, unless it was her impression that Miss Howe's dress was cut a trifle too low in the neck, that she was almost too effective in that cream and yellow to be quite right. Alicia remembered afterwards to smile at it, that her first ten minutes of intercourse with Hilda Howe were dominated by a lively desire to set Celine at her - with such a foundation to work upon what could Celine not have done? She remembered her surprise, too, at the ordinary things Hilda said in that rich voice, even in the tempered drawing-room tones of which resided a hint of the seats nearest the exit under the gallery, and her wonder at the luxury of gesture that went with them, movements which seemed to imply blank verse and to be thrown away upon two women and a little furniture. A consciousness stood in the room between them, and their commonplaces about the picturesqueness of the bazar rode on long absorbed regards, one reading, the other anxious to read; yet the encounter was so conventionally creditable to them both that they might have smiled past each other under any circumstances next day and acknowledged no demand for more than the smile.

The cutlets had come before Hilda's impression was at the back of her head, her defences withdrawn, her eyes free and content, her elbow on the table. They had found a portrait-painter.

"He has such an eye," said Alicia, "for the possibilities of character."

"Such an eye that he develops them. I know one man he painted. I suppose when the man was born he had an embryo soul, but in the meantime he and everybody else had forgotten about it. All but Salter. Salter re-created it on the original lines, and brought it up, and gave it a lodging behind the man's, wrinkles. I saw the picture. It was fantastic - psychologically."

"Pyschology has a lot to say to portrait-painting, I know," Alicia said. "Do let him give you a little more. It's only Moselle." She felt quite direct and simple too in uttering her postulate. Her eyes had a friendly, unembarrassed look, there was nothing behind them but the joy of talking intelligently about Salter.

Hilda did not even glance away. She looked at her hostess instead, with an expression of candour so admirable that one might easily have mistaken it to be insincere. It was part of her that she could swim in any current, and it was pleasant enough, for the moment, to swim in Alicia's. Both the Moselle and the cutlets, moreover, were of excellent quality.

"It's everything to everything, don't you think? And especially, thank Heaven, to my trade." Her voice softened the brusqueness of this; the way she said it gave it a right to be said in any terms. That was the case with flagrancies of hers sometimes.

"To discover motives and morals and passions and ambitions and to make a picture of them with your own body - your face and hands and voice - compare our plastic opportunity with the handling of a brush to do it, or a pen or a chisel!"

"I know what you mean," said Alicia. She had a little flush, and an excited hand among the wineglasses. "No, I don't want any; please don't bother me!" to the man at her elbow with something in aspic. "It's much more direct - your way."

"And, I think, so much more primitive, so much earlier sanctioned, abiding so originally among the instincts! Oh yes! if we are lightly esteemed it is because we are bad exponents. The ideal has dignity enough. They charge us, in their unimaginable stupidity, with failing to appreciate our lines, especially when they are Shakespeare's - with being unliterary. You might - good Heavens! - as well accuse a painter of not being a musician! Our business lies behind the words - they are our mere medium! Rosalind wasn't literary - why should I be? But don't indulge me in my shop, if it bores you," Hilda added lightly, aware as she was that Miss Livingstone was never further from being bored.

"Oh, please go on! If you only knew," her lifted eyebrows confessed the tedium of Calcutta small talk. "But why do you say you are lightly esteemed? Surely the public is a touchstone - and you hold the public in the hollow of your hand!"

Hilda smiled. "Dear old public! It does its best for us, doesn't it? One loves it, you know, as sailors love the sea, never believing in its treachery in the end. But I don't know why I say we are lightly esteemed, or why I dogmatise about it at all. I've done nothing - I've no right. In ten years perhaps - no, five - I'll write signed articles for the New Review about modern dramatic tendencies. Meanwhile you'll have to consider that the value of my opinions is prospective."

"But already you have succeeded - you have made a place."

"In Coolgardie, in Johannesburg, I think they remember me in Trichinopoly too, and - yes, it may be so - in Manila. But that wasn't legitimate drama," and Hilda smiled again in a way that coloured her unspoken reminiscence, to Alicia's eyes, in rose and gold. She waited an instant for these tints to materialise, but Miss Howe's smile slid discreetly into her wineglass instead.

"There's immense picturesqueness in the Philippines," she went on, her look of thoughtful criticism contrasting in the queerest way with her hat. "Real ecclesiastical tyranny with pure traditions. One wonders what America will do with those friars, when she does go there."

"Do you think she is going?" asked Alicia vaguely. It

Mrs. Everard Cotes

was the merest politeness - she did not wait for a reply. With a courageous air which became her charmingly, she went on, "Don't you long to submit yourself to London? I should."

"Oh, I must. I know I must. It's in the path of duty and conscience - it's not to be put off for ever. But one dreads the chained slavery of London" - she hesitated before the audacity of adding, "the sordid hundred nights," but Alicia divined it, and caught her breath as if she had watched the other woman make a hazardous leap.

"You are magnificently sure," she said. Alicia herself felt curiously buoyed up and capable, conscious of vague intuitions of immediate achievement. The lunch-table still lay between the two, but it had become in a manner intangible; the selves of them had drawn together, and regarded each other with absorbent eyes. In Hilda's there was an instant of consideration before she said - "I might as well tell you - you won't misunderstand - that I AM sure. I expect things of myself. I hold a kind of mortgage on my success; when I foreclose it will come, bringing the long, steady, grasping chase of money and fame, eyes fixed, never a day to live in, only to accomplish, every moment straddled with calculation, an end to all the byways where one finds the colour of the sun. The successful London actress, my dear - what existence has she? A straight flight across the Atlantic in a record-breaker, so many nights in New York, so many in Chicago, so many in a Pullman car, and the net result in every newspaper - an existence of pure artificiality infested by reporters. It's like living in the shell of your personality. It's the house for ever on your back; at the last you are buried in it, smirking in your coffin with a half-open eye on the floral offerings. There never was reward so qualified by its conditions."

"Surely there would be some moments of splendid compensation?"

"Oh yes; and for those in the end we are all willing to perish! But then you know all, you have done all; there is nothing afterwards but the eternal strain to keep even with yourself. I don't suppose I could begin to make you see the joys of a strolling player - they aren't much understood even in the profession - but there are so many, honestly, that London being at the top of the hill, I'm not panting up. My way of going has twice wound round the world already. But I'm talking like an illustrated interview. You will grant the impertinence of all I've been saying when I tell you that I've never yet had an illustrated interview."

"Aren't they almost always vulgar?" Alicia asked. "Don't they make you sit the wrong way on a chair, in tights?"

Hilda threw her head back and laughed, almost, Alicia noted, like a man. She certainly did not hide her mouth with her hands or her handkerchief, as women often do in bursts of hilarity; she laughed freely, and as much as she wanted to, and it was as clear as possible that tights presented themselves quite preposterously to any discussion of her profession. They were things to be taken for granted, like the curtain and the wings; they had no relation to clothing in the world.

Alicia laughed too. After all, they were absurd - her outsider's prejudices. She said something like that, and Hilda seemed to soar again for her point of view about the illustrated interviews. "They ARE atrocities," she said. "On their merits they ought to be cast out of even the suburbs of art and literature. But they help to make the atmosphere that gives us power to work, and if they do that, of course - " and the pursed seriousness of her lips gave Alicia the impression that, though the whole world took offence, the expediency of the illustrated interview was beyond discussion.

The servant brought them coffee. "Shall we smoke here," said Miss Livingstone, "or in the drawing-room?"

"Oh, do you want to? Are you quite sure you like it? Please don't on my account - you really mustn't. Suppose it should mike you ill?" If Hilda felt any tinge of amusement she kept it out of her face. Nothing was there but cheerful concern.

"It won't make me ill." Alicia lifted her chin with delicate assertiveness. "I suppose you do smoke, don't you?"

"Occasionally - with some people. Honestly, have you ever done it before?"

"Four times," said Alicia, and then turned rose-colour with the apprehension that it sounded amateurish to have counted them. "I thought it was one of your privileges to do it always, just as you - "

"Go to bed with our boots on and put ice down the back of some Serene Highness's neck. I suppose it is, but now and then I prefer to dispense with it. In my bath, for instance, and almost always in omnibuses."

"How absurd you are! Then we'll stay here."

Miss Howe softly manipulated her cigarette and watched Alicia sacrifice two matches.

"There's Rosa Norton of our company," she went on. "Poor, dear old Rosy! She's fifty-three - grey hair smooth back, you know, and a kind of look of anxious mamma. And it gets into her eyes and chokes her, poor dear; but blow her, if she won't be as Bohemian as anybody. I've seen her smoke in a bonnet with strings tied under her chin. I got up and went away."

"But I can't possibly affect you in that way," said Alicia, putting her cigarette down to finish, as an afterthought, a marron glace. "I'm not old and I'm not grotesque."

"No, but - oh, all right. After you with the matches, please."

"I BEG your pardon. How thoughtless of me! Dear me, mine has gone out. Do you suppose anything is wrong with them? Perhaps they're damp."

"Trifle dry, if anything," Hilda returned, with the cigarette between her lips, "but in excellent order, really." She took it between her first and second finger for a glance at the gold letters at the end, leaned back and sent slow, luxurious spirals through her nostrils. It was rather, Alicia reflected, like a horse on a cold day - she hoped Miss Howe wouldn't do it again. But she presently saw that it was Miss Howe's way of doing it.

"No, you're not old and grotesque," Hilda said contemplatively; "you're young and beautiful." The freedom seemed bred, imperceptibly and enjoyably, from the delicate cloud in the air. Alicia flushed ever so little under it, but took it without wincing. She had less than the common palate for flattery of the obvious kind, but this was something different - a mere casual and unprejudiced statement of fact.

"Fairly," she said, not without surprise at her own calmness; and there was an instant of silence, during which the commonplace seemed to be dismissed between them.

"You made a vivid impression here last year," said Alicia. She felt delightfully terse and to the point.

"You mean Mr. Lindsay. Mr. Lindsay is very impressionable. Do you know him well?"

Alicia closed her lips, and a faint line graved itself on each side of them. Her whole face sounded a retreat, and her eyes were cold - it would have annoyed her to know how cold - with distance.

"He is an old friend of my brother's," she said. Hilda had the sensation of coming unexpectedly, through the lightest loam, upon a hard surface. She looked attentively at the red heart of her cigarette crisped over with grey, in its blackened calyx.

"Most impressionable," she went on, as if Alicia had not spoken. "As to the rest of the people - bah! you can't rouse Calcutta. It is sunk in its torpid liver, and imagines itself superior. It's really funny, you know, the way hepatic influences can be idealised - made to serve ennobling ends. But Mr. Lindsay is - different."

"Yes?" Miss Livingstone's intention was neutral, but, in spite of her, the asking note was in the word.

"We have done some interesting things together here. He has shown me the queerest places. Yesterday he made me go with him to Wellesley Square, to look at his latest enthusiasm standing in the middle of it."

"A statue?"

"No, a woman, preaching and warbling to the people. She wasn't new to me - I knew her before he did - but the picture was, and the performance. She stood poised on a coolie's basket in the midst of a rabble of all colours, like a fallen angel - I mean a dropped one. Light seemed to come from her, from her hair or her eyes or something. I almost expected to see her sail away over the palms into the sunset when it was ended."

"It sounds most unusual," Alicia said, with a light smile. Her interest was rather obviously curbed.

"It happens every day, really, only one doesn't stop and look; one doesn't go round the corner."

There was another little silence, full of the unwillingness of Miss Livingstone's desire to be informed.

Hilda knocked the ash of her cigarette into her finger-bowl, and waited. The pause grew so stiff with embarrassment that she broke it herself.

"And I regret to say it was I who introduced them," she said.

"Introduced whom?"

"Mr. Lindsay and Miss Laura Filbert of the Salvation Army. They met at Number Three; she had come after my soul. I think she was disappointed," Hilda went on tranquilly, "because I would only lend it to her while she was there."

"Of the Salvation Army! I can't imagine why you should regret it. He is always grateful to be amused."

"Oh, there is no reason to doubt his gratitude. He is rather intense about it. And - I don't know that my regret is precisely on Mr. Lindsay's account. Did I say so?" They were simple, amiable words, and their pertinence was very far from insistent; but Alicia's crude blush - everything else about her was so perfectly worked out - cried aloud that it was too sharp a pull up. "Perhaps though," Hilda hurried on with a pang, "we generalise too much about the men."

What Miss Livingstone would have found to say - she had certainly no generalisation to offer about Duff Lindsay - had not a servant brought her a card at that moment, is embarrassing to consider. The card saved her the necessity. She looked at it blankly for an instant, and then exclaimed, "My cousin, Stephen Arnold! He's a reverend - a Clarke Mission priest, and he will come straight in here. What shall we do with our cigarettes?"

Miss Howe had a pleasurable sense that the situation was developing.

"Yours has gone out again, so it doesn't much matter, does it? Drown the corpse in here, and I'll pretend it belongs to me." She pushed the finger-bowl across, and Alicia's discouraged remnant went into it. "Don't ask me to sacrifice mine," she added, and there was no time for remonstrance; Arnold's voice was lifting itself at the door.

"Pray may I come in?" he called from behind the portiere.

Hilda, who sat with her back to it, smiled in enjoying recognition of the thin, high academic note, the prim finish of the inflection. It reminded her of a man she knew who "did" curates beautifully.

Arnold walked past her with his quick, humble, clerical gait, and it amused her to think that he bent over Alicia's hand as if he would bless it.

"You can't guess how badly I want a cup of coffee." He flavoured what he said, and made it pretty, like a woman. "Let me confess at once, that is what brought me." He stopped to laugh; there was a hint of formality and self-sacrifice even in that. "It is coffee-time, isn't it?" Then he turned and saw Hilda, and she was, at the moment, flushed with the luxury of her sensations, a vision as splendid as she must have been to him unusual. But he only closed his lips and thrust his chin out a little, with his left hand behind him in one of his intensely clerical attitudes, and so stood waiting. Hilda reflected afterwards that she could hardly have expected him to exclaim, "Whom have we here?" with upraised hands, but she had to acknowledge her flash of surprise at his self-possession. She noted, too, his grave bow when Alicia mentioned them to each other, that there was the habit of deference in it, yet that it waved her courteously, so to speak, out of his life. It was all as interesting as the materialisation of a quaint tradition, and she decided not, after all, to begin a trivial comedy for herself and Alicia, by asking the Reverend Stephen Arnold whether he objected to tobacco. She had an instant's circling choice of the person she would represent to this priest in the little intermingling half-hour of their lives that lay shaken out before them, and dropped unerringly. It really hardly mattered, but she always had such instants. She was aware of the shadow of a regret at the opulence of her personal effect; her hand went to her throat and drew the laces closer together there. An erectness stole into her body as she sat, and a look into her eyes that divorced her at a stroke from anything that could have spoken to him of too general an accessibility, too unthinking a largesse. She went on smoking, but almost immediately her cigarette took its proper note of insignificance. Alicia, speaking of it once afterwards to Arnold, found that he had forgotten it.

"Even in College Street you have heard of Miss Howe," Alicia said, and the negative, very readable in Arnold's silent bow, brought Hilda a flicker of happiness at her hostess's expense.

"I don't think the posters carry us as far as College Street," she said, "but I am not difficult to explain, Mr. Arnold. I act with Mr. Stanhope's Company. If you lived in Chowringhee you couldn't help knowing all about me, the letters are so large." The bounty of her well-spring of kindness was in it under the candour and the simplicity; it was one of those least of little things which are enough.

Arnold smiled back at her, and she saw recognition leap through the armour-plate of his ecclesiasticism.

He glanced away again quickly, and looked at the floor as he said he feared they were terribly out of it in College Street, for which, however, he had evidently no apology to offer. He continued to look at the floor with a careful air, as if it presented points pertinent to the situation. Hilda felt herself - it was an odd sensation - too sunny upon the nooked, retiring current that flowed in him. He might have turned to the cool accustomed shadow that Alicia made, but she was aware that he did not, that he was struggling through her strangeness and his shyness for something to say to her. He stirred his coffee, and once or twice his long upper lip trembled as if he thought he had found it; but it was Alicia who talked, making light accusations against the rigours of the Mission House, complaining of her cousin that he was altogether given over to bonds and bands, that she personally would soon cease to hold him in affection at all; she saw so little of him it wasn't really worth while.

This was old fencing ground between them, and Stephen parried her pleasantly enough, but his eyes strayed speculatively to the other end of the table, where, however, they rose no higher than the firm, lightly-moulded hand that held the cigarette.

"If I could found a monastic order," Hilda said, "one of the rules should be a week's compulsory retirement into the world four times a year." She spoke with a kind of grave brightness; it was difficult to know whether she was altogether in jest.

"There would be secession all over the place," Arnold responded, with his repressed smile. "You would get any number of probationers; I wonder whether you would keep them!"

"During that week," Hilda went on, "they should be compelled to dine and dance every night, to read a 'Problem' novel every morning before luncheon, to marry and be given in marriage, and to go to all the variety entertainments. Think of the austere bliss of the return to the cloisters! All joy lies in a succession of sensations, they say. Do you remember how Lord Ormont arranged his pleasures? Oh yes, my brother-hood would be popular, as soon as it was understood."

Alicia hurried in with something palliating - she could remember flippancies of her own that had been rebuked - but there was no sign or token of disapproval in Arnold's face. What she might have observed there, if she had been keen enough in vision, was a slight disarrangement, so to speak, of the placid priestly mask, and something like the original undergraduate looking out from beneath.

Hilda began to put on her gloves. The left one gaped at two finger-ends; she buttoned it with the palm thrown up and outward, as if it were the daintiest spoil of the Avenue de l'Opera.

"Not yet!" Alicia cried.

"Thanks, I must. To-night is our last full rehearsal, and I have to dress the stage for the first act before six o'clock. And, after pulling all that furniture about, I shall want an hour or two in bed."

"You! But it's monstrous. Is there nobody else?"

"I wouldn't let anybody else," Hilda laughed. "Don't forget, please, that we are only strolling players, odds and ends of people, mostly from the Antipodes. Don't confound our manners and customs with anything you've heard about the Lyceum. Good-bye. It has been charming. Goodbye, Mr. Arnold."

But Alicia held her hand. "The papers say it is to be The Offence of Galilee, after all," she said.

"Yes. Hamilton Bradley is all right again, and we've found a pretty fair local Judas - amateur. We couldn't possibly put it on without Mr. Bradley. He takes the part of" - Hilda glanced at the hem of the listening priestly robe - "of the chief character, you know."

"That was the great Nonconformist success at home last year, wasn't it?" Arnold asked; "Leslie Patullo's play? I knew him at Oxford. I can't imagine - he's a queer chap to be writing things like that."

"It works out better than you - than one might suppose," Hilda returned, moving toward the door. "Some of the situations are really almost novel, in spite of all your centuries of preaching." She sent a disarming smile with that, looking over her shoulder in one of her most effective hesitations, one hand holding back the portiere.

"And next week?" cried Alicia.

"Oh, next week we do L'Amourette de Giselle - Frank Golding's re-vamp. Good-bye! Good-bye!"

"I wonder very much what Patullo has done with The Offence of Galilee," Arnold said, after she had gone.

"Come and see, Stephen. We have a box, and there will be heaps of room. It's - suitable, isn't it?"

"Oh, quite."

"Then dine with us - the Yardleys are coming - and go on. Why not?"

"Thanks very much indeed. It is sure to reward one. I think I shall be able to give myself that pleasure."

Arnold made a longer visit than usual; his cup of coffee, indeed, became a cup of tea; and his talk, while he stayed, seemed to suffer less from the limitations of his Order than it usually did. He was fluent and direct; he allowed it to appear that he read more than his prayers; that his glance at the world had still a speculation in it; and when he went away, he left Alicia with flushed cheeks and brightened eyes, murmuring a vague inward corollary upon her day -

"It pays! It pays!"

CHAPTER V

Mr. Llewellyn Stanhope's Company was not the only combination that offered itself to the entertainment of Calcutta that December Saturday night. The ever-popular Jimmy Finnigan and his "Surprise Party" - he sailed up the Bay as regularly as the Viceroy descended from the hills - had been advertising "Side-splitting begins at 9.30. Prices as usual" with reference to this particular evening for a fortnight. In the Athenian Theatre - it had a tin roof and nobody could hear the orchestra when it rained - the Midgets were presenting the earlier collaborations of Messrs. Gilbert and Sullivan, every Midget guaranteed under nine years of age. Colonel Pike's Great Occidental Circus had been in full blast on the Maidan for a week. It became a great Occidental circus when Colonel Pike married the proprietress. They were both staying at the Grand Oriental Hotel at Singapore when she was made a relict through cholera, and he had more time than he knew what to do with, to say nothing of moustaches that predestined him to a box-office. And certainly circumstances justified the lady's complaisance, for while hitherto hers had been but a fleeting show, it was now, in the excusably imaginative terms of Colonel Pike, an architectural feature of the cold weather. There was the Mystic Bower, too, in an octagonal tent under a pipal tree, which gave you by an arrangement of looking-glasses the most unaccountable sensations

Mrs. Everard Cotes

for one rupee; and a signboard cried "Know Thyself!" where a physiological display lurked from the eyes of the police behind a perfectly respectable skeleton at one end of Peri Chandra's Gully. Llewellyn Stanhope saw that there was competition, sighed to think how much, as he stood in the foggy vestibule of the Imperial Theatre wrapped in the impressive folds of his managerial cape, and pulled his moustache and watched the occasional carriage that rolled his way up the narrow lane from Chowringhee. He thought bitterly, standing there, of Calcutta's recognition of the claims of legitimate drama, for the dank darkness was full of the noise of wheels and the flashing of lamps on the way to accord another season's welcome to Jimmy Finnigan. "I might've learned this town well enough by now," he reflected, "to know that a bally minstrel show's about the size of it." Mr. Stanhope had not Mr. Finnigan's art of the large red lips and the twanging banjo; his thought was scornful rather than envious. He aspired, moreover, to be known as the pilot of stars, at least in the incipience of their courses, to be taken seriously by association, since nature had arranged that he never could be on his intrinsic merits. His upper lip was too short for that, his yellow moustache too curly, while the perpetual bullying he underwent at the hands of leading ladies gave him an air of deference to everybody else which was sometimes painfully misunderstood. The stars, it must be said regretfully, in connection with so laudable an ambition, nearly always betrayed him, coming down with an unmistakably meteoric descent, stony-broke in the uttermost ends of the earth, with a strong inclination to bring the cause of that misfortune before the Consular Courts. They seldom succeeded in this design, since Llewellyn was usually able to prove to them in advance that it would be fruitless and expensive, but the paths of Eastern capitals were strewn with his compromises, in Japanese yen, Chinese dollars, Indian rupees, for salaries which no amount of advertising could wheedle into the box-office. When the climax came, Llewellyn usually went to hospital and received the reporters of local papers in pathetic audience there, which counteracted the effect of the astounding statements the stars made in letters to the editor, and yet gave the public clearly to understand that owing to its coldness and neglect a number of ladies and gentlemen of very superior talents were subsisting in their midst mainly upon brinjals and soda-water. "I'm in hospital," Mr. Stanhope would say to the reporters, "and I'm d - glad of it," - he always insisted on the oath going in, it appealed so sympathetically to the domiciled Englishman grown cold to superiority, - "for, upon my soul, I don't know where I'd turn for a crust if I weren't." In the end the talented ladies and gentlemen usually went home by an inexpensive line as the voluntary arrangement of a public to whom plain soda was a ludicrous hardship, and native vegetables an abomination at any price. Then Llewellyn and Rosa Norton - she had a small inalienable income, and they were really married though they preferred for some inexplicable reason to be thought guilty of less conventional behaviour - would depart in another direction, full of gratification for the present and of confidence for the future. Llewellyn usually made a parting statement to the newspapers that although his aims were unalterably high he was not above profiting by experience, and that next season he could be relied upon to hit the taste of the community with precision. This year, as we know, he had made a serious effort by insisting that at least a proportion of his ladies and gentlemen should be high-kickers and equal to an imitation, good enough for the Orient, of most things done by the illustrious Mr. Chevalier. But the fact that Mr. Stanhope had selected The Offence of Galilee to open with tells its own tale. He was convinced, but not converted, and he stood there with his little legs apart, chewing a straw above the three uncut emeralds that formed the chaste decoration of his shirt-front, giving the public of Calcutta one more chance to redeem itself.

It began to look as if Calcutta were not wholly irredeemable. A ticca-gharry deposited a sea-captain; three carriages arrived in succession; an indefinite number of the Duke's Own, hardly any of them drunk, filed in to the rupee seats under the gallery: an overflow from Jimmy Finnigan, who could no longer give his patrons even standing room. When this occurred Llewellyn turned and swung indifferently away in the direction of the dressing-rooms. When Jimmy Finnigan closed his doors so early there was no further cause for anxiety. Calcutta was abroad and stirring, and would turn for amusement even to The Offence of Galilee.

Eventually - that is, five minutes before the curtain rose - the representatives of the leading Calcutta journals decided that they were justified in describing the house as a large and fashionable audience. The Viceroy had taken a box, and sent an Aide-de-Camp to sit in it, also a pair of M.P.'s from the North of England, whom he was expected to attend to in Calcutta, and the governess. The Commander-in-Chief had not been solicited to be present, the theatrical season demanding an economy in such personalities if they were to go round; but a Judge of the High Court had a party in the front row, and a Secretary to the Bengal Government sat behind him. To speak of unofficials, there must have been quite forty lakhs of tea and jute and indigo in the house, very genial and prosperous, to say nothing of hides and seeds, and the men who sold money and bought diamonds with the profits, which shone in their wives' hair. A duskiness prevailed in the bare arms and shoulders; much of the hair was shining and abundant, and very black. A turn of the head showed a lean Greek profile, an outline bulbous and Armenian, the smooth creamy mask of a Jewess, while here and there glimmered something more opulent and inviting still, which proclaimed, if it did not confess, the remote motherhood of the zenana and the origin of the sun. An audience of fluttering fans and wrinkled shirt collars - the evening was warm under the gas-lights - sensuous, indolent, already amused with itself. Not an old woman in it from end to end, hardly a man turned fifty, and those who were had the air and looked to have the habits of twenty-five - an audience that might have got up and stretched itself but for good manners, and walked out in childish boredom at having to wait for the rise of the curtain, but sat on instead, diffusing an atmosphere of affluence and delicate scents, and suggesting, with imperious chins, the use of quick orders in a world of personal superiority.

Thus the stalls - they were spindling cane-bottomed chairs - and the boxes, in one of which the same spindling cane-bottomed chairs supported, in more expensive seclusion, Surgeon-Major and Miss Livingstone, the Reverend Stephen Arnold, and two or three other people. The Duke's Own sat under the gallery, cheek by jowl with all the flotsam and jetsam of an Eastern port, well on the look-out for offensive personalities from the men of the ships, and spitting freely. Here, too, was an ease of shoulder and a freedom from the cares of life - at a venture the wives were taking in washing in Brixton, and the children sent to Board School at the expense of the nation. And in a climate like this it was a popular opinion that a man must either enjoy himself or commit suicide.

The Sphinx on the crooked curtain looked above and beyond them all. It was a caricature of the Sphinx, but could not confine her gaze.

Hilda's audience that night knew all about The Offence of Galilee from the English illustrated papers. The illustrated papers had a great way of ministering to the complacency of Calcutta audiences; they contained photographs of almost every striking scene, composed at the leisure of the cast, but so vividly supplemented with descriptions of the leading lady's clothes that it hardly required any effort of the imagination to conjure up the rest. The postures and the chief garments of Pilate - he was eating pomegranates when the curtain rose, and listening to scandal from his slave-maidens about Mary Magdalene - were at once recognised in their resemblance to those of the photographs, and in the thrill of this satisfaction any discrepancies in cut and texture passed generally unobserved. A silent curiosity settled upon the house, half reverent, as if with the Bible names came thronging a troop of sacred associations to cluster about personalities brusquely torn out of church, and people listened for familiar sentences with something like the composed gravity with which they heard on Sundays the reading of the second lesson. But as the stage-talk went on, the slave-maidens announcing themselves without delay comfortably modern and commonplace, and Pilate a cynic and a decadent, though as distinctively from Melbourne, it was possible to note the breaking up of this sentiment. It was plain after all that no standard of ideality was to be maintained or struggled after. The relief was palpable; nevertheless, when Pilate's wife cast a shrewish gibe at him over the shoulder of her exit, the audience showed but a faint inclination to be amused. It was to be a play evidently like any other play, the same coarse fibre, the same vivid and vulgar appeals. It is doubtful whether this idea was critically present to anyone but Stephen Arnold, but people unconsciously tasted the dramatic substance offered them, and leaned back in their chairs with the usual patient acknowledgment that one mustn't expect too much of a company that found it worth while to come to Calcutta. The house grew submissive and stolid, but one could see half-awakened prejudices sitting in the dress-circle. The paper-chasing Secretary said to the most intelligent of his party that on the whole he liked his theology neat, forgetting that the preference belonged to Mr. Andrew Lang in connection with a notable lady novelist; and the most intelligent - it was Mrs. Barberry - replied that it did seem strange. The depths under the gallery were critically attentive, though Llewellyn Stanhope felt them hostile and longing for verbal brick-bats; and the Reverend Mr. Arnold shrank into the farthest corner of Surgeon-Major Livingstone's box, and knew all the misery of outrage. Pilate and the slave-maidens, Pilate's fat wife, and an unspeakable comic centurion, offered as yet hardly more than a prelude, but the monstrosity of the whole performance was already projected upon Arnold's suffering imagination. This, then, was what Patullo had done with it. But what other, he asked himself in quiet anger, could Patullo have been expected to do? the fellow he remembered. Arnold tilted his chair back and stared, with arms folded and sombre brows, at the opposite wall. He looked once at the door, but some spirit of self-torture kept him in his seat. If so much offence could be made with the mere crust and envelope, so to speak, of the sacred story, what sacrilege might not be committed with the divine personalities concerned? He remembered, with the touch of almost physical nausea that assailed him when he saw them, one or two pictures in recent Paris exhibitions where the coveted accent of surprise had been produced by representing the sacred figure in the trivial monde of the boulevards, and fixed upon them as the source of Patullo's intolerable inspiration. Certain muscles felt responsive at the thought of Patullo which Arnold had forgotten he possessed; it was so seldom that a missionary priest, even of athletic traditions, came in contact with anybody who required to be kicked.

Alicia was in front with the Yardleys, dropping her unfailing plummet into the evening's experience. Arnold, hesitating over the rudeness of departure, thought she was sufficiently absorbed; she would hardly mind. The centurion slapped his tin armour, and made a jest, which reached Stephen over his hostess's shoulder, and seemed to brand him where he sat. He looked about for his hat and some excuse that would serve, and while he looked the sound of applause rose from the house. It was a demonstration without great energy, hardly more than a flutter from stall to stall, with a vague, fundamental noise from the gallery; but it had the quality which acclaimed something new. Arnold glanced at the stage, and saw that while Pilate and the hollow-chested slaves and the tin centurion were still on, they had somehow lost significance and colour, and that all the meaning and the dominance of the situation had gathered into the person of a woman of the East who danced. She was almost discordant in her literalness, in her clear olive tints and the kol smudges under her eyes, the string of coins in the mass of her fallen hair, and her unfettered body. Beside her the slave-girls, crouching, looked like painted shells. She danced before Pilate in strange Eastern ways, in plastic weavings and gesturings that seemed to be the telling of a tale; and from the orchestra only one unknown instrument sobbed out to help her. The women of the people have ever bought in Palestine, buy to-day in the Mousky, the coarse, thick grey-blue cotton that fell about her limbs, and there was audacity in the poverty of her beaten silver anklets and armlets. These shone and twinkled with her movements; but her softly splendid eyes and reddened lips had the immobility of the bazar. People looked at their playbills to see whether it was really Hilda Howe or some nautch-queen borrowed from a native theatre. By the time she sank before Pilate and placed his foot upon her head a new spirit had breathed upon the house. Under the unexpectedness of the representation it sat up straight, and there was a keenness of desire to see what would happen next which plainly curtailed the applause, as it does with children at a pantomime.

"Have you ever seen anything like it before?" Alicia asked Captain Yardley; and he said he thought he had once, in Algiers, but not nearly so well done. Arnold rose again to go, but the Magdalene had begun the well-known passage with Pilate, about which the newspapers absurdly reported later that if Miss Howe had not been a Protestant, and so impervious the Pope would have excommunicated her, and as he looked his movement imperceptibly changed to afford him a better place. He put an undecided hand upon a prop of the box that rose behind Alicia's shoulder, and so stood leaning and looking, more conspicuous in the straight lines and short shoulder cape of the frock of his Order than he knew. Hilda, in one of those impenetrable regards which she threw straight in front of her, while Pilate yawped and posed nearer and nearer the desire of the Magdalene to be admitted to his household, was at once aware of him. Presently he sat down again - it was still the profane, the fabulous, the horrible Patullo, but a strain of pure gold had come into the fabric worth holding in view, impossible, indeed, to close the eyes upon. Far enough it was from any semblance to historical fact, but almost possible, almost admissible, in the form of the woman, as historical fiction. She dared to sit upon the floor now, in the ungraceful huddled Eastern fashion, clasping her knees to her breast, with her back half turned to her lord, the friend of Caesar, so that he could not see the design that sat behind the mask of her sharp indifference. She rested her chin upon her knees, and let the blankness of her beauty exclaim upon the subtlety of her replies, plainly measuring the power of her provocation against the impoverished quality that camp and grove, court and schools, might leave upon august Roman sensibilities. It was the old, old sophistication, so perfect in its concentration behind the kol-brushed eyes and the brown breasts, the igniting, flickering, raging of an instinct upon the stage. Alicia, when it was over, said to Mrs. Yardley, "How the modern woman goes off upon side issues!" to which that lady nodded a rather suspicious assent.

Long before Hilda had begun to act for Arnold, to play to his special consciousness, he was fastened to his chair, held down, so to speak, by a whirlpool of conflicting impulses. She did so much more than "lift" the inventive vulgarisation of the Bible story in the common sense; she inspired and transfused it so that whenever she appeared people irresistibly forgot the matter for her, or made private acknowledgments to the effect that something was to be said even for an impious fantasy which gave her so unique an opportunity. To Arnold her vivid embodiment of an incident in that which was his morning and evening meditation made special appeal, and though it was in a way as if she had thrust her heathen torch into his Holy of Holies, he saw it lighted with fascination, and could not close the door upon her. The moment of her discovery of this came early, and it is only she, perhaps, who could tell how the strange bond wove itself that drew her being - the Magdalene's - to the priest who sat behind a lady in swansdown and chiffon in the upper box nearest to the stage on the right. The beginnings of such things are untraceable, but the fact may be considered in connection with this one that Hamilton Bradley, who represented, as we have been told he would, the Chief Character, did it upon lines very recognisably those of the illustrations of sacred books, very correct as to the hair and beard and pictured garment of the Galilean; with every accent of hollow-eyed pallor and inscrutable remoteness, with all the thin vagueness, too, of a popular engraving, the limitations and the depression. Under it one saw the painful inconsistency of the familiar Hamilton Bradley of other presentations, and realised with irritation, which must have been tenfold in Hilda, how he rebelled against the part. Perhaps this was enough in itself to send her dramatic impulse to another focus, and the strangeness of the adventure was a very thing she would delight in. Whatever may be said about it, while yet the shock of the woman's earthly passion with its divine object was receding from Arnold's mind before the exquisite charm and faithfulness of the worshipping Magdalene, he became aware that in some special way he sat judging and pitying her. She had hardly lifted her eyes to him twice, yet it was he, intimately he, who responded as if from afar off, to the touch of her infinite solicitude and abasement, the joy and the shame of her love. As he watched and knew, his lips tightened and his face paled with the throb of his own renunciation, he folded his celibate arms in the habit of his brotherhood, and was caught up into a knowledge and an imitation of how the spotless Original would have looked upon a woman suffering and transported thus. The poverty of the play faded out; he became almost unaware of the pinchbeck and the fustian of Patullo's invention, and its insufferable mixture with the fabric of which every thread was precious beyond imagination. He looked down with tender patience and compassion upon the development of the woman's intrigue in the palace, through the very flower of her crafts and guiles, to save Him who had transfigured her from the hands of the rabble and the high priests; he did not even shrink from the inexpressibly grating note of the purified Magdalene's final passionate tendering of her personal sacrifice to the enamoured Pilate as the price of His freedom, and when at the last she wept at His feet where He lay bound and delivered, and wrapped them, in the agony of her abandonment, in the hair of her head, the priest's lips almost moved in words other than those of the playwright - words that told her he knew the height and the depth of her sacrifice and forgave it, "Neither do I condemn thee . . ." In his exultation he saw what it was to perform miracles, to remit sins. The spark of divinity that was in him glowed to a white heat; the woman on the stage warmed her hands at it in two consciousnesses. She was stirred through all her artistic sense in a new and delicious way, and wakened in some dormant part of her to a knowledge beautiful and surprising. She felt in every nerve the exquisite quality of that which lay between them, and it thrilled her through all her own perception of what she did, and all the applause at how she did it. It was as if he, the priest, was borne out upon a deep broad current that made toward solar spaces, toward infinite bounds, and as if she, the actress, piloted him. . . .

The Sphinx on the curtain - it had gone down in the old crooked lines - again looked above and beyond them all. I have sometimes fancied a trace of malignancy about her steady eyeballs, but perhaps that is the accident or the design of the scene-painter; it does not show in photographs. The audience was dispersing a trifle sedately; the performance had been, as Mrs. Barberry told Mr. Justice Horne, interesting but, depressing. "I hope," said Alicia to Stephen, fastening the fluffy-white collar of the wrap he put round her, "that I needn't be sorry I asked you to come. I don't quite know. But she did redeem it, didn't she? That last scene - "

"Can you not be silent?" Arnold said, almost in a whisper; and her look of astonishment showed her that there were tears in his eyes. He left the theatre and walked light-headedly across Chowringhee and out into the starlit empty darkness of the Maidan, where presently he stumbled upon a wooden bench under a tree. There, after a little, sleep fell upon his amazement, and he lay unconscious for an hour or two, while the breeze stole across the grass from the river and the mast-head lights watched beside the city. He woke chilled and normal, and when he reached the Mission House in College Street his servant was surprised at the unusual irritation of a necessary rebuke.

CHAPTER VI

While Alicia Livingstone fought with her imagination in accounting for Lindsay's absence from the theatre on the first night of a notable presentation by Miss Hilda Howe, he sat with his knees crossed on the bench farthest back and the corner obscurest of the Salvation Army Headquarters in Bentinck Street. It had become his accustomed place; sitting there he had begun to feel like the adventurer under Niagara, it was the only spot from which he could observe, try to understand and cope with the torrential nature of his passion. Nearer to the fair charm of his kneeling Laura, in the uncertain flare of the kerosene lamp and the sound of the big drum, he grew blind, lost count, was carried away. His persistent refusal of a better place also profited him in that it brought to Ensign Sand and the other "officers" the divination that he was one of those shyly anxious souls who have to be enticed into the Kingdom of Heaven with wariness, and they made a great pretence of not noticing him, going on with the exercises just as if he were not there, a consideration which he was able richly to enhance when the plate came round. After his first contribution, Mrs. Sand regarded his spiritual interests with almost superstitious reverence, according them the fullest privacy of which she was capable. The gravity which the gentleman attached to his situation was sufficiently testified by the "amount"; Mrs. Sand never wanted better evidence than the amount. Even

Laura, acting doubtless under instructions, seemed disposed to hold away from him in her prayers and exhortations; only a very occasional allusion passed her lips which Duff could appropriate. These, when they fell, he gathered and set like flowers in his tenderest consciousness, to visit and water them after the sun went down and for twenty-four hours he would not see her again. Her intonation went with them and her face; they lived on that. They stirred him, I mean, least of all in the manner of their intention. After the first quarter of an hour, it is to be feared, Lindsay suffered no more apprehensions on the score of emotional hypnotism. He recognised his situation plainly enough, and there was no appeal in it of which the Reverend Stephen Arnold, for example, could properly suspect the genuineness or the permanence.

On this Saturday night he sat through the meeting as he had sat through other meetings, absorbed in his exquisite experience which he meditated mostly with his eyes on the floor. His attitude was one quite adapted to deceive Ensign Sand; if he had been occupied with the burden of his transgressions it was one he might very well have fallen into. When Laura knelt or sang he sometimes looked at her, at other times he looked at the situation in the brightness of her presence at the other end of the room. She gave forth there, for Lindsay, an illumination by which he almost immediately began to read his life; and it was because he thought he had done this with accuracy and intelligence that he came up behind her that evening when the meeting was over as she followed the rest, with her sari drawn over her head, out into the darkness of Bentinck Street, and said with directness, "I should like to come and see you. When may I? Any time that suits you. Have you half an hour to spare to-morrow?"

It was plain that she was tired, and that the brightness with which she welcomed his advance was a trifle taught and perfunctory. Not the frankness though, or the touch of "Now we are getting to business," that stood in her expression. She looked alert and pleased.

"You would like to have a little talk, wouldn't you?" she said. Her manner took Lindsay a trifle aback; it suggested that she conferred this privilege so freely. "To-morrow - let me see, we march in the morning, and I have an open-air at four in the afternoon - the Ensign takes the evening meeting. Yes, I could see you to-morrow about two or about seven, after I get back from the Square." It was not unlike a professional appointment.

Lindsay considered. "Thanks," he said, "I'll come at about seven - if you are sure you won't be too exhausted to have me after such a day."

He saw that her lids as she raised them to answer were slightly reddened at the edges, testifying to the acridity of Calcutta's road dust, and a dry crack crept into the silver voice with which she said matter-of-factly, "We are never too exhausted to attend to our Master's business."

Lindsay's face expressed an instant's hesitation; he looked gravely the other way. "And the address?" he said.

"Almost next door - we all live within bugle-call. The entrance is in Crooked Lane. Anybody will tell you."

At the door Ensign Sand was conspicuously waiting. Lindsay said "Thanks" again, and passed out - she seemed to be holding it for him - and picked his way over the gutters to the shop of his Chinaman opposite. From there he watched the little company issue forth and turn into Crooked Lane, where the entrance was. It gave him a sense that she had her part in this squalor, which was not altogether distressful in that it also localised her in the warm, living, habitable world, and helped to make her thinkable and attainable. Then he went to his room at the club and found there a note from Miss Howe, written apparently to forgive him in advance, to say that she had not expected him. "Friendly creature!" he said as he turned out the lamp, and smiled in the dark to think that already there was one who guessed, who knew.

One gropes in Crooked Lane after the lights of Bentinck Street have done all that can be expected of them. There are various things to avoid, washer-men's donkeys and pariah dogs, unyoked ticca-gharries, heaps of rubbish, perhaps a leprous beggar. Lindsay, when he had surmounted these, found himself at the entrance to a quadrangle which was positively dark. He waylaid a sweeper slinking out, and the man showed him where an open staircase ran down against the wall in one corner. It was up there, he said, that the "tamasho-mems"* lived. There were three tamasho-mems, he continued, responding to Lindsay's trivial coin, and one sahib, but this was not the time for the tamasho - it was finished. Lindsay mounted the first flight by faith, and paused at the landing to avoid collision with a heavy body descending. He inquired Miss Filbert's whereabouts from this person, who providentially lighted a cigar, disclosing himself a bald Armenian in tusser silk trousers and a dirty shirt, presumably, Lindsay thought, the landlord. At all events he had the information, Lindsay was to keep straight on, it was the third storey. Duff kept straight on in a spirit of caution, and just missed treading upon the fattest rat in the heathen parish of St. John's. At the top he saw a light and hastened; it shone from an open door at the side of a passage. The partition in which the door was came considerably short of the ceiling, and from the top of it to the window opposite stretched a line of garments to dry, of pungent odour and infantile pattern. Lindsay dared no farther, but lifted up his voice in the Indian way to summon a servant, "Qui hai?"# he called, "Qui hai?"

* Festival-making women.

"Whoever is there?"

He heard somewhere within the noise of a chair pushed back, and a door farther down the passage opened outwards, disclosing Laura Filbert with her hand upon the handle. She made a supple, graceful picture. "Good-evening, Mr. Lindsay," she said as he advanced. "Won't you come in?" She clung to the handle until he had passed into the room, then she closed the door after him. "I was expecting you," she said. "Mr. Harris, let me make you acquainted with Mr. Lindsay. Mr. Lindsay, Mr. Harris."

Mr. Harris was sitting sideways on one of the three cheap little chairs. He was a clumsily built youth, and he wore the private's garb of the Salvation Army. It was apparent that he had been reading a newspaper; he had a displeasing air of possession. At Laura's formula he looked up and nodded without amiability, folded his journal the other side out and returned to it.

"Please take a seat," Laura said, and Lindsay took one. He had a demon of self-consciousness that possessed him often, here he felt dumb. Nor did he in the very least expect Mr. Harris. He crossed his legs in greater discomfort than he had dreamed possible, looking at Laura, who sat down like a third stranger, curiously detached from any sense of hospitality.

"Mr. Lindsay is anxious about his soul, Mr. Harris," she said pleasantly. "I guess you can tell him what to do as well as I can."

"Oh!" Lindsay began, but Mr. Harris had the word. "Is he?" said Mr. Harris, without looking up from his paper. "Well, what I've got to say on that subject I say at the evenin' meetin', which is a proper an' a public place. He can hear it there any day of the week."

"I think I have already heard," remarked Lindsay, "what you have to say."

"Then that's all right," said Mr. Harris, with his eyes still upon his newspaper. He appeared to devour it. Laura looked from one to the other of them and fell upon an expedient.

"If you'll excuse me," she said, "I'll just get you that bicycle story you were kind enough to lend me, Mr. Harris, and you can take it with you. The Ensign's got it," and she left the room. Lindsay glanced round, and promptly announced to himself that he could not come there again. It was taking too violent an advantage. The pursuit of an angel does not imply that you may trap her in her corner under the Throne. The place was divided by a calico curtain, over which plainly showed the top of a mosquito curtain - she slept in there. On the walls were all tender texts about loving and believing and bearing others' burdens, interspersed with photographs, mostly of women with plain features and enthusiastic eyes, dressed in some strange costume of the Army in Madras, Ceylon, China. A little wooden table stood against the wall holding an album, a Bible and hymn-books, a work-basket and an irrelevant Japanese doll which seemed to stretch its absurd arms straight out in a gay little ineffectual heathen protest. There was another more embarrassing table: it had a coarse cloth; and was garnished with a loaf and butter-dish, a plate of plantains and a tin of marmalade, knives and teacups for a meal evidently impending. It was atrociously, sordidly intimate, with its core in Harris, who when Miss Filbert had well gone from the room looked up. "If you're here on private business," he said to Lindsay, fixing his eyes, however, on a point awkwardly to the left of him, "maybe you ain't aware that the Ensign" - he threw his head back in the direction of the next room - "is the person to apply to. She's in command here. Captain Filbert's only under her."

"Indeed?" said Lindsay. "Thanks."

"It ain't like it is in the Queen's army," Harris volunteered, still searching Lindsay's vicinity for a point upon which his eyes could permanently rest, "where, if you remember, Ensigns are the smallest officer we have."

"The commission is, I think, abolished," replied Lindsay, governing a deep and irritated frown.

"Maybe so. This Army don't pretend to pattern very close on the other - not in discipline anyhow," said Mr.

Harris with ambiguity. "But you'll find Ensign Sand very willing to do anything she can for you. She's a hard-working officer."

A sharp wail smote the air from a point close to the lath and canvas partition, on the other side, followed by hasty hushings and steps in the opposite direction. It enabled Lindsay to observe that Mrs. Sand seemed at present to be sufficiently engaged, at which Mr. Harris shifted one heavy limb over the other, and lapsed into silence, looking sternly at an advertisement. The air was full of their mutual annoyance, although Duff tried to feel amused. They were raging as primitively, under the red flannel shirt and the tan-coloured waistcoat with white silk spots, as two cave-men on an Early British coast; their only sophistication lay in Harris's newspaper and Lindsay's idea that he ought to find this person humorous. Then Laura came back and resolved the situation.

"Here it is," she said, handing the volume to Mr. Harris; "we have all enjoyed it. Thank you very much." There was in it the oddest mixture of the supreme feminine and the superior officer. Harris, as he took the book, had no alternative.

"Good-evening, then, Captain," said he, and went, stumbling at the door.

"Mr. Harris," said Laura equably, "found salvation about a month ago. He is a very steady young man - foreman in one of the carriage works here. He is now struggling with the tobacco habit, and he often drops in in the evening."

"He seems to be a - a member of the corps,"

said Lindsay.

"He would be, only for the carriage works. He says he doesn't find himself strong enough in grace to give up his situation yet. But he wears the uniform at the meetings to show his sympathy, and the Ensign doesn't think there's any objection."

Laura was sitting straight up in one of the cheap little chairs, her sari drawn over her head, her hands folded in her lap. The native dress clung to her limbs in sculpturable lines, and her consecrated ambitions seemed more insistent than ever. She had nothing to do with anything else, nothing to do with her room or its arrangements, nothing, Lindsay felt profoundly, to do with him. Her personal zeal for him seemed to resolve itself, at the point of contact, into something disappointingly thin; he saw that she counted with him altogether as a unit in a glorious total, and that he himself had no place in her knowledge or her desire. This brought him, with something like a shock, to a sense of how far he had depended on her interest for his soul's sake to introduce her to a wider view of him.

"But you have come to tell me about yourself," she said, suddenly it seemed to Lindsay, who was wrapped in the contemplation of her profile. "Well, is there any special stumbling-block?"

"There are some things I should certainly like you to know," replied Lindsay; "but you can't think how difficult - " he glanced at the lath and plaster partition, but she to whom publicity was a condition salutary, if not essential, to spiritual experience, naturally had no interpretation for that.

"I know it's sometimes hard to speak," she said; "Satan ties our tongues."

The misunderstanding was absurd, but he saw only its difficulties, knitting his brows.

"I fear you will find my story very strange and very mad," he said. "I cannot be sure that you will even listen to it."

"Oh," Laura said simply, "do not be afraid! I have heard confessions! I work at home, you see, a good deal among the hospitals, and - we do not shrink, you know, in the Army, from things like that."

"Good God!" he exclaimed, staring, "you don't think - you don't suppose - "

"Ah! don't say that! It's so like swearing."

As he sat in helpless anger, trying to formulate something intelligible, the curtain parted, and a sallow little Eurasian girl of eighteen, also in the dress of the Army, came through from the bedroom part. She smiled in a conscious, meaningless way, as she sidled past them. At the door her smile broadened, and as she closed it after her she gave them a little nod.

"That's my lieutenant," said Laura.

"The place is like a warren," Lindsay groaned. "How can we talk here?"

Laura looked at him gravely, as one making a diagnosis. "Do you think," she said, "a word of prayer would help you?"

"No," said Lindsay. "No, thank you. What is making me miserable," he added quietly, "is the knowledge that we are being overheard. If you go into the next room, I am quite certain you will find Mrs. Sand listening by the wall."

"She's gone out! She and the Captain and Miss De Souza, to take the evening meeting. Nobody is in there except the two children, and they are asleep." Her smile, he thought, made a Madonna of her. "Indeed, we are quite alone, you and I, in the flat now. So please don't be afraid, Mr. Lindsay! Say whatever is in your heart, and the mere saying - "

"Oh," Lindsay cried, "stop! Don't, for Heaven's sake, look at me in that light any longer. I'm not penitent. I'm not - what do you call it? - a soul under conviction. Nothing of the sort." He waited with considerateness for this to have its effect upon her; he could not go on until he saw her emerge, gasping, from the inundation of it. But she was not even staggered by it. She only looked down at her folded hands with an added seriousness and a touch of sorrow.

"Aren't you?" she said. "But at least you feel that you ought to be. I thought it had been accomplished. But I will go on praying."

"Shall you be very angry if I tell you that I'd rather you didn't? I want to come into your life differently - sincerely."

She looked at him with such absolute blankness that his resolution was swiftly overturned, and showed him a different face.

"I won't tell you anything about what I feel and what I want to-night except this - I find that you are influencing all my thoughts and all my days in what is to me a very new and a very happy way. You hear as much as that often, and from many people, don't you? So there is nothing in it that need startle you or make you uncomfortable." He paused, and she nodded in a visible effort to follow him.

"So I am here to-night to ask you to let me do something for you just for my own pleasure - there must be some way of helping you, and being your friend - "

"As Mr. Harris is," she interrupted. "I do influence Mr. Harris for good, I know. He says so."

"Influence me," he begged, "in any way you like."

"I will pray for you," she said. "I promise that."

"And you will let me see you sometimes?" he asked, conceding the point.

"If I thought it would do you any good" - she looked at him doubtfully, clasping and unclasping her hands; "I will see; I will ask for guidance. Perhaps it is one of His own appointed ways. If you have no objection, I will give you this little book, Almost Persuaded. I am sure you are almost persuaded. Above all, I hope you will go on coming to the meetings."

And in the course of the next two or three moments Lindsay found himself, somewhat to his astonishment, again in the night of the staircase, dismissed exactly as Mr. Harris had been, by the agency of a printed volume. Only in his case a figure of much angelic beauty stood at the top, holding a patent kerosene lamp high, to illumine his way. He refrained from looking back lest she should see something too human in his face, and vanish, leaving him in darkness which would be indeed impenetrable.

CHAPTER VII

There was a panic in Dhurrumtolla; a "ticca-gharry" - the shabby oblong box on wheels, dignified in municipal regulations as a hackney carriage - was running away. Coolie mothers dragged naked children up on the pavement with angry screams; drivers of ox-carts dug their lean beasts in the side, and turned out of the way almost at a trot; only the tram-car held on its course in conscious invincibility. A pariah tore along beside the vehicle barking; crows flew up from the rubbish heaps in the road by half-dozens, protesting shrilly; a pedlar of blue bead necklaces just escaped being knocked down. Little groups of native clerks and money-lenders stood looking after, laughing and speculating; a native policeman, staring also, gave them sharp orders to disperse, and they said to him, "Peace, brother." To each other they said, "Behold, the driver is a 'mut-wallah'" (or drunken person); and presently, as the thing whirled farther up the emptied perspective, "Lo! the syce has fallen." The driver was certainly very drunk; his whip circled perpetually above his head; the syce clinging behind was stiff with terror, and fell off like a bundle of rags. Inside, Hilda Howe, with a hand in the strap at each side and her feet against the opposite seat, swayed violently and waited for what might happen, breathing short. Whenever the gharry thrashed over the tram-lines, she closed her eyes. There was a point near Cornwallis Street where she saw the off front wheel make sickeningly queer revolutions; and another, electrically close, when two tossing roan heads with pink noses appeared in a gate to the left, heading smartly out, all unawares, at precisely right angles to her own derelict equipage. That was the juncture of the Reverend Stephen Arnold's interference, walking and discussing with Amiruddin Khan, as he was, the comparative benefits of Catholic and Mohammedan fasting. It would be easy to magnify what Stephen did in that interruption of the considerate hearing he was giving to Amiruddin. The ticca-gharry ponies were almost spent, and any resolute hand could have impelled them away from the carriage-pole with which the roans threatened to impale their wretched sides. The front wheel, however, made him heroic, going off at a tangent into a cloth merchant's shop, and precipitating a crash while he still clung to the reins. The door flew open on the under side, and Hilda fell through, grasping at the dust of the road; while the driver, discovering that his seat was no longer horizontal, entered suddenly upon sobriety, and clamoured with tears that the cloth-merchant should restore his wheel - was he not a poor man? Hilda, struggling with her hat-pins, felt her dress brushed by various lean hands of the bazar, and observed herself the central figure in yet another situation. When she was in a condition to see, she saw Arnold soothing the ponies; Amiruddin, before the vague possibility of police complication having slipped away. Stephen had believed the gharry empty. The sight of her, in her disordered draperies, was a revelation and a reproach.

"Is it possible!" he exclaimed, and was beside her. "You are not hurt?"

"Only scraped, thanks. I am lucky to get off with this."

She held up her right palm, broadly abraded round the base, where her hand had struck the road. Arnold took it delicately in his own thin fingers to examine it; an infinity of contrast rested in the touch. He looked at it with anxiety so obviously deep and troubled, that Hilda silently smiled. She who had been battered, as she said, twice round the world, found it disproportionate.

"It's the merest scratch," she said, grave again to meet his glance.

"Indeed, I fear not." The priest made a solicitous bandage with his handkerchief, while the circle about them solidified. "It is quite unpleasantly deep. You must let me take you at once to the nearest chemist's and get it properly washed and dressed, or it may give you a vast amount of trouble - but I am walking."

"I will walk too," Hilda said readily. "I should prefer it, truly." With her undamaged hand she produced a rupee from her pocket, where a few coins chinked casually, looked at it, and groped for another. "I really can't afford any more," she said. "He can get his wheel mended with that, can't he?"

"It is three times his fare," Arnold said austerely, "and he deserved nothing - but a fine, perhaps." The man was suppliant before them, cringing, salaaming, holding joined palms open. Hilda lifted her head and looked over the shoulders of the little rabble, where the sun stood golden upon the roadside and two naked children played with a torn pink kite. Something seemed to gather into her eyes as she looked, and when she fixed them softly upon Arnold, to speak, as it had spoken before.

"Ah," she said. "Our deserts."

It was the merest echo, and she had done it on purpose, but he could not know that, and as she dropped the rupees into the craving hands, and turned and walked away with him, he was held in a frightened silence. There was nothing perhaps that he wanted to talk of more than of his experience at the theatre; he longed to have it simplified and explained; yet in that space of her two words the impossibility of mentioning it had sprung at him and overcome him. He hoped, with instant fervour, that she would refrain from any allusion to The Offence of Galilee. And for the time being she did refrain. She said, instead, that her hand was smarting absurdly already, and did Arnold suppose the chemist would use a carbolic lotion? Stephen, with a guarded look, said very possibly not, but one never knew; and Hilda, thinking of the far-off day when the little girl of her was brought tactfully to disagreeable necessities; covered a preposterous impulse to cry with another smile.

A thudding of bare feet overtook them. It was the syce, with his arms full of thin paper bags, the kind that hold cheap millinery. "Oh, the good man!" Hilda exclaimed. "My parcels!" and looked on equably, while Arnold took them by their puckered ends. "I have been buying gold lace and things from Chunder Dutt for a costume," she explained. The bags dangled helplessly from Arnold's fingers; he looked very much aware of them. "Let me carry at least one," she begged. "I can perfectly with my parasol hand;" but he refused her even one. "If I may be permitted to take the responsibility," he said happily, and she rejoined, "Oh, I would trust you with things more fragile." At which, such is the discipline of these Orders, he looked steadily in front of him, and seemed deaf with modesty.

"But are you sure," said Hilda, suddenly considerate, "that it looks well?"

"Is the gold lace then so very meretricious?"

"It goes doubtfully with your cloth," she laughed, and instantly looked stricken with the conviction that she might better have said something else. But Arnold appeared to take it simply and to see no gibe in it, only a pleasant commonplace.

"It might look queer in Chowringhee," he said, "but this is not a censorious public." Then, as if to palliate the word, he added, "They will think me no more mad to carry paper bags than to carry myself, when it is plain that I might ride - and they see me doing that every day."

All the same the paper bags swinging beside the girdled black skirt did impart a touch of comedy, which was in a way a pity, since humour goes so far to destroy the picturesque. Hilda without the paper bags would have been vastly enough for contrast. She walked - one is inclined to dwell upon her steps and face the risk of being unintelligible - in a wide-sleeved gown of peach-coloured silk, rather frayed at the seams; a trifle spent in vulnerable places, surmounted by an extravagant collar and a Paris hat. The dress was of artistic intention inexpensively carried out, the hat had an accomplished chic; it had fallen to her in the wreck and ruin of a too ambitious draper of Coolgardie. As a matter of fact it was the only one she had. The wide sleeves ended a little below the elbow, and she carried in compensation a pair of long suede gloves, a compromise which only occasionally discovered itself buttonless, and a most expensive umbrella, the tribute of a gentleman in that line of business in Cape Town, whose standing advertisement is now her note of appreciation. Arnold in his unvarying gait paced beside her; he naturally shrank, so close to her opulence, into something less impressive than he was; a mere intelligence he looked, in a quaint uniform, with his long lip drawn down and pursed a little in this accomplishment of duty, and his eyes steadily in front of him. Hilda's lambent observation was everywhere, but most of all on him; a fleck of the dust from the road still lay upon the warm bloom of her cheek, a perpetual happy curve clung about her mouth. So they passed in streets of the thronging people, where yards of new-dyed cotton, purple and yellow, stretched drying in the sun, where a busy tom-tom called the pious to leave coppers before a blood-red, golden-tongued Kali, half visible through the door of a mud hut - where all the dealers in brass dishes and glass armlets and silver-gilt stands for the comfortable hubble-bubble, squatted in line upon their thresholds and accepted them with indifference. So they passed, worthy of a glance from that divinity who shapes our ends.

They talked of the accident. "You stopped the horses, didn't you?" Hilda said, and the speculation in her eyes was concerned with the extent to which a muscular system might dwindle, in that climate, under sacerdotal robes worn every day.

"I told them to stop, poor things," Arnold said; "they had hardly to be persuaded."

"But you didn't save my life or anything like that, did you?" she adventured like a vagrant in the sun. The blood was warm in her. She did not weigh her words. "I shouldn't like having my life saved. The necessity for feeling such a vast emotion - I shouldn't know how to cope with it."

"I will claim to have saved your other hand," he smiled. "You will be quite grateful enough for that."

She noted that he did not hasten, behind blushes, into the shelter of a general disavowal. The cassock seemed to cover an obligation to acknowledge things.

"I see," she said, veering round. "You are quite right to circumscribe me. There is nothing so boring as the gratitude that will out. It is only the absence of it, too plainly expressed, that is unpleasant. But you won't find that in me either." She gave him a smile as she lowered her parasol to turn into the shop of Lahiri Dey, licensed to sell European drugs, that promised infinite possibilities of friendship; and, he, following, took pleased and careful possession of it.

An hour later, as they approached Number Three, Lal Behari's Lane, Miss Howe looked pale, which is not surprising since they had walked and talked all the way. Their talk was a little strenuous too; it was as if they had fallen upon an opportunity, and, mutually, consciously made the most of it.

"You must have some tea immediately," Arnold said, before the battered urns and the dusty crotons of her dwelling.

"A little whisky and soda, I think. And you will come

up, please, and have some too. You must."

"Thanks," he said, looking at his watch. "If I do - "

"You'll have the soda without the whisky! All right!" she laughed, and led the way.

"This is vicious indulgence," Arnold said of his beverage, sitting under the inverted Japanese umbrellas. "I haven't been pitched out of a ticca-gharry."

It is doubtful whether the indulgence was altogether in the soda, which is, after all, ascetic in its quality, and only suitably effervescent, like ecclesiastical humour. It may very probably be that there was no indulgence; indeed, one is convinced that the word, like so many words, says too much. The springs of Arnold's chair were bursting through the bottom, and there were stains on its faded chintz-arms, but it was comfortable, and he leaned back in it, looking up at the paper umbrellas. You know the room; I took you into it with Duff Lindsay, who did not come there from rigidities and rituals, and who had a qualified pleasure in it. But there were lines in the folds of the flowered window-curtains dragging half a yard upon the floor, which seemed to disband Arnold's spirit, and a twinkle in the blue bead of a bamboo screen where the light came through that released it altogether. The shabby violent-coloured place encompassed him like an easy garment, and the lady with her feet tucked up on a sofa and a cushion under her tumbled head, was an unembarra-ssing invitation to the kind of happy things he had not said for years. They sat in the coolness of the room for half an hour, and then, after a little pause, Hilda said suddenly -

"I am glad you saw me in The Offence of Galilee on Saturday night. We shall not play it again."

"It has been withdrawn?"

"Yes. The rights, you know, really belong to Mr. Bradley; and he can't endure his part."

"Is there no one else to - "

"He objects to anyone else. We generally play together." This was inadvertent, but Stephen had no reason to imagine that she contracted her eyebrows in any special irritation. "It is an atrocious piece," she added.

"Is it?" he said absently, and then, "Yes, it is an atrocious piece. But I am glad, too, that I saw you."

He looked away from her, reddening deeply, and stood up. He bade her a measured and precise farewell. It seemed as if he hurried. She only half rose to give him her unwounded hand, and when he was gone she sank back again thoughtfully.

CHAPTER VIII

"I have outstayed all the rest," Lindsay said, with his hat and stick in his hand, in Alicia Livingstone's drawing-room, "because I want particularly to talk to you. They have left me precious little time," he added, glancing at his watch.

She had wondered when he came, early in the formal Sunday noon hour for men's calls, since he had more casual privileges; and wondered more when he sat on with composure, as one who is master of the situation, while Major-Generals and Deputy-Secretaries came and went. There was a mist in her brain as she talked to the Major-Generals and Deputy-Secretaries - it did not in the least obscure what she found to say - and in the midst of it the formless idea that he must wish to attach a special importance to his visit. This took shape and line when they were alone, and he spoke of out-sitting the others. It impelled her to walk to the window and open it. "You might stay to lunch," she said, addressing a pair of crows in altercation on the verandah.

"There is nearly half an hour before lunch," he said. "Can I convince you in that time, I wonder, that I'm not an absolute fool?"

Alicia turned and came back to her sofa. She may have

had a prevision of the need of support. "I hardly think," she said, drawing the long breath with which we try to subdue a tempest within, "that it would take so long." She looked with careful criticism at the violets in his buttonhole.

"I've had a supreme experience," he said, "very strange and very lovely. I am living in it, moving in it, speaking in it," he added quickly, watching her face; "so don't, for Heaven's sake, touch it roughly."

She lifted her hand in nervous, involuntary deprecation. "Why should you suppose I would touch it roughly?" There was that in her voice which cried out that she would rather not touch it at all; but Lindsay, on the brink of his confidence, could not suppose it, did not hear it. He knew her so well.

"A great many people will," he said. "I can't bear the thought of their fingers. That is one reason that brings me to you."

She faced him fully at this; her eyelids quivered, but she looked straight at him. It nerved her to be brought into his equation, even in the form which should finally be eliminated. She contrived a smile.

"I believe you know already," Lindsay cried.

"I have heard something. Don't be alarmed - not from people, from Miss Howe."

"Wonderful woman! I haven't told her."

"Is that always necessary? She has intuitions. In this case," Alicia went on, with immense courage, "I didn't believe them."

"Why?" he asked enjoyingly. Anything to handle his delight - he would even submit it to analysis.

She hesitated - her business was in great waters, the next instant might engulf her. "It's so curiously unlike you," she faltered. "If she had been a duchess - a very exquisite person, or somebody very clever - remember I haven't seen her."

"You haven't, so I must forgive you invidious comparisons." Lindsay visaged the words with a smile, but they had an articulated hardness.

Alicia raised her eyebrows.

"What do you expect one to imagine?" she asked, with quietness.

"A miracle," he said sombrely.

"Ah, that's difficult!"

There was silence for a moment between them, then she added perversely -

"And, you know, faith is not what it was."

Duff sat biting his lips. Her dryness irritated him. He was accustomed to find in her fields of delicately blooming enthusiasms, and running watercourses where his satisfactions were ever reflected. Suddenly she seemed to emerge to her own consciousness, upon a summit from which she could look down upon the turmoil in herself and beyond it, to where he stood.

"Don't make a mistake," she said. "Don't." She thrust her hand for a fraction of an instant toward him, and then swiftly withdrew it, gathering herself together to meet what he might say.

What he did say was simple, and easy to hear. "That's what everybody will tell me; but I thought you might understand." He tapped the toe of his boot with his stick as if he counted the strokes. She looked down and counted them too.

"Then you won't help me to marry her?" he said, definitely, at last.

"What could I do?" She twisted her sapphire ring. "Ask somebody else."

"Don't expect me to believe there is nothing you could do. Go to her as my friend. It isn't such a monstrous thing to ask. Tell her any good you know of me. At present her imagination paints me in all the lurid colours of the lost."

The face she turned upon him was all little sharp white angles, and the cloud of fair hair above her temples stood out stiffly, suggesting Celine and the curling tongs. She did not lose her elegance; the poise of her chin and shoulders was quite perfect, but he thought she looked too amusedly at his difficulty. Her negative, too, was more unsympathetic than he had any reason to expect.

"No," she said. "It must be somebody else. Don't ask me. I should become involved - I might do harm." She had surmounted her emotion; she was able to look at the matter with surprising clearness and decision. "I should do harm," she repeated.

"You don't count with her effect on you."

"You can't possibly imagine her effect on me. I'm not a man."

"But won't you take anything - about her - from me? You know I'm really not a fool - not even very impressionable?"

"Oh no!" she said impatiently. "No - of course not."

"Pray why?"

"There are other things to reckon with." She looked coldly beyond him out of the window. "A man's intelligence when he is in love - how far can one count on it?"

There was nothing but silence for that, or perhaps the murmured, "Oh, I don't agree," with which Lindsay met it. He rode down her logic with a simple appeal. "Then after all," he said, "you're not my friend."

It goaded her into something like an impertinence. "After you have married her," she said, "you'll see."

"You will be hers then," he declared.

"I will be yours." Her eyes leaped along the prospect and rested on a brass-studded Tartar shield at the other end of the room.

"And I thought you broad in these views," Lindsay said, glancing at her curiously. Her opportunity for defence was curtailed by a heavy step in the hall, and the lifted portiere disclosed Surgeon Major Livingstone, looking warm. He, whose other name was the soul of hospitality, made a profound and feeling remonstrance against Lindsay's going before tiffin, though Alicia, doing something to a bowl of nasturtiums, did not hear it. Not that her added protest would have detained Lindsay, who took his perturbation away with him as quickly as might be. Alicia saw the cloud upon him as he shook hands with her, and found it but slightly consoling to reflect that his sun would without doubt re-emerge in all effulgence on the other side of the door.

Mrs. Everard Cotes

CHAPTER IX

That same Sunday, Alicia had been able to say to Lindsay about Hilda Howe, "We have not stood still - we know each other well now," and when he commented with some reserve upon this to follow it up. "But these things have so little to do with mere length of time or number of opportunities," she declared. "One springs at some people."

A Major-General, interrupting, said he wished he had the chance; and they talked about something else. But perhaps this is enough to explain a note which went by messenger from the Livingstones' pillared palace in Middleton Street to Number Three, Lal Behari's Lane, on Monday morning. It was a short note, making a definite demand with an absence of colour and softness and emotion which was almost elaborate. Hilda, at breakfast, tore off the blank half sheet, and wrote in pencil -

"I think I can arrange to get her here about five this afternoon. No rehearsal - they're doing something to the gas-pipes at the theatre, so you will find me, anyway. And I'll be delighted to see you."

She twisted it up and addressed it, reconsidered that, and made the scrap more secure in a yellow envelope. It had an embossed post-office stamp, which she sacrificed with resignation. Then she went back to an extremely uninteresting vegetable curry, with the reflection - "Can she possibly imagine that one doesn't see it yet?"

Alicia came before five. She brought a novel of Gissing's, in order apparently that they might without fail talk about Gissing. Hilda was agreeable; she would talk about Gissing, or about anything, tipped on the edge of her bed - Alicia had surmounted that degree of intimacy at a bound by the declaration that she could no longer endure the blue umbrellas - and clasping one knee, with an uncertain tenure of a chipped bronze slipper deprived of its heel. Wonderful silk draperies fell about her, with ink-spots on the sleeves; her hair was magnificent.

"It's so curious to me," she was saying of the novel, "that anyone should learn all that life as you do, at a distance, in a book. It's like looking at it through the little end of an opera-glass."

"I fancy that the most desirable way," said Alicia, glancing at the door.

"Don't you believe it. The best way is to come out of it, to grow out of it. Then all the rest has the charm of novelty and the value of contrast, and the distinction of being the best. You, poor dear, were born an artificial flower in a cardboard box. But you couldn't help it."

"Everybody doesn't grow out of it." The concentration in Alicia's eyes returned again with vacillating wings.

"She can't be here for a quarter of an hour yet." The slipper dropped at this point, and Hilda stooped to put it on again. She kept her foot in her hands, and regarded it pensively.

"Shoes are the one thing one shouldn't buy in the native quarter," she continued; "at all events, ready-made."

"You have an audacity - " Alicia ended abruptly in a wan smile.

"Haven't I? Are you quite sure he wants to marry her?"

"I know it."

"From him?"

"From him."

"Oh!" - Hilda deliberated a moment nursing her slipper - "Really? Well, we can't let that happen."

"Why not?"

"You have a hardihood! Is no reason plain to you? Don't you see anything?"

Alicia smiled again painfully, as if against a tension of her lips. "I see only one thing that matters - he wants it," she said.

"And won't be happy till he gets it! Rubbish, my dear! We are an intolerably self-sacrificing sex." Hilda felt about for pillows, and stretched her length along the bed. "They've taught us well, the men; it's a blood disease now, running everywhere in the female line. You may be sure it was a barbarian princess that hesitated between the lady and the tiger. A civilised one would have introduced the lady and given her a dot, and retired to the nearest convent. Bah! It's a deformity, like the dachshund's legs."

Alicia looked as if this would be a little troublesome, and not quite worth while, to follow.

"The happiness of his whole life is involved," she said simply.

"Oh dear yes - the old story! And what about the happiness of yours? Do you imagine it's laudable, admirable, this attitude? Do you see yourself in it with pleasure? Have you got a sacred satisfaction of self-praise?"

Contempt accumulated in Miss Howe's voice, and sat in her eyes. To mark her climax she kicked her slippers over the end of the bed.

"It is idiotic - it's disgusting," she said.

Alicia caught a flash from her. "My attitude!" she cried. "What in the world do you mean? Do you always think in poses? I take no attitude. I care for him, and in that proportion I intend that he shall have what he wants - so far as I can help him to it. You have never cared for anybody - what do you know about it?"

Hilda took a calm, unprejudiced view of the ceiling. "I assure you I'm not an angel," she cried. "Haven't I cared! Several times."

"Not really - not lastingly."

"I don't know about really; certainly not lastingly. I've never thought the men should have a monopoly of nomadic susceptibilities. They entail the prettiest experiences."

"Of course, in your profession - "

"Don't be nasty, sweet lady. My affections have never taken the opportunities of our profession. They haven't even carried me into matrimony, though I remember once, at Sydney, they brought me to the brink! We must contrive an escape for Duff Lindsay."

"You assume too much - a great deal too much. She must be beautiful - and good."

"Give me a figure. She's a lily, and she draws the kind of beauty that lilies have from her personal chastity and her religious enthusiasm. Touch those things and bruise them, as - as marriage would touch and bruise them - and she would be a mere fragment of stale vegetation. You want him to clasp that to his bosom for the rest of his life?"

"I won't believe you. You're coarse and you're cruel."

Tears flashed into Miss Livingstone's eyes with this. Hilda, still regarding the ceiling, was aware of them, and turned an impatient shoulder while they should be brushed undetected away.

"I'm sorry, dear," she said. "I forgot. You are usually so intelligent, one can be coarse and cruel with comfort, talking to you. Go into the bathroom and get my salts - they're on the washhand-stand - will you? I'm quite faint with all I'm about to undergo."

Laura Filbert came in as Alicia emerged with the salts. Ignoring the third person with the bottle, she went directly to the bedside and laid her hand on Hilda's head.

"Oh Miss Howe, I am so sorry you are sick - so sorry," she said. It was a cooing of professional concern, true to an ideal, to a necessity.

"I am not very bad," Hilda improvised. "Hardly more than a headache."

"She makes light of everything," Miss Filbert said, smiling toward Alicia, who stood silent, the prey of her impression. Discovering the blue salts bottle, Laura walked over to her and took it from her hands.

"And what," said the barefooted Salvation Army girl to Miss Livingstone, "might your name be?"

There was an infinite calm interest in it - it was like a conventionality of the other world, and before its assurance Alicia stood helpless.

"Her name is Livingstone," called Hilda from the bed, "and she is as good as she is beautiful. You needn't be troubled about HER soul - she takes Communion every Sunday morning at the Cathedral."

"Hallelujah!" said Captain Filbert, in a tone of dubious congratulation.

"Much better," said Hilda cheerfully, "to take it at the Cathedral, you know, than nowhere."

Miss Filbert said nothing to this, but sat down upon the

edge of the bed, looking serious, and stroked Hilda's hair.

"You don't seem to have much fever," she said. "There was a poor fellow in the Military Hospital this morning with a temperature of one hundred and seven. I could hardly bear to touch him."

"What was the matter?" asked Hilda idly, occupied with hypotheses about the third person in the room.

"Oh, I don't know exactly. Some complication, I suppose, of Satan's tribute - "

"Divinest Laura!" Hilda interposed quickly, drawing her head back. "Do take a chair. It will be even more soothing to see you comfortable."

Captain Filbert spoke again to Alicia, as she obeyed. "Miss Howe is more thoughtful for others than some of our converted ones," she said, with vast kindness. "I have often told her so. I have had a long day."

"It may improve me in that character," Hilda said, "to suggest that if you will go about such people, a little carbolic disinfectant is a good thing, or a crystal or two of permanganate of potash in your bath. Do you use those things?"

Laura shook her head. "Faith is better than disinfectants. I never get any harm. My Master protects me."

"My goodness!" Hilda said. And in the silence that occurred, Captain Filbert remarked that the only thing she used carbolic acid for was a decayed tooth. Presently Alicia made a great effort. She laid hands on

Hilda's previous reference as a tangibility that remained with her.

"Do you ever go to the Cathedral?" she said.

The faintest shade of dogmatism crossed Captain Filbert's features, as when on a day of cloud fleeces the sun withdraws for an instant from a flower. Since her sect is proclaimed beyond the boundaries of dogma it may have been some other obscurity, but that was the effect.

"No. I never go there. We raise our own Ebenezer; we are a tabernacle to ourselves."

"Isn't it exquisite - her way of speaking!" cried Hilda from the bed, and Laura glanced at her with a deprecating, reproachful smile, in reproof of an offence admittedly incorrigible. But she went on as if she were conscious of a stimulus.

"Wherever the morning sky bends or the stars cluster is sanctuary enough," she said; "a slum at noonday is as holy for us as daisied fields; the Name of the Lord walks with us. The Army is His Army, He is Lord of our hosts."

"A kind of chant," murmured Hilda, and Miss Livingstone became aware that she might if she liked play with the beginnings of magnetism. Then that impression was carried away as it were on a puff of air, and it is hardly likely that she thought of it again.

"I suppose all the elite go to the Cathedral?" Laura said. The sanctity of her face was hardly disturbed, but a curiosity rested upon it, and behind the curiosity a far-off little, leaping tongue of some other thing. Hilda on the bed named it the constant feminine, and narrowed her eyes.

"Dear me, yes," she said for Alicia. "His Excellency the Viceroy and all his beautiful A.D.C.'s, no end of military and their ladies, Secretaries to the Government of India in rows, fully choral, Under-Secretaries so thick they're kept in the vestibule till the bells stop. 'And make Thy chosen people joyful'!" she intoned. "Not forgetting Surgeon-Major and Miss Alicia Livingstone, who occupy the fourth pew to the right of the main aisle, advantageously near the pulpit."

"You know already what a humbug she is," Alicia said, but Captain Filbert's inner eye seemed retained by that imaginary congregation.

"Well, it wouldn't be any attraction for me," she said, rising to go through the little accustomed function of her departure. "I'll be going now, I think. Ensign Sand has fever again, and I have to take her place at the Believers' Meeting." She took Hilda's hand in hers and held it for an instant. "Good-bye, and God bless you - in the way you most need," she said, and turned to Alicia, "Good-bye. I am glad to know that we will be one in the glad hereafter though our paths may diverge" - her eye rested with acknowledgment upon Alicia's embroidered sleeves - "in this world. To look at you I should have thought you were of the bowed down ones, not yet fully assured, but perhaps you only want a little more oxygen in the blood of your religion. Remember the word of the Lord - 'Rejoice! again I say unto you, rejoice!' Goodbye."

She drew her head-covering farther forward, and

moved to the door. It sloped to her shoulders and made them droop; her native clothes clung about her breast and her hips in the cringing Oriental way. Miss Howe looked after her guest with a curl of the lip as uncontrollable as it was unreasonable. "A saved soul, perhaps. A woman - oh, assuredly," she said in the depths of her hair.

The door had almost closed upon Captain Filbert when Alicia made something like a dash at an object about to elude her. "Oh," she exclaimed, "wait a minute. Will you come and see me? I think - I think you might do me good. I live at Number Ten, Middleton Street. Will you come?"

Laura came back into the room. There was a little stiffness in her air, as if she repressed something.

"I have no objection," she said.

"To-morrow afternoon - at five? Or - my brother is dining at the club - would you rather come to dinner?"

"Whichever is agreeable to you will suit me." She spoke carefully, after an instant's hesitation.

"Then do come and dine - at eight," Alicia said; and it was agreed.

She stood staring at the door when Laura finally closed it, and only turned when Hilda spoke.

"You are going to have him to meet her," she said. "May I come too?"

"Certainly not." Alicia's grasp was also by this time on

the door handle.

"Are you going too? You daren't talk about her!" Hilda cried.

"I'm going too. I've got the brougham. I'll drive her home," said Alicia, and went out swiftly.

"My goodness!" Hilda remarked again. Then she got up and found her slippers and wrote a note, which she addressed to the Reverend Stephen Arnold, Clarke Mission House, College Street. "Thanks immensely," it ran, "for your delightful offer to introduce me to Father Jordan and persuade him to show me the astronomical wonders he keeps in his tower at St. Simeon's. An hour with a Jesuit is an hour of milk and honey, and belonging to that charming Order, he won't mind my coming on a Sunday evening - the first clear one."

Miss Howe signed her note and bit consideringly at the end of her pen. Then she added: "If you have any influence with Duff Lindsay, it may be news to you that you can exert it with advantage to keep him from marrying a cheap ethereal little religieuse of the Salvation Army named Filbert. It may seem more fitting that you should expostulate with her, but I don't advise that."

CHAPTER X

The door of Ensign Sand's apartment stood open with a purposeful air when Captain Filbert reached headquarters that evening; but in any case it is likely that she would have gone in. Mrs. Sand walked the floor, carrying a baby, a pale sticky baby with blotches, which had inherited from its maternal parent a conspicuous lack of buttons. Mrs. Sand's room was also ornamented with texts, but they had apparently been selected at random, and they certainly hung that way. The piety of the place seemed at the control of an older infant, who sat on the floor and played with his father's regimental cap. On the other side of the curtain Captain Sand audibly washed himself and brushed his hair.

"What kind of meetin' did you have?" asked Mrs. Sand. "There - there now; he shall have his bottle, so he shall!"

"A beautiful meeting. Abraham Lincoln White, the Savannah negro, you know, came as a believer for the first time, and so did Miss Rozario from Whiteaway and Laidlaw's. We had such a happy time."

"What sort of collection?"

Laura opened a knotted handkerchief and counted out

Mrs. Everard Cotes

some copper coins.

"Only seven annas three pice! And you call that a good meeting! I don't believe you exhorted them to give!"

"Oh, I think I did!" Laura returned mechanically.

"Seven annas and three pice! And you know what the Commissioner wrote out about our last quarter's earnings! What did you say?"

"I said - I said the collection would now be taken up," Laura faltered.

"Oh dear! oh dear! Leopold, stop clawing me! Couldn't you think of anythin' more tellin' or more touchin' than that? Fever or no fever, it does not do for me to stay away from the regular meetin's. One thing is plain - HE wasn't there!"

"Who?"

"Well, you've never told me his name, but I expect you've got your reasons." Mrs. Sand's tone was not arch, but slightly resentful. "I mean the gentleman that attends so regular and sits behind, under the window. A society man, I should say, to look at him, though the officers of this Army are no respecters of persons, and I don't suppose the Lord takes any notice of his clothes."

"His name is Mr. Lindsay. No, he wasn't there."

The girl's tone was distant and cold. The rebuke about the collection had gone home to a place raw with similar reproaches.

"I hope you haven't been discouraging him?"

Captain Filbert looked at her superior officer with astonishment.

"I have entreated him to come to the meetings. But he never attends a Believers' Rally. Why should he?"

"What's his state of mind? He came to see you, didn't he, the other night?"

"Yes, he did. I don't think he's altogether careless."

"Ain't he seeking?"

"He wouldn't admit it, but he may not know himself. The Lord has different ways of working. What else should bring him, night after night?"

Mrs. Sand glanced meaningly at a point on the floor, with lifted eyebrows, then at her officer, and finally hid a badly-disciplined smile behind her baby's head. When she looked back again Laura had flushed all over, and an embarrassment stood between them, which she felt was absurd.

"My!" she said, - scruples in breaking it could hardly perhaps have been expected of her, - "you do look nice when you've got a little colour. But if you can't see that it's you that brings him to the meetin's, you must be blind, that's all."

Captain Filbert's confusion was dispelled, as by the wave of a wand.

"Then I hope I may go on bringing him," she said. "He

Mrs. Everard Cotes

couldn't come to a better place."

"Well, you'll have to be careful," said Mrs. Sand, as if with severe intent. "But I don't say discourage him; I wouldn't say that. You may be an influence for good. It may be His will that you should be pleasant to the young man. But don't make free with him. Don't, on any account, have him put his arm round your waist."

"Nobody has done that to me," Laura replied austerely, "since I left Putney, and so long as I am in the Army nobody will. Not that Mr. Lindsay" (she blushed again) "would ever want to. The class he belongs to look down on it."

"The class he belongs to do worse things. The Army doesn't look down on it. It's only nature, and the Army believes in working with nature. If it was Mr. Harris I wouldn't say a word - he marches under the Lord's banner."

Captain Filbert listened without confusion; her expression was even slightly complacent.

"Well," she said, "I told Mr. Harris last evening that the Lieutenant and I couldn't go on giving him so much of our time, and he seemed to think he'd been keeping company with me. I had to tell him I hadn't any such idea."

"Did he seem much disappointed?"

"He said he thought he would have more of the feeling of belonging to the Army if he was married in it; but I told him he would have to learn to walk alone."

Mrs. Sand speculatively bit her lips.

"I don't know but what you did right," she said. "By the grace of God you converted him, and he hadn't ought to ask more of you. But I have a kind of feeling that Mr. Lindsay 'll be harder to convince."

"I daresay."

"It would be splendid, though, to garner him in. He might be willing to march with us and subscribe half his pay, like poor Captain Corby, of the Queen's army, did in Rangoon."

"He might be proud to."

"We must all try and bring sin home to him," Mrs. Sand remarked with rising energy; "and don't you go saying anything to him hastily. If he's gone on you - "

"Oh Ensign! let us hope he is thinking of higher things! Let us both pray for him. Let Captain Sand pray for him too, and I'll ask the Lieutenant. Now that she's got Miss Rozario safe into the kingdom, I don't think she has any special object."

"Oh yes, we'll pray for him," Ensign Sand returned, as if that might have gone without saying, "but you - "

"And give me that precious baby. You must be completely worn out. I should enjoy taking care of him; indeed I should."

"It's the first - the very first - time she ever took that draggin' child out of my arms for an instant," the Ensign remarked to her husband and next in command later in the evening, but she resigned the infant without protest at the time. Laura carried him into her own room with something like gaiety, and there repeated to him more nursery rhymes, dating from secular Putney, than she would have believed she remembered.

The Believers' Rally, as will be understood, was a gathering of some selectness. If the Chinaman came, it was because of the vagueness of his perception of the privileges he claimed; and his ignorance of all tongues but his own left no medium for turning him out. Qualms of conscience, however, kept all Miss Rozario's young lady friends away, and these also doubtless operated to detain Duff Lindsay. One does not attend a Believers' Rally unless one's personal faith extends beyond the lady in command of it, and one specially refrains if one's spiritual condition is a delicate and debatable matter with her. In Wellesley Square, later in the evening, the conditions were different. It would not be easy to imagine a scene that suggested greater liberality of sentiment. The moon shed her light upon it, and the palms threw fretted shadows down. Beyond them, on four sides, lines of street-lamps shone, and tram-drivers whistled bullock-carts off the lines, and street pedlars lifted their cries. A torch marked the core of the group of exhorters; it struck pale gold from Laura's hair, and made glorious the buttons of the man who beat the drum. She talked to the people in their own language; the "open air" was designed for the people. "Kiko! Kiko!" (Why! Why!) Lindsay heard her cry, where he stood in the shadow, on the edge of the crowd. He looked down at a coolie-woman with shrivelled breasts crouched on her haunches upon the ground, bent with the toil of half a century, and back at the girl beside the torch. "Do not delay until to-morrow!" Laura besought them. "Kul ka dari mut karo!" A sensation of disgust assailed him; he turned away. Then, in an impulse of atonement - he felt already so responsible for her - he went back and dropped a coin into the coolie creature's lap. But he grew more miserable as he stood, and finally walked deliberately to a wooden bench at a distance where he could not hear her voice. Only the hymn pursued him; they sang presently a hymn. In the chorus the words were distinguishable, borne in the robust accents of Captain Sand -

"Us ki ho tarif,
Us ki ho tarif!"

The strange words, limping on the familiar air, made a barbarous jangle, a discordance of a specially intolerable sort.

"Glory to His name!
Glory to His name!"

Lindsay wondered, with a poignancy of pity, whether the coolie-woman were singing too, and found something like relief in the questionable reflection that if she wasn't, in view of the rupee, she ought to be.

His "Good-evening!" when the meeting was over, was a cheerful, general salutation, and the familiarity of the sight of him was plain in the response he got, equally general and equally cheerful. Lieutenant Da Cruz's smile was even further significant, if he had thought of interpreting it, and there was overt amiability in the manner in which Ensign Sand put her hymn-books together and packed everybody, including her husband, whose arm she took, out of the way.

"Wait for me," Laura said, to whom a Eurasian beggar made elaborate appeal, as they moved off.

"I guess you've got company to see you home," Mrs. Sand called out, and they did not wait. As Lindsay came closer the East Indian paused in his tale of the unburied wife for whom he could not afford a coffin, and slipped away.

"The Ensign knows she oughtn't to talk like that," Laura said. Lindsay marked with a surge of pleasure that she was flushed, and seemed perturbed.

"What she said was quite true," he ventured.

"But - anybody would think - "

"What would anybody think? Shall we keep to this side of the road? It's quieter. What would anybody think?"

"Oh, silly things." Laura threw up her head with a half laugh. "Things I needn't mention."

Lindsay was silent for an instant. Then "Between us?" he asked, and she nodded.

Their side of the street, along the square, was nearly empty. He found her hand and drew it through his arm. "Would you mind so very much," he said, "if those silly things were true?" He spoke as if to a child. His passion was never more clearly a single object to him, divorced from all complicating and non-essential impressions of her. "I would give all I possess to have it so," he told her, catching at any old foolish phrase that would serve.

"I don't believe you mean anything like all you say, Mr. Lindsay." Her head was bent and she kept her hand within his arm. He seemed to be a circumstance that brought her reminiscences of how one behaved sentimentally toward a young man with whom there was no serious entanglement. It is not surprising that he saw only one thing, walls going down before him, was aware only of something like invitation. Existence narrowed itself to a single glowing point; as he looked it came so near that he bounded to meet it.

"Dear," he said, "you can't know - there is no way of telling you - what I mean. I suppose every man feels the same thing about the woman he loves; but it seems to me that my life had never known the sun until I saw you. I can't explain to you how poor it was, and I won't try; but I fancy God sends every one of us, if we know it, some one blessed chance, and He did more for me - He lifted the veil of my stupidity and let me see it, passing by in its halo, trailing clouds of glory. I don't want to make you understand, though - I want to make you promise. I want to be absolutely sure from to-night that you'll marry me. Say that you'll marry me - say it before we get to the crossing. Say it, Laura." She listened to his first words with a little half-controlled smile, then made as if she would withdraw her hand, but he held it with his own, and she heard him through, walking beside him formally on her bare feet, and looking carefully at the asphalt pavement as they do in Putney.

"I don't object to your calling me by my given name," she said when he had done, "but it can't go any further than that, Mr. Lindsay, and you ought not to bring God into it - indeed you ought not. You are no son or servant of His - you are among those whose very light is darkness, and how great is your darkness!"

"Don't," he said shortly. "Never mind about that - now. You needn't be afraid of me, Laura - there are decent chaps, you know, outside your particular Kingdom of Heaven, and one of them wants you to marry him, that's how it is. Will you?"

"I don't wish to judge you, Mr. Lindsay, and I'm very much obliged, but I couldn't dream of it."

"Don't dream of it; consider it, accept it. Why, dear creature, you are mine already - don't you feel that?"

Her arm was certainly warm within his and he had the possession of his eyes in her. Her tired body even clung to him. "Are you quite sure you haven't begun to think of loving me?" he demanded.

"It isn't a question of love, Mr. Lindsay, it's a question of the Army. You don't seem to think the Army counts for anything."

One is convinced that it wasn't a question of love, the least in the world; but Lindsay detected an evasion in what she said, and the flame in him leaped up.

"Sweet, when love is concerned there is no other question."

"Is that a quotation?" she asked. She spoke coldly, and this time she succeeded in withdrawing her hand. "I daresay you think the Army very common, Mr. Lindsay, but to me it is marching on a great and holy crusade, and I march with it. You would not ask me to give up my life-work?"

"Only to take it into another sphere," Duff said unreflectingly. He was checked, but not discouraged; impatient, but in no wise cast down. She had not flown, she walked beside him placidly. She had no intention of flight. He tried to resign himself to the task of beating down her trivial objections, curbing his athletic impulse to leap over them.

"Another sphere," - he caught a subtle pleasure in her enunciation. "I suppose you mean high society; but it would never be the same."

"Not quite the same. You would have to drive to see your sinners in a carriage and pair, and you might be obliged to dine with them in - what do ladies generally dine in? - white satin and diamonds, or pearls. I think I would rather see you in pearls." He was aware of the inexcusableness of the points he made, but he only stopped to laugh inwardly at their impression, watching the absorbed turn of her head.

"We might think it well to be a little select in our sinners - most of them would be on Government House list, just as most of your present ones are on the lists of the charitable societies or the police magistrates. But you would find just as much to do for them."

"I should not even know how to act in such company."

"You can go home for a year, if you like, to be taught, to some people I know; delightful people, who will understand. A year! You will learn in three months - what odds and ends there are to know. I couldn't spare you for a year."

Lindsay stopped. He had to. Captain Filbert was

murmuring the cadences of a hymn. She went through two stanzas, and covered her eyes for a moment with her hand. When she spoke it was in a quiet, level, almost mechanical way. "Yes," she said. "The Cross and the Crown, the Crown and the Cross. Father in heaven, I do not forget Thy will and Thy purpose, that I should bring the word of Thy love to the poor and the lowly, the outcast and those despised. And what I say to this man, who offers me the gifts and the gladness of a world that had none for Thee, is the answer Thou hast put in my heart - that the work is Thine and that I am Thine, and he has no part or lot in me, nor can ever have. Here is Crooked Lane. Good-night, Mr. Lindsay." She had slipped into the devious darkness of the place before he could find any reply, before he quite realised, indeed, that they had reached her lodging. He could only utter a vague "Goodnight," after her, formulating more definite statements to himself a few minutes later, in Bentinck Street.

CHAPTER XI

Miss Howe was walking in the business quarter of Calcutta. It was the business quarter, yet the air was gay with the dimpling of piano notes, and looking up one saw the bright sunlight fall on yellow stuccoed flats above the shops and the offices. There the pleasant north wind blew banners of muslin curtains out of wide windows, and little gardens of palms in pots showed behind the balustrades of the flat roofs whenever a storey ran short. Everywhere was a subtle contagion of momentary well-being, a sense of lifted burden. The stucco streets were too slovenly to be purely joyous, but a warm satisfaction brooded in them, the pariahs blinked at one genially, there was a note of cheer even in the cheeling of the kites where they sat huddled on the roof-cornices or circled against the high blue sky. It was enjoyable to be abroad, in the brushing fellowship of the pavements, in touch with brown humility half-clad and going afoot, since even brown humility seemed well affected toward the world, alert and content. The air was full of the comfortable flavour of food-stuffs and spiced luxuries, and the incense of wayside trees; it was as if the sun laid a bland compelling hand upon the city, bidding strange flowers bloom and strange fruits increase. Brokers' gharries rattled past, each holding a pale young man preoccupied with a notebook; where the bullock-carts gathered themselves together and

Mrs. Everard Cotes

blocked the road the pale young men put excited heads out of the gharry windows and used remarkable imprecations. One of them, as Hilda turned into the compound of the Calcutta Chronicle, leaned out to take off his hat, and sent her up to the office of that journal in the pleasant reflection of his infinite interest in life. "Upon my word," she said to herself as she ascended the stairs behind the lean legs of a Mussulman servant in a dirty shirt and an embroidered cap, "he's so lighthearted, so genial, that one doubts the very tremendous effect even of a failure like the one he contemplates."

She sent her card in to the manager-sahib by the lean Mussulman, and followed it past the desks of two or three Bengali clerks, who hardly lifted their well-oiled heads from their account-books to look at her - so many mem sahibs to whose enterprises the Chronicle gave prominence came to see the manager-sahib, and they were so much alike. At all events they carried a passport to indifference in the fact that they all wanted something, and it was clear to the meanest intelligence that they appeared to be more magnificent than they were, visions in dazzling complexions and long kid gloves, rattling up in third-class ticca-gharries, with a wisp of fodder clinging to their skirts. It was less interesting still when they belonged to the other class, the shabby ladies, nearly always in black, with husbands in the Small Cause Court, or sons before the police magistrate, who came to get it, if possible, "kept out of the paper." Successful or not these always wept on their way out, and nothing could be more depressing. The only gleam of entertainment to be got out of a lady visitor to the manager-sahib occurred when the female form enshrined the majestic personality of a boarding-house madam, whose asylum for respectable young men in leading Calcutta firms had been maliciously traduced in the local columns of the Chronicle - a lady who had never known what a bailiff looked like in the lifetime of her first husband, or her second either. Then at the sound of a pudgy blow upon a table, or high abusive accents in the rapid elaborate cadences of the domiciled East Indian tongue, Hari Babu would glance at Gobind Babu with a careful smile, for the manager-sahib who dispensed so much galli* was now receiving the same, and defenceless.

* Abuse.

The manager sat at his desk when Hilda went in. He did not rise - he was one of those highly sagacious little Scotchmen that Dundee exports in such large numbers to fill small posts in the East, and she had come on business. He gave her a nod, however, and an affectionate smile, and indicated with his blue pencil a chair on the other side of the table. He had once made three hundred rupees in tea shares, and that gave him the air of a capitalist and speculator gamely shrewd. Tapping the table with his blue pencil he asked Miss Howe how the world was using HER.

"Let me see," said Hilda, a trifle absent-mindedly, "were you here last cold weather - I rather imagine you were, weren't you?"

"I was; I had the pleasure of - "

"To be sure. You got the place in December, when that poor fellow Baker died. Baker was a country-bred I know, but he always kept his contracts, while you got your po-lish in Glesca, and your name is Macphairson

- isn't it?"

"I was never in Glasgow in my life, and my name is Macandrew," said the manager, putting with some aggressiveness a paper-weight on a pile of bills.

"Never mind," said Hilda, again wrapped in thought, "don't apologise - it's near enough. Well, Mr. Macandrew," - her tone came to a point, - "what is the Stanhope Company's advertisement worth a month to the Chronicle?"

"A hundred rupees maybe - there or thereabouts;" and Mr. Macandrew, with a vast show of indifference, picked up a letter and began to tear at the end of it.

"One hundred and fifty-five I think, to be precise. That communication will wait, won't it? What is it - Kally Nath Mitter's paper and stores bill? You won't be able to pay it any quicker if we withdraw our advertisement."

"Why should ye withdraw it?"

"It was given to you on the understanding that notices should appear of every Wednesday and Saturday's performance. For two Wednesdays there has been no notice, and last Saturday night you sent a fool."

"So Muster Stanhope thinks o' withdrawin' his advertisement?"

"He is very much of that mind."

The manager put his thumbs in the armholes of his waistcoat, leaned back in his chair, and demonstrated the principle that had given him a gold watch chain - "never be bluffed."

"Ye can withdraw it," he said, with a warily experimental eye upon her.

"How reasonable of you not to make a fuss! We'll have the order to discontinue in writing, please. If you'll give me a pen and paper - thanks - and I'll keep a copy."

"Stanhope has wanted to transfer it to the Market Gazette for some time," she went on as she wrote.

"That's not a newspaper. You'll get no notices there."

"Cheaper on that account, probably."

"They charge like the very deevil. D'ye know the rates of them?"

"I can't say I do."

"There's a man on our staff that doesn't like your show. We'll be able to send him every night now."

"When we withdraw our advertisement?"

"Just then."

"All right," said Hilda. "It will be interesting to point out in the Indian Empire the remarkable growth of independent criticism in the Chronicle since Mr. Stanhope no longer uses the space at his disposal. I hope your man will be very nasty indeed. You might as well hand over the permanent passes - the gentleman will expect, I suppose, to pay."

"They'll be in the yeditorial department," said Mr. Macandrew, but he did not summon a messenger to go for them. Instead he raised his eyebrows in a manner that expressed the necessity of making the best of it, and humorously scratched his head.

"We have four hundred pounds of new type coming out in the Almora - she's due on Thursday," he said. "Entirely for the advertisements. We'll have a fine display next week. It's grand type - none of your Calcutta-made stuff."

"Pays to bring it out, does it?" asked Hilda inattentively, copying her letter.

"Pays the advertisers." There were ingratiating qualities in the managerial smile. Hilda inspected them coldly.

"There's your notice of withdrawal," she said. "Good-morning."

"Think of that new type, and how lovely Jimmy Finnigan's ad will look in it."

"That's all right. Good-morning." Miss Howe approached the door, the blue glance of Macandrew pursuant.

"No notices for two Wednesdays, eh? We'll have to see about that. I was thinkin' of transferrin' your space to the third page; it's a more advantageous position - and no extra charge - but ye'll not mention it to Jimmy."

Miss Howe lifted an arrogant chin. "Do I understand you'll do that, and guarantee regular notices, if we leave the advertisement with you?"

Mr. Macandrew looked at her expressively, and tore, with a gesture of moderated recklessness, the notice of withdrawal in two.

"Rest easy," he said, "I'll see about it. I'd go the len'th of attendin' myself to-night, if ye could spare two three extra places."

"Moderate Macandrew!"

"Moderate enough. I've got some frien's stayin' in the same place with me from Behar - indigo people. I was thinkin' I'd give them a treat, if three places c'd be spared next to the Chronicle seats."

"We do Lady Whippleton to-night and the booking's been heavy. Five is too many, Mr. Macandrew, even if you promised not to write the notice yourself."

"I might pay for one;" Macandrew drew red cartwheels on his blotting-pad.

"Those seats are sure to be gone. I'll send you a box. Stanhope's as bad as he can be with dysentery - you might make a local out of that. Be sure to mention he can't see anybody - it's absurd the way Calcutta people want to be paid."

"A box'll be Grand," said Mr. Macandrew. "I'll see ye get plenty of ancores. Can ye manage the door? Good-day, then."

Hilda stepped out on the landing. The heavy, regular thud of the presses came up from below. They were printing the edition that took the world's news to planters' bungalows in the jungle of Assam and the lonely policeman on the edge of Manipore. The smell of the newspaper of to-day and of yesterday, and of a year ago, stood in the air; through an open door she saw the dusty, uneven edges of files of them, piled on the floor. Three or four messengers squatted beside the wall, with slumbrous heads between their knees. Occasionally a shout came from the room inside, and one of them, crying "Hazur!" with instant alacrity, stretched himself mightily, loafed upon his feet and went in, emerging a moment later carrying written sheets, with which he disappeared into the regions below. The staircase took a lazy curve and went up; under it, through an open window, the sun glistened upon the shifting white and green leaves of a pipal tree, and a crow sat on the sill and thrust his grey head in with caws of indignant expostulation. A Government peon in scarlet and gold ascended the stair at his own pace, bearing a packet with an official seal. The place, with its ink-smeared walls and high ceilings, spoke between dusty yawns of the languor and the leisure which might attend the manipulation of the business of life, and Hilda paused for an instant to perceive what it said. Then she walked behind her card into the next room, where a young gentleman, reading proofs in his shirt sleeves, flung himself upon his coat and struggled into it at her approach. He seemed to have the blackest hair and the softest eyes and the neatest moustache available, all set in a complexion frankly olive, amiable English cut, in amiable Oriental colour, and the whole illumined, when once the coat was on and the collar perfectly turned down, by the liveliest, most engaging smile. Standing with his head slightly on one side and one hand resting on the table, while the other saw that nothing was disarranged between collar and top waistcoat button, he was an interjection point of invitation and attention.

"The Editor of the Chronicle?" Hilda asked with diffident dignity, and very well informed to the contrary.

"NOT the editor - I am sorry to say." The confession was delightfully vivid - in the plenitude of his candour it was plain that he didn't care who knew that he was sorry he was not the editor. "In journalistic parlance, the sub editor," he added. "Will you be seated, Miss Howe?" and with a tasteful silk pocket handkerchief he whisked the bottom of a chair for her.

"Then you are Mr. Molyneux Sinclair," Hilda declared. "You have been pointed out to me on several first nights. Oh, I know very well where the Chronicle seats are!"

Mr. Sinclair bowed with infinite gratification, and tucked the silk handkerchief back so that only a fold was visible. "We members of the Fourth Estate are fairly well known, I'm afraid, in Calcutta," he said. "Personally, I could sometimes wish it were otherwise. But certainly not in this instance."

Hilda gave him a gay little smile. "I suppose the editor," she said, with a casual glance about the room, "is hammering out his leader for to-morrow's paper. Does he write half and do you write half, or how do you manage?"

A seriousness overspread Mr. Sinclair's countenance,

which nevertheless irradiated, as if he could not help it, with beaming eyes. "Ah, those are the secrets of the prison-house, Miss Howe. Unfortunately it is not etiquette for me to say in what proportion I contribute the leading articles of the Chronicle. But I can tell you in confidence that if it were not for the editor's prejudices - rank prejudices - it would be a good deal larger."

"Ah, his prejudices! Why not be quite frank, Mr. Sinclair, and say that he is just a little tiny bit jealous of his staff. All editors are, you know." Miss Howe shook her head in philosophical deprecation of the peccadillo, and Mr. Sinclair cast a smiling, embarrassed glance at his smart brown leather boot. The glance was radiant with what he couldn't tell her as a sub-editor of honour about those cruel prejudices, but he gave it no other medium.

"I'm afraid you know the world, Miss Howe," he said, with a noble reserve, and that was all.

"A corner of it here and there. But you are responsible for the whole of the dramatic criticism," - Hilda charged him roundly, - "the editor can't claim any of THAT."

An inquiring brown face under an embroidered cap appeared at the door; a brown hand thrust in a bunch of printed slips. Mr. Sinclair motioned both away, and they vanished in silence.

"That I can't deny," he said. "It would be useless if I wished to do so - my style betrays me - I must plead guilty. It is not one of my legitimate duties - if I held this position on the Times, or say the Daily Telegraph, our London contemporaries, it would not be required of me. But in this country everything is piled upon the sub-editor. Many a night, Miss Howe, I send down the last slips of a theatre notice at midnight and am here in this chair" - Mr. Sinclair brought his open palm down upon the arm of it - "by eleven the following day!" Mr. Sinclair's chin was thrust passionately forward, moisture dimmed the velvety brightness of those eyes which, in more dramatic moments, he confessed to have inherited from a Nawab great-grandfather. "But I don't complain," he said, and drew in his chin. It seemed to bring his argument to a climax, over which he looked at Hilda in warm, frank expansion.

"Overworked, too, I daresay," she said, and then went on a trifle hurriedly. "Well, I must tell you, Mr. Sinclair, how kind your criticism always is, and how much I personally appreciate it. None of the little points and effects one tries to make seem to escape you, and you are always generous in the matter of space too."

Molyneux impartially threw out his hand. "I believe in it!" he exclaimed. "Honour where honour is due, Miss Howe, and the Stanhope Company has given me some very enjoyable evenings. And you'll hardly believe me, but it is a fact, I assure you, I seldom get a free hand with those notices. Suicidal to the interests of the paper as it is, the editor insists as often as not on cutting down my theatre copy!"

"Cuts it down, does he? The brute!" said Miss Howe.

"I've known him sacrifice a third of it for an indigo market report. Now, I ask you, who reads an indigo market report? Nobody. Who wants to know how

Jimmy Finnigan's - how the Stanhope Company's latest novelties went off? Everybody. Of course, when he does that sort of thing, I make it warm for him next morning?"

The door again opened and admitted a harassed little Babu in spectacles, bearing a sheaf of proof slips, who advanced timidly into the middle of the room and paused.

"In a few minutes, Babu," said Mr. Sinclair; "I am engaged."

"It iss the Council isspeech of the Legal Member, sir, and it iss to go at five p.m. to his house for last correction."

"Presently, Babu. Don't interrupt. As I was saying, Miss Howe, I make it warm for him till he apologises. I must say he always apologises, and I don't often ask more than that. But I was obliged to tell him the last time that if it happened again one of us would have to go."

"What did he say to that?"

"I don't exactly remember. But it had a tremendous effect - tremendous. We became good friends almost immediately."

"Quite so. We miss you when you don't come, Mr. Sinclair - last Saturday night, for example."

"I HAD to go to the Surprise Party. Jimmy came here with tears in his eyes that morning. 'My show is tumbling to pieces,' he said. 'Sinclair, you've got to come to-night.' Made me dine with him - wouldn't let me out of his sight. We had to send a reporter to you and Llewellyn that night."

"Mr. Sinclair, the notice made me weep."

"I know. All that about the costumes. But what can you expect? The man is as black as your hat."

"We have to buy our own costumes," said Hilda, with a glance at the floor, "and we haven't any too much, you know, to do it on."

"The toilets in Her Second Son were simply magnificent. Not to be surpassed on the boards of the Lyceum in tasteful design or richness of material. They were ne plus ultra!" cried Mr. Sinclair. "You will remember I said so in my critique."

"I remember. If I were you I wouldn't go so far another time. There's a lot of cotton velvet and satin about it, you know, between ourselves, and Finnigan's people will be getting the laugh on us. That's one of the things I wanted to mention. Don't be quite so good to us. See? Otherwise - well, you know how Calcutta talks, and what a pretty girl Beryl Stace is, for example. Mrs. Sinclair mightn't like it, and I don't blame her."

"As I said before, Miss Howe, you know the world," Mr. Sinclair replied, with infinite mellow humour, and as Miss Howe had risen he rose too, pulling down his waistcoat.

"There was just one other thing," Hilda said, holding out her hand. "Next Wednesday, you know, Rosa Norton takes her benefit. Rosy's as well known here as the Ochterlony monument; she's been coming every cold weather for ten years, poor old Rosy. Don't you think you could do her a bit of an interview for Wednesday's paper? She'll write up very well - get her on variety entertainments in the Australian bush."

Mr. Molyneux Sinclair looked pained to hesitate. "Personally," he said confidentially, "I should like it immensely, and I daresay I could get it past the editor. But we're so short-handed."

Miss Howe held up a forefinger which seemed luminous with solution. "Don't you bother," she said, "I'll do it for you; I'll write it myself. My 'prentice hand I'll try on Rosy, and you shall have the result ready to print on Tuesday morning. Will that do?"

That would do supremely. Mr. Sinclair could not conceal the admiration he felt for such a combination of talents. He did not try; he accompanied it to the door, expanding and expanding until it seemed more than ever obvious that he found the sub-editorial sphere unreasonably contracted. Hilda received his final bow from the threshold of what he called his "sanctum," and had hardly left the landing in descent when a square-headed, collarless, red-faced male in shirt sleeves came down, descending, as it seemed, in bounds from parts above. "Damn it, Sinclair!" she heard, as he shot into the apartment she had left, "here's the whole council meeting report set up and waiting three-quarters of an hour - press blocked; and the printer Babu says he can get nothing out of you. What the devil . . . If the dak's* missed again, by thunder! . . . paid to converse with itinerant females . . . seven columns . . . infernal idiocy" . . .

* Country post.

Hilda descended in safety and at leisure, reflecting with amusement as she made her way down that Mr. Sinclair was doubtless waiting until his lady visitor was well out of earshot to make it warm for the editor.

CHAPTER XII

I find myself wondering whether Calcutta would have found anything very exquisitely amusing in the satisfactions which exchanged themselves between Mr. Llewellyn Stanhope's leading lady and the Reverend Stephen Arnold, had it been aware of them; and I conclude reluctantly that it would not. Reluctantly, because such imperviousness argues a lack of perception, of flair in directions which any Continental centre would recognise as vastly tickling, regrettable in a capital of such vaunted sophistication as that which sits beside the Hooghly. It may as well be shortly admitted, however, that to stir Calcutta's sense of comedy you must, for example, attempt to corner, by shortsightedness or faulty technical equipment, a civet cat in a jackal hunt, or, coming out from England to assume official duties, you must take a larger view of your dignities than the clubs are accustomed to admit. For the sex that does not hunt jackals it is easier - you have only to be a little frivolous and Calcutta will invent for you the most side-shaking nickname, as in the case of three ladies known in a viceroyalty of happy legend as the World, the Flesh, and the Devil. I should be sorry to give the impression that Calcutta is therefore a place of gloom. The source of these things is perennial, and the noise of laughter is ever in the air of the Indian capital. Between the explosions, however, it is natural enough that the affairs of a priest of College Street and an actress of no address at all should slip unnoticed, especially as they did not advertise it. Stephen mostly came, on afternoons when there was no rehearsal, to tea. He, Stephen, had a perception of contrasts which answered fairly well the purposes of a sense of humour, and nobody could question hers; it operated obscurely to keep them in the house.

She told him buoyantly once or twice that he had been sent to her to take the place of Duff Lindsay, who had fallen to the snare of beauty; although she mentioned to herself that he took it with a difference, a vast temperamental difference which she was aware of not having yet quite sounded. The depths of his faith of course - there she could only scan and hesitate, but this was a brink upon which she did not often find herself, away from which, indeed, he sometimes gently guided her. The atmospheres of their talk were the more bracing ones of this world, and it was here that Hilda looked when she would make him a parallel for Lindsay, and here that she found her measure of disappointment. He warmed himself and dried his wings in the opulence of her spirit, and she was not on the whole the poorer by any exchange they made, but she was sometimes pricked to the reflection that the freemasonry between them was all hers, and the things she said to him had still the flavour of adventure. She found herself inclined - and the experience was new - to make an effort for a reward which was proble-matical and had to be considered in averages, a reward put out in a thin and hesitating hand under a sacerdotal robe, with a curious concentrated quality, and a strange flavour of incense and the air of cold churches. There was also the impression - was it too fantastic? - of words carried over a medium, an invisible wire which brought the soul of them and left the body by the way. Duff Lindsay, so eminently responsive and calculable, came running with open arms; in his rejoiceful eye-beam one saw almost a midwife to one's idea. But the comparison was irritating, and after a time she turned from it. She awoke once in the night, moreover, to declare to the stars that she was less worried by the consideration of Arnold's sex than she would have thought it possible to be - one hardly paused to consider that he was a man at all; a reflection which would certainly not have occurred to her about poor dear Duff. With regard to Stephen Arnold, it was only, of course, another way of saying that she was less oppressed, in his company, by the consideration of her own. Perhaps it is already evident that this was her grievance with life, when the joy of it left her time to think of a grievance, the attraction of her personal lines, the reason of the hundred fetiches her body claimed of her and found her willing to perform, the fact that it meant more to her, for all her theories, that she should be looking her best when she got up in the morning than was justifiable from any point of view except the biological. She had no heroic quarrel with these conditions - her experience had not been upon that plane - but she bemoaned them with sincerity as too fundamental, too all pervading; one came upon them at every turn, grinning in their pretty chains. It was absurd, she construed, that a world of mankind and woman kind with vastly interesting possibilities should be so essentially subjected. So primitive, it was, she argued in her vivid candour, and so interfering - so horribly interfering! Personally she did not see herself one of the fugitive half of the race; she had her defences; but the necessity of using them was matter for complaint when existence might have been so delightful a boon without it, full of affinities and communities in every direction. She had not, I am convinced, any of the notions of a crusader upon this popular subject, nor may I portray her either shocked or revolted, only rather bored, being a creature whom it was unkind to hamper; and she would have explained quite in these simple terms the reason why Stephen Arnold's saving neutrality of temperament was to her a pervasive charm of his society.

She had not yet felt at liberty to tell him that she could not classify him, that she had never known anyone like him before; and there was in this no doubt a vague perception that the confession showed a limitation of experience on her part for which he might be inclined to call her to account; since cultured young Oxonians with an altruistic bias, if they do not exactly abound, are still often enough to be discovered if one happens to belong to the sphere which they haunt, they and their ideals. Not that any such consideration led her to gloss or to minimise the disabilities of her own. She sat sometimes in gravest wonder, pinching her lips, and watched the studiously modified interest of his glance following her into its queer byways - her sphere's - full of spangles and limelight, and the first-class hysteria of third-class rival artistry. There was a fascination in bringing him out of his remoteness near to those things, a speculation worth making as to what he might do. This remained ungratified, for he never did anything. He only let it appear by the most indefinite signs possible, that he saw what she saw, peering over his paling, and she in the picturesque tangle outside found it enough.

He was there when she came back from the Chronicle office, patient under the blue umbrellas; he had brought her a book, and they had told him she would not be long in returning. He had gone so far as to order tea for her, and it was waiting with him. "Make it," she commanded; "why haven't you had some already?" and while he bent over the battered Britannia metal spout she sank into the nearest seat and let her hat make a frame for her face against the back of it. She was too tired, she said, to move, and her hands lay extended, one upon each arm of her chair, with the air of being left there to be picked up at her convenience. Arnold, over the teapot, agreed that walking in Calcutta was an insidious pleasure - one gathered a lassitude - and brought her cup. She looked at him for an instant as she took it.

"But I am not too tired to hear what you have on your mind," she said. "Have Kally Nath Mitter's relations prevailed over his convictions? Won't your landlord let you have your oratory on the roof after all?"

"You get these things so out of perspective," Stephen said, "that I don't think I should tell you if they were so. But they're not. Kally Nath is to be baptized to-morrow. We are certain to get our oratory."

"I am very glad," Hilda interrupted. "When one prays for so long a time together it must be better to have fresh air. It will certainly be better for Brother Colquhoun. He seems to have such a weak chest."

"It will be better for us all." Arnold seemed to reflect, across his teacup, how much better it would be. Then he added, "I saw Lindsay last night."

"Again? And - "

"I think it is perfectly hopeless. I think he is making way."

"Sickening! I hoped you would not speak to him again. After all - another man - it's naturally of no use!"

"I spoke as a priest!"

"Did he swear at you?"

"Oh dear no! He was rather sympathetic. And I went very far. But I could get him to see nothing - to feel nothing."

"How far did you go?"

"I told him that she was consecrated, that he proposed to commit sacrilege. He seemed to think he could make it up to her."

"If anyone else had said that to me I should have laughed - you don't suspect the irony in it" Hilda said. "Pray who is to make it up to him?"

"I suppose there is that point of view."

"I should think so, indeed! But taking it, I despair with you. I had her here the other day and tried to make the substance of her appear before him. I succeeded too - he gave me the most uncomfortable looks - but I might as well have let it alone. The great end of nature," Hilda went on, putting down her cup, "reasonable beings in their normal state would never lend themselves to. So she invents these temporary insanities. And therein is nature cruel, for they might just as well be permanent. That's a platitude, I know," she added, "but it's irresistibly suggested."

Stephen looked with some fixedness at a point on the other side of the room. The platitude brought him, by some process of inversion, the vision of a drawing-room in Addison Gardens, occupied by his mother and sisters, engaged with whatever may be Kensington's substitutes at the moment for the spinet and the tambour frame; and he had a disturbed sense that they might characterise such a statement differently, if, indeed, they would consent to characterise it at all. He looked at the wall as if, being a solid and steadfast object, it might correct the qualm - it was really something like that - which the wide sweep of her cynicism brought him.

"From what he told me last week I thought we shouldn't see it. He seemed determined enough but depressed, and not hopeful. I fancied she was being upheld - I thought she would easily pull through. Indeed, I wasn't sure that there was any great temptation. Somebody must be helping him."

"The devil, no doubt," Hilda replied concisely; "and with equal certainty, Miss Alicia Livingstone."

Arnold gave her a look of surprise. "Surely not my cousin!" he protested. "She can't understand."

"Oh, I beg of you, don't speak to HER! I think she understands. I think she's only too tortuously intelligent."

Stephen kept an instant of nervous silence. "May I ask? - " he began, formally.

"Oh yes! It is almost an indecent thing to say of anyone so exquisitely self-contained, but your cousin is very much in love with Mr. Lindsay herself. It seems almost a liberty, doesn't it, to tell you such a thing about a member of your family?" she went on, at Arnold's blush; "but you asked me, you know. And she is making it her ecstatic agony to bring this precious union about. I think she is taking a kindergarten method with the girl - having her there constantly and showing her little scented, luxurious bits of what she is so possessed to throw away. People in Alicia's condition have no sense of immorality."

"That makes it all the more painful," said Arnold; but the interest in his tone was a little remote, and his gesture, too, which was not quite a shrug, had a relegating effect upon any complication between Alicia and Lindsay. He sat for a moment without saying more, covering his eyes with his hand.

"Why should you care so much?" Hilda asked gently. "You are at the very antipodes of her sect. You can't endorse her methods - you don't trust her results."

"Oh, all that! It's of the least consequence." He spoke with a curious, governed impulse coming from beneath his shaded eyes. "It's seeing another ideal pulled down, gone under, something that held, as best it could, a ray from the source. It's another glimpse of the strength of the tide - terrible. It's a cruel hint that one lives above it in the heaven of one's own hopes, by some mere blind accident. To have set one's feeble hand to the spiritualising of the world and to feel the possibility of that - "

"I see," said Hilda, and perhaps she did. But his words

oppressed her. She got up with a movement which almost shook them off, and went to a promiscuous looking-glass to remove her hat. She was refreshed and vivified - she wanted to talk of the warm world. She let a decent interval elapse, however; she waited till he took his hand from his eyes. Even then, to make the transition easier, she said, "You ought to be lifted up to-day, if you are going to baptize Kally Nath to-morrow."

"The Brother Superior will do it. And I don't know - I don't know. The young woman he is to marry withdraws, I believe, if he comes over to us - "

"The, young woman he is to marry! Oh my dear and reverend friend! Avec ces gens la! I have had a most amusing afternoon," she went on quickly. "I have taken off my hat, now let me remove your halo." She was safe with her conceit; Arnold would always smile at any imputation of saintship. He held himself a person of broad indulgences, and would point openly to his consumption of tea-cakes. But this afternoon a miasma hung over him. Hilda saw it, and bent herself, with her graphic recital, to dispel it, perceived it thicken and settle down upon him, and went bravely on to the end. Mr. Macandrew and Mr. Molyneux Sinclair lived and spoke before him. It was comedy enough, in essence, to spread over a matinee.

"And that is the sort of thing you store up and value," he said, when she had finished. "These persons will add to your knowledge of life?"

"Extremely," she replied to all of it.

"I suppose they will in their measure. But personally I

could wish you had not gone. Your work has no right to make such demands."

"Be reasonable," she said, flushing. "Don't talk as if personal dignity were within the reach of everybody. It's the most expensive of privileges. And nothing to be so very proud of - generally the product of somebody else's humiliations, handed down. But the humiliations must have been successful, handed down in cash. My father drove a cab and died in debt. His name was Cassidy. I shall be dignified some day - some day! But you see I must make it possible myself, since nobody has done it for me."

"Well, then, I'll alter my complaint. Why should you play with your sincerity?"

"I didn't play with it," she flashed; "I abandoned it. I am an actress."

They often permitted themselves such candours; to all appearance their discussion had its usual equable quality, and I am certain that Arnold was not even aware of the tension upon his nerves. He fidgeted with the tassel of his ceinture, and she watched his moving fingers. Presently she spoke quietly, in a different key.

"I sometimes think," she said, "of a child I knew, in the other years. She had the simplest nature, the finest instincts. Her impulses, within her small limits, were noble - she was the keenest, loyalest little person; her admirations rather made a fool of her. When I look at the woman she is now I think the uses of life are hard, my friend - they are hard."

He missed the personal note; he took what she said on

its merits as an illustration.

"And yet," he replied, "they can be turned to admirable purpose."

"I wonder!" Hilda exclaimed brightly. She had turned down the leaf of that mood. "But we are not cheerful - let us be cheerful. For my part I am rejoicing as I have not rejoiced since the first of December. Look at this!"

She opened a small black leather bag, and poured money out of it, in notes and currency, into her lap.

"Is it a legacy?"

"It's pay," she cried, with pleasure dimpling about her lips. "I have been paid - we have all been paid! It's so unusual - it makes me feel quite generous. Let me see. I'll give you this, and this, and this," - she counted into her open palm ten silver rupees, - "all those I will give you for your mission. Prends!" and she clinked them together and held them out to him.

He had risen to go, and his face looked grey and small. Something in him had mutinied at the levity, the quick change of her mood. He could only draw into his shell; doubtless he thought that a legitimate and inoffensive proceeding.

"Thanks, no," he said, "I think not. We desire people's prayers, rather than their alms."

He went away immediately, and she glossed over his scandalous behaviour, and said farewell to him as she always did, in spite of the unusual look of consciousness in her eyes. She continued to hold the ten rupees carefully and separately, as if she would later examine them in diagnosing her pain. It was keener and profounder than any humiliation, the new voice, crying out, of a trampled tenderness. She stood and looked after him for a moment with startled eyes and her hand, in a familiar gesture of her profession, upon her heart. Then she went to her room, and deliberately loosened her garments and lay down upon her bed, first to sob like that little child she remembered, and afterwards to think, until the world came and knocked at her door and bade her come out of herself and earn money.

CHAPTER XIII

The compulsion which took Stephen Arnold to Crooked Lane is hardly ours to examine. It must have been strong, since going up to Mrs. Sand involved certain concessions, doubtless intrinsically trifling, but of exaggerated discomfort to the mind spiritually cloistered, whatever its other latitude. Among them was a distinctly necessary apology, difficult enough to make to a lady of rank so superior and authority so voyant in the Church militant, by a mere fighting soul without such straps and buttons as might compel recognition upon equal terms. It is impossible to know how far Stephen envisaged the visit as a duty - the priestly horizon is perhaps not wholly free from mirage - or to what extent he confessed it an indulgence. He was certainly aware of a stronger desire than he could altogether account for that Captain Filbert should not desert her post. The idea had an element of irritation oddly personal; he could not bear to reflect upon it. It may be wondered whether in any flight of venial imagination Arnold saw himself in a parallel situation with a lady. I am sure he did not. It may be considered, however, that among mirages there are unaccountable resemblances - resemblances without shape or form. He might fix his gaze, at all events, upon the supreme argument that those who were given to holy work, under any condition, in any degree, should make no rededication of themselves. This had to support him as best it could against the conviction that had Captain Filbert been Sister Anastasia, for example, of the Baker Institution, and Ensign Sand the Mother Superior of its Calcutta branch, it was improbable that he would have ventured to announce his interest in the matter by his card, or in any other way.

It was a hesitating step, therefore, that carried him up to the quarters, and a glance of some nervous distress that made him aware, as he stood bowing upon her threshold, clasping with both hands his soft felt hat to his breast, that Mrs. Sand was not displeased to see him. She hastened, indeed, to give him a chair; she said she was very glad he'd dropped in, if he didn't mind the room being so untidy - where there were children you could spend the whole day picking up. They were out at present, with Captain Sand, in the perambulator, not having more servants than they could help. A sweeper and a cook they did with; it would surprise the people in this country, who couldn't get along with less than twenty, she often said.

Mrs. Sand's tone was casual; her manner had a quality somewhat aggressively democratic. It said that under her welcome lay the right to criticise, which she would have exercised with equal freedom had her visitor been the Lord Bishop John Calcutta himself; and it made short work of the idea that she might be over-gratified to receive Holy Orders in any form. She was not unwilling, however, to show, as between Ensign and man, reasonable satisfaction; presently, in fact, she went so far as to say, still vaguely remarking upon his appearance there, that she often thought there ought to be more sociability between the different religious bodies; it would be better for the cause. There was nothing narrow, she said, about her, nor yet about

Captain Sand. And then, with the distinct intimation that that would do, that she had gone far enough, she crossed her hands in her lap and waited. It became her to have it understood that this visit need have no further object than an exchange of amiabilities; but there might be another, and Mrs. Sand's folded hands seemed to indicate that she would not necessarily meet it with opposition.

Stephen made successive statements of assent. He sat grasping his hat between his knees, his eyes fixed upon an infant's sock which lay upon the floor immediately in front of him, looking at Mrs. Sand as seldom and as briefly as possible, as if his glance took rather an unfair advantage, which he would spare her.

"Yes, yes," he said. "Yes, certainly," revolving his hat in his hands. And when she spoke of the fraternity that might be fostered by such visits, he looked for an instant as if he had found an opening, which seemed, however, to converge and vanish in Mrs. Sand's folded hands. He flushed to think afterwards, that it was she who was obliged to bring his resolution to a head, her scent of his embarrassment sharpening her curiosity.

"And is there anything we Army officers can do for you, Mr. Arnold?" she inquired.

There was a hint in her voice that, whatever it was, they would have done it more willingly if she had not been obliged to ask.

"I am afraid," he said, "my mission is not quite so simple. I could wish it were. It is so easy to show our poor needs to one another; and I should have confidence - " He paused, amazed at the duplicity that grinned at him in his words. At what point more remote within the poles was he likely to show himself with a personal request?

"I have nothing to ask for myself," he went on, with concentration almost harsh. "I am here to see if you will consent to speak with me about a matter which threatens your - your community - about your possible loss of Miss Filbert."

Mrs. Sand looked blank. "The Captain isn't leavin' us, as far as I know," she said.

"Oh - is it possible that you are not aware that - that very strong efforts are being made to induce her to do so?"

Mrs. Sand looked about her as if she expected to find an explanation lying somewhere near her chair. Light came to her suddenly, and brought her a conscious smile; it only lacked force to be a giggle. She glanced at her lap as she smiled; her air was deprecating and off-putting, as if she had detected in what Arnold said some suggestion of a gallant nature aimed at herself. Happily, he was not looking.

"You mean Mr. Lindsay!" she exclaimed, twisting her wedding-ring and its coral guard.

"I hope - I beg - that you will not think me meddlesome or impertinent. I have the matter very much at heart. It seems to lie in my path. I must see it. Surely you perceive some way of averting the disaster in it!"

"I'm sure I don't know what you refer to." Mrs. Sand's

tone was prudish and offended. "She hasn't said a word to me - she's a great one for keeping things to herself - but if Mr. Lindsay don't mean marriage with her - "

"Why, of course!" Arnold, startled, turned furiously red, but Mrs. Sand in her indignation did not reflect the tint. "Of course! Is not that," he went on after an instant's pause, "precisely what is to be lamented - and prevented?"

Mrs. Sand looked at her visitor with dry suspicion. "I suppose you are a friend of his," she said.

"I have known him for years. Pray don't misunderstand me. There is nothing against him - nothing whatever."

"Oh, I don't suppose there is, except that he is not on the Lord's side. But I don't expect any of his friends are anxious for him to marry an officer in the Salvation Army. Society people ain't fond of the Army, and never will be."

"His people - he has only distant relatives living - are all at home," Stephen said vaguely. The situation had become slightly confused.

"Then you speak for them, I suppose?"

"Indeed not. I am in no communication with them whatever. I fancy they know nothing about it. I am here entirely - ENTIRELY of my own accord. I have come to place myself at your disposition if there is anything I can do, any word I can say, to the end of preventing this catastrophe in a spiritual life so pure and devoted; to ask you at all events to let me join my prayers to yours that it shall not come about."

The squalor of the room seemed to lift before his eyes and be suffused with light. At last he had made himself plain. But Mrs. Sand was not transfigured. She seemed to sit, with her hands folded, in the midst of a calculation.

"Then he HAS put the question. I told her he would," she said.

"I believe he has asked her to marry him and she has refused, more than once. But he is importunate, and I hear she needs help."

"Mr. Lindsay," said Mrs. Sand, "is a very takin' young man."

"I suppose we must consider that. There is position too, and wealth. These things count - we are all so human - even against the Divine realities into possession of which Miss Filbert must have so perfectly entered."

"I thought he must be pretty well off. Would he be one of them Government officials?"

"He is a broker."

"Oh, is he indeed?" Mrs. Sand's enlightenment was evidently doubtful. "Well, if they get married Captain Filbert 'll have to resign. It's against the regulations for her to marry outside of the Army."

"But is she not vowed to her work; isn't her life turned for ever into that channel? Would it not be horrible to you to see the world interfere?"

"I won't say but what I'd be sorry to see her leave us. But I wouldn't stand in her way either, and neither would Captain Sand."

"Stand in her way! In her way to material luxury, poverty of spirit, the shirking of all the high alternatives, the common moral mediocrity of the world. I would to God I could be that stumbling block! I have heard her - I have seen the light in her that may so possibly be extinguished."

"I don't deny she has a kind of platform gift, but she's losin' her voice. And she doesn't understand briskin' people up, if you know what I mean."

"She will be pulled down - she will go under!" Arnold repeated in the depths of his spirit. He stood up, fumbling with his hat. Mrs. Sand and her apartment, her children out of doors in the perambulator, and the whole organisation to which she appertained had grown oppressive and unnecessary. He was aware of a desire to put his foot again in his own world, where things were seen, were understood. He thought there might be solace in relating the affair to Brother Colquhoun.

"It's a case," said Mrs. Sand judicially, "where I wouldn't think myself called on to say one word. Such things everyone has a right to decide for themselves. But you oughtn't to forget that a married woman" - she looked at Arnold's celibate habit as if to hold it accountable for much - "can have a great influence for good over him that she chooses. I am pretty sure Captain Filbert's already got Mr. Lindsay almost persuaded. I shouldn't be at all surprised if he joined the Army himself when she's had a good chance at him."

Arnold put on his hat with a groan, and began the descent of the stairs. "Good-afternoon then," Mrs. Sand called out to him from the top. He turned mechanically and bared his head. "I beg your pardon," he said. "Good-afternoon."

CHAPTER XIV

Mrs. Sand found it difficult to make up her mind upon several points touching the visit of the Reverend Stephen Arnold. Its purport, of which she could not deny her vague appreciation, drew a cloud across a rosy prospect, and in this light his conduct showed unpardonable; on the other hand it implied a compliment to the corps, it made the spiritual position of an officer of the Army, a junior too, a matter of moment in a wider world than might be suspected; and before this consideration Mrs. Sand expanded. She reflected liberally that salvation was not necessarily frustrated by the laying-on of hands; she had serene fancies of a republic of the redeemed. She was a prey to further hesitations regarding the expediency of mentioning the interview to Laura, and as private and confidential it ministered for two days to her satisfactions of superior officer. In the end, however, she had to sacrifice it to the girl's imperturbable silence. She chose an intimate and a private hour, and shut the door carefully upon herself and her captain, but she had not at all decided, when she sat down on the edge of the bed, what complexion to give to the matter, nor had she a very definite idea, when she got up again, of what complexion she had given it. Laura, from the first word, had upset her by an intense eagerness, a determination not to lose a syllable. Captain Filbert insisted upon hearing all before she would acknowledge anything; she hung upon the sentences Mrs. Sand repeated, and joined them together as if they were parts of a puzzle; she finally had possession of the conversation much as I have already written it down. As Mrs. Sand afterward told her husband, Miss Filbert sat there growing whiter and whiter, more and more worked up, and it was impossible to take any comfort in talking to her. It seemed as if she, the Ensign, might save herself the trouble of giving an opinion one way or the other, and not a thing could she get the girl to say except that it was true enough that the gentleman wanted to marry her, and she was ashamed of having let it go so far. But she would never do it - never! She declared she would write to this Mr. Arnold and thank him, and ask him to pray for her, "and she as much as ordered me to go and do the same," concluded Mrs. Sand, with an inflection which made its own comment upon such a subversion of discipline.

Stephen, under uncomfortable compulsion, sent Laura's letter - she did write - to Lindsay. "I cannot allow you to be in the dark about what I am doing in the matter," he explained; "though if I had not this necessity for writing you might reasonably complain of an intrusive and impertinent letter. But I must let you know that she has appealed to me, and that as far as I can I will help her."

Duff read both communications - Laura's to the priest was brief and very technical - between the business quarters of Ralli Brothers and the Delhi and London Bank, with his feet in the opposite seat of his office-gharry and his forehead puckered by an immediate calculation forward in rupee paper. His irritation spoiled his transaction - there was a distinct edge in the manager's manner when they parted, and it was perhaps a pardonable weakness that led him to dash in blue pencil across the page covered with Arnold's minute handwriting, "Then you have done with pasty compromises - you have gone over to the Jesuits. I congratulate you," and readdressed the envelope to College Street. The brown tide of the crowd brought him an instant messenger, and he stood in the doorway for a moment afterwards frowning upon the yellow turbans that swung along in the sunlight against the white wall opposite, across the narrow commercial road. The flame of his indignation set forth his features with definiteness and relief, consuming altogether the soft amused well-being which was nearly always there. His lips set themselves together, and Mrs. Sand would have been encouraged in any scheme of practical utility by the lines that came about his mouth. A brother in finance of some astuteness, who saw him scramble into his gharry, divined that with regard to a weighty matter in jute mill shares pending, Lindsay had decided upon a coup, and made his arrangements accordingly. He also went upon his way with a fresh impression of Lindsay's undeniable good looks, as sometimes in a coin new from the mint one is struck with the beauty of a die dulled by use and familiarity.

Stephen Arnold, receiving his answer, composed himself to feel distress, but when he had read it, that emotion was lightened in him by another sentiment.

"A community admirable in many ways," he murmured, refolding the page. "Does he think he is insulting me?"

Whatever degree of influence, Jesuitical or other, Lindsay was inclined to concede to Stephen's intermediary, he was compelled to recognise without delay that Captain Filbert, in the exercise of her profession, had not neglected to acquire a knowledge of defensive operations. She retired effectively, the quarters in Crooked Lane became her fortified retreat, whence she issued only under escort and upon service strictly obligatory. Succour from Arnold doubtless reached her by the post; and Lindsay felt it an anomaly in military tactics that the same agency should bring back upon him with a horrid recoil the letters with which he strove to assault her position. Nor could Alicia induce any sortie to Middleton Street. Her notes of invitation to quiet teas and luncheons were answered on blue-lined paper, the pen dipped in reticence and the palest ink, always with the negative of a formal excuse. They loosed the burden of her complicity from Miss Livingstone's shoulders, these notes which bore so much the atmosphere of Crooked Lane, and at the same time they formed the indictment against her which was, perhaps, best calculated to weigh upon her conscience. She saw it, holding them at arm's length, in enormous characters that ever stamped and blotted out the careful, taught-looking writing, and the invariable "God bless you, yours truly," at the end. They were all there, aridly complete, the limitations of the lady to whom she was helping Lindsay to bind himself without a gleam of possibility of escape or a rift through which tiniest hope could creep, to emerge smiling upon the other side. When she saw him, in fatalistic reverie, going about ten years hence attached to the body of this petrification, she was almost disposed to abandon the pair, to let them take their wretched chance. But this was a climax which did not occur often; she returned, in most of her waking moments, to devising schemes by which Laura might be delivered into the hands she was so likely to encumber. The new French poet, the American novelist of the year, and a work by Mr. John Morley lay upon Alicia's table many days together for this reason. She sometimes remembered what she expected of these volumes, what plein air sensations or what profound plunges, and did not quite like her indifference as to whether her expectations were fulfilled. She discovered herself intellectually jaded - there had been tiring excursions - and took to daily rides which carried her far out among the rice-fields, and gave her sound nights to sustain the burden of her dreaming days. She had ideas about her situation; she believed she lived outside of it. At all events she took a line; the new Arab was typical, and there were other measures which she arranged deliberately with the idea that she was making a physical fight. Life might weigh one down with a dragging ball and chain, but one could always measure the strength of one's pinions against these things. She made it her sorry and remorseless task to separate from her impulses those that she found lacking in philosophy, hinting of the foolish woman, and to turn a cruel heel upon them. She stripped her meditations of all colour and atmosphere; she would not accept from her grief the luxury of a rag to wrap herself in. If this gave hers a skeleton to live with, she had what gratification there was in observing that it was anatomically as it should be. The result that one saw from the outside was chiefly a look of delicate hardness, of tissue a little frayed, but showing a quality in the process. We may hope that some unconfessed satisfaction was derivable from her continued reception of Duff's confidences - it has long been evident that he found her persuadable - her unflinching readiness to consult with him; granting the analytic turn we may almost suppose it. Starvation is so monotonous a misery that a gift of personal diagnosis might easily lend attraction to poisoned food as an alternative, if one may be permitted a melodramatic simile in a case which Alicia kept conventional enough. She did not even abate the usual number of Duff's invitations to dinner when there was certainly nothing to repay her for regarding him across a gulf of flowers and silver, and a tide of conversation about the season's paper-chasing, except the impoverished complexion which people acquire who sit much in Bentinck Street, desirous and unsatisfied.

It may very well be that she regretted her behaviour in this respect, for it was eventually after one of these parties that Surgeon-Major Livingstone, pressing upon his departing guest in the hall the usual whisky and soda, found it necessary instead to give him another kind of support, and to put him immediately and authoritatively to bed. Lindsay was very well content to submit; he confessed to fever off and on for four or five days past, and while the world went round the pivotal staircase, as Dr. Livingstone gave him an elbows up, he was indistinctly convinced that the house of a friend was better than a shelf at the club.

The next evening's meeting saw his place empty under the window of the hall in Crooked Lane, noticeably for the first time in weeks of these exercises. The world shrank, for Laura, to the compass of the kerosene lamps; there was no gaze from its wider sphere against which she must key herself to indifference. When on the second and third evening she was equally undisturbed, it was borne in upon her that either she or Mr. Arnold, or both, had prevailed, and she offered up thanks. On the fourth she reflected recurrently and anxiously that it was not after all a very glorious victory if the devil had carried off the wounded; if

Lindsay, after all the opportunities that had been his, should slip back without profit to the level from which she had striven - they had all striven - to lift him. Mrs. Sand, not satisfied to be buffeted by such speculations, sent a four-anna bit to the head bearer at the club on her own account and obtained information.

Alicia saw no immediate privilege in the complication, though the circumstances taken together did present a vulgar opportunity which Mrs. Barberry came for hours to take advantage of. There were the usual two nurses as well as Mrs. Barberry; Alicia could take the Arab farther afield than ever, and she did. One can imagine her cantering fast and far with a sense of conscious possession in spite of Mrs. Barberry and the two nurses. There may be a certain solace in the definite and continuous knowledge available about a person hovering on the brink of enteric under your own roof-tree. It was as grave as that; Surgeon-Major Livingstone could not make up his mind. Alicia knew only of this uncertainty; other satisfactions were reserved for the nurses and Mrs. Barberry. She could see that her brother was anxious, he was so uniformly cheerful, so brisk and fresh and good-tempered coming from Lindsay's room in the morning, to say at breakfast that the temperature was the same, hadn't budged a point, must manage to get it down somehow in the next twenty-four hours, and forthwith to envelop himself in the newspapers. Those arbitrary and obstinate figures, which stood for apprehension to the most casual ear, stamped themselves on most things as the day wore on, and at tea-time Mrs. Barberry gave her other details, thinking her rather cold in the reception of them. But she plainly preferred to be out of it, avoiding the nurses on the stairs, refraining from so much as a glance at the boiled milk preparations of the butler. "And you know," said Mrs. Barberry, recountant, "how these people have to be watched." To Mrs. Barberry she was really a conundrum, only to be solved on the theory of a perfectly preposterous delicacy. There was so little that was preposterous in Miss Livingstone's conduct as a rule that it is not quite fair to explain her attitude either by this exaggeration or by an equally hectic scruple about her right to take care of her guest, such a right dwindling curiously when it has been given in the highest to somebody else. These pangs and penalties may have visited her in their proportion, but they did not take the importance of motives. She rather stood aside with folded hands, and in an infinite terror of prejudicing fate, devoured her heart by way of keeping its beating normal. Perhaps, too, she had a vision of a final alternative to Lindsay's marriage, one can imagine her forcing herself to look at it.

Remove herself as she chose, Alicia could not avoid passing Lindsay's room, for her own lay beyond it. In the seven o'clock half light of a February evening, in the middle of the week, she went along the matted upper hall on tiptoe, and stumbled over a veiled form squatted in the native way, near his door, profoundly asleep. "Ayah!" she exclaimed, but the face that looked confusedly up at her was white, whiter than common, Captain Filbert's face. Alicia drew her hand away and made an imperceptible movement in the direction of her skirts. She stood silent, stricken in the dusk with astonishment, but the sense that was strongest in her was plainly that of having made a criminal discovery. Laura stumbled upon her feet, and the two faced each other for an instant, words held from them equally by the authority of the sickroom door. Then Alicia beckoned as imperiously as if the other had in fact been the servant she took her for, and Laura followed to where, farther on, a bedroom door stood open, which presently closed upon them both. It was a spacious room, with pale high-hung draperies, a scent of flowers, such things as an etching of Greuze, an ivory and ebony crucifix over the bed. Captain Filbert remembered the crucifix afterward with a feeling almost intense, also some silver-backed brushes on the toilet-table. Across the open window a couple of bars of sunset glowed red and gold, and a tall palm of the garden cut all its fronds sharply against the light.

"Well?" said Alicia, when the door was shut.

Captain Filbert put out a deprecating hand.

"I intended to ask if you had any objection, miss, but you had gone out. And the nurse was in the room; I couldn't get to her. There was nobody but the servants about."

"Objection to what?"

"To my being there. I came to pray for Mr. Lindsay."

"Did you make any noise?"

Miss Filbert looked professionally touched. "It was silent prayer, of course," she said.

Alicia, standing with one hand upon the toilet-table, had an air of eagerness, of successful capture. The yellow sky in the window behind her made filmy lights round her hair, and outlined her tall figure, in the gracefulness of which there was a curious crisped effect, like a conventional pose taken easily, from habit. Laura Filbert thought she looked like a princess.

"I seem to hear of nothing but petitions," she said. "Isn't somebody praying for you?"

The blood of any saint would have risen in false testimony at such a suggestion. Laura blushed so violently that for an instant the space between them seemed full of the sound of her protest.

"I hope so, miss," she said, and looked as if for calming over Alicia's shoulder away into the after-sunset bars along the sky. The colour sank back out of her face, and the light from the window rested on it ethereally. The beautiful mystery drew her eyes to seek, and their blue seemed to deepen and dilate, as if the old splendour of the uplifted golden gates rewarded them.

"Why do you use that odious word?" Alicia explained. "You are not my maid! Don't do it again - don't dream of doing it again!"

"I - I don't know." The girl was still plainly covered with confusion at being found in the house uninvited. "I suppose I forgot. Well, good-evening," and she turned to the door.

"Don't go," Alicia commanded. "Don't. You never come to see me now. Sit down." She dragged a chair forward and almost pushed Laura into it. "I will sit down too - what am I thinking of?"

Laura reflected for a moment, looking at her folded hands. "I might as well tell you," she said, "that I have not been praying that Mr. Lindsay should get better.

Only that he should be given time to find salvation and die in Jesus."

"Don't - don't say those things to me. How light you are - it's wicked!" Alicia returned with vehemence, and then as Captain Filbert stared, half comprehending, "Don't you care?" she added curiously.

It was so casual that it was cruel. The girl's eyes grew wider still during the instant she fixed them upon Alicia in the effort of complete understanding. Then her lip trembled.

"How can I care?" she cried; "how can I?" and burst into weeping. She drew her sari over her face and rocked to and fro. Her dusty bare foot protruded from her cotton skirt. She sat huddled together, her head in its coverings sunk between weak shaking shoulders. Alicia considered her for an instant as a pitiable and degraded spectacle. Then she went over and touched her.

"You are completely worn out," she said, "and it is almost dinner-time. The ayah will bring you a hot bath and then you will come down and have some food quietly with me. My brother is dining out somewhere. I will go away for a little while and then I know you will feel better. And after dinner," she added gently, "you may come up if you like and pray again for Mr. Lindsay. I am sure he would - "

The faintest break in her own voice warned her, and she hurried out of the room.

It was a foolish thing, and the Livingstones' old Karim Bux much deplored it, but the miss-sahib had forgotten to give information that the dinner of eight commanded a fortnight ago would not take place - hence everything was ready in its sequence for this event, with a new fashion of stuffing quails and the first strawberries of the season from Dinapore. The feelings of Karim Bux in presenting these things to a woman in the dress of a coolie are not important; but Alicia, for some reason, seemed to find the trivial incident gratifying.

CHAPTER XV

Under the Greek porch of Number Ten, Middleton
Street, in the white sunlight between the shadows of
the stucco pillars, stood a flagrant ticca-gharry. The
driver lay extended on the top of it, asleep, the syce
squatted beneath the horse's nose, and fed it
perfunctorily with hay from a bundle tied under the
vehicle behind. A fringe of palms and ferns in pots ran
between the pillars, and orchids hung from above,
shutting out the garden where heavy scents stood in the
sun, and mynas chattered on the drive. The air was full
of ease, warm, fretillante, abandoned to the lavish
energy of growing things; beyond the discoloured wall
of the compound rose the tender cloud of a leafing
tamarisk against the blue. A long time already the
driver had slept immovably, and the horse, uncomp-
laining but uninterested, had dragged at the wisps of
hay.

Inside there was no longer a hint of Mrs. Barberry,
even a dropped handkerchief agreeably scented. The
night nurse had realised herself equally superfluous
and had gone; the other, a person of practical views,
could hardly retain her indignation at being kept from
day to day to see her patient fed, and hand him books
and writing materials. She had not even the duty of
debarring visitors, but sat most of the time in the
dressing-room where echoes fell about her of the

stories with which riotous young men, in tea and wheat and jute, hastened Mr. Lindsay's convalescence. There she tapped her energetic fat foot on the floor in vain, to express her views upon such waste of scientific training. She had Surgeon Major Livingstone's orders; and he on this occasion had his sister's.

There was an air of relief, of tension relaxed, between the two women in the drawing-room; it was plain that Alicia had communicated these things to her visitor, in their main import. Hilda was already half disengaged from the subject, her eye wandered as if in search for the avenue to another. By a sudden inclination Alicia began the story of Laura Filbert on her knees at Lindsay's door. She told it in a quiet, steady, colourless way, pursuing it to the end - it came with the ease of frequent private rehearsals - and then with her elbows on her knees and her chin in her palms she stopped and gazed meditatively in front of her. There was something in the gaze to which Hilda yielded an attention unexpectedly serious, something of the absolute in character and life impervious to her inquiry. Yet to analysis it was only the grey look of eyes habituated to regard the future with penetration and to find nothing there.

"Have you told him?" Hilda asked after an instant's pause, during which she conceded something, she hardly knew what; she meant to find out later.

"I haven't seen him. But I will tell him, I promise you."

"I have no doubt you will! But don't promise ME. I won't even witness the vow!" Hilda cried.

"What does it matter? I shall certainly tell him." The

words fell definitely like pebbles. Hilda thoughtfully picked them up.

"On the whole," she said, "perhaps it would be as well. Yes, it is my advice. It is quite likely that he will be revolted. It may be curative."

Alicia turned away her head to hide the faint frown that nevertheless crept into her voice. "I don't think so," she said. "How you do juggle with things! I don't know why I talk to you about this - this matter. I am sure I ought not."

"I was going to say," pursued Hilda, indifferent to her scruple, "that I shouldn't be at all surprised if his illness leaves him quite emotionally sane. The poison has worked itself out of his blood - perhaps the passion and the poison were the same."

"I wonder!" Alicia said. She said it mechanically, as the easiest comment.

"When I knew you first your speculation would have been more active, my dear. You would have looked into the possibility and disputed it. What has become of your modernity?"

It was the tenderest malice, but it obtained no concessive sign. Alicia seemed to weigh it. "I think I like theories better than illustrations," she said in defence.

"One can look at theories as one looks at the sky, but an illustration wants a careful point of view. For this one perhaps you are a little near."

"Perhaps," Alicia assented, "I am a little near." She glanced quickly down as she spoke, but when she raised her eyes they were dry and clear.

"I can see it better," Hilda went on, with immense audacity, "much better."

"Isn't it safer to feel?"

"Jamais de la vie! The nerves lie always."

They were on the edge of the vortex of the old dispute. Alicia leaned back among the cushions and regarded the other with an undecided eye.

"You are not sure," said Hilda, "that you won't ask me, at this point, to look at the pictures in that old copy of the Persian classic - I forget its lovely name - or inquire what sort of house we had last night. Well, don't be afraid of hurting my feelings. Only, you know, between us as between more doubtful people, the door must be either open or shut. I fancy you take cold easily; perhaps you had better shut the door."

"Not for worlds," Alicia said, with promptitude. Then she added, rather cleverly, "That would be spoiling my one view of life."

Hilda smiled. "Isn't there any life where you live?" She glanced round her, at the tapestried elegance of the room, with sudden indifference. "After all," she said, "I don't know what I am doing here, in your affairs. As the world swings no one could be more remote from them or you. I belong to its winds and its highways - how have you brought me here, a tramp-actress, to your drawing-room?"

Alicia laid a detaining hand upon Miss Howe's skirt. "Don't go away," she said. Hilda sat at the other end of the sofa; there was hardly a foot between them. She went on with a curious excitement.

"My kind of life is so primitive, so simple; it is one pure impulse, you don't know. One only asks the things that minister - one goes and finds and takes them; one's feet in the straw, one's head under any roof. What difference does it make? The only thing that counts, that rules, is the chance of seeing something else, feeling something more, doing something better."

Alicia only looked at her and tightened the grasp of her fingers on the actress's skirt. Hilda made the slightest, most involuntary movement. It comprehended the shaking off of hindrance, the action of flight. Then she glanced about her again with a kind of appraisement, which ended with Alicia and embraced her. What she realised seemed to urge her, I think, in some weak place of her sex, to go on intensely, almost fiercely.

"Everything here is aftermath. You are a gleaner, Alicia Livingstone. We leave it all over the world for people of taste, like you, in the glow of their illusions. I couldn't make you understand our harvest; it is of the broad sun and the sincerity of things."

"I know I must seem to you dreadfully out of it," Alicia said, wearing, as it were, across her heaviness a lighter cloud of trouble.

But the other would not be stayed; she followed by compulsion her impulse to the end. "Shall I be quite candid?" she said. "I find the atmosphere about you, dear, a trifle exhausted."

Alicia with a face of astonishment made a half movement towards the window before she understood. There was some timidity in her glance at Hilda and in her mechanical smile. "Oh," she said, "I see what you mean; and I don't wonder. I am so literal - I have so little imagination."

"Don't talk of it as if it were money or fabric - something you could add up or measure," Hilda cried remorselessly. "You have none!"

As if something slipped from her Alicia threw out locked hands. "At least I had enough to know you when you came!" she cried. "I felt you, too, and it's not my fault if there isn't enough of me to - to respond properly. And I can't give you up. You seem to be the one valuable thing that I can have - the only permanent fact that is left."

Hilda had a rebound of immense discomfort. "Who said anything about giving up?" she interrupted.

"Why, you did! But I'm quite willing to believe you didn't mean it, if you say so." She turned the appeal of her face and saw a sudden pitiful consideration in Hilda's, and as if it called them forth two tears sprang to her eyes and fell, as she lowered her delicate head upon her lap.

"Dear thing! I didn't indeed. If I meant anything it was that I'm overstrung. I've been horribly harried lately." She possessed herself of one of Alicia's hands and stroked it. Alicia kept her head bent for a moment and

Mrs. Everard Cotes

then let it fall, in sudden abandonment, upon the other woman's shoulder. Her defences crumbled so utterly that Hilda felt guilty of using absurdly heavy artillery. They sat together for a moment or two in silence with only that supervening sense of successful aggression between them, and the humiliation was Hilda's. Presently it grew heavy, embarrassing. Alicia got up and began a slow, restless pacing up and down before the alcove they sat in. Hilda watched her - it was a rhythmic progress - and when she came near with a sound of brushing silk and a faint fragrance which seemed a personal emanation, drew a long breath as if she were an essence to be inhaled, and so, in a manner obtained, assimilated.

"Oh yes," Miss Livingstone said, rehabilitating herself with a smile, "I must keep you. I'll do anything you like to make myself more - worth while. I'll read for the pure idea. I think I'll take up modelling. There's rather a good man here just now."

"Yes," Hilda assented. "Read for the pure idea - take up modelling. It is most expedient, especially if you marry. Women who like those things sometimes have geniuses for sons. But for me, so far as I count - oh, my dear, do nothing more. You are already an achieved effect - a consummation of the exquisite in every way. Generations have been chosen among for you; your person holds the inheritance of all that is gracious and tender and discriminating in a hundred years. You are as rare as I am, and if there is anything you would take from me, I would make more than one exchange for the mere niceness of your fibre - the feeling you have for fine shades of morality and taste - all that makes you a lady, my dear."

"Such niminy piminy things," said Alicia, contradicting the light of satisfaction in her eyes. The sound of a step came from the room overhead, and the light died out. "And what good do they do me?" she cried in soft misery. "What good do they do me!"

"Considerably less than they ought. Why aren't you up there now? What simple, honester opportunity do you want than a sick-room in your own house?"

Alicia, with a frightened glance at the ceiling, flew to her side. "Oh, hush!" she cried. "Go on!"

"It ought to be there beside him, the charm of you. The room should be full of cool refreshing hints of what you are. Your profile should come between him and the twilight with a scent of violets."

"It sounds like a plot," Alicia murmured.

"It IS a plot. Why quibble about it? If you smile at him it's a plot. If you put a rose in your hair it's a deep-laid scheme, deeper than you perceive - the scheme the universe is built on. We wouldn't have lent ourselves to the arrangement, we women, if we had been consulted; we're naturally too scrupulous, but nobody asked us. 'Without our aid He did us make,' you know."

"But - deliberately - to go so far! I couldn't, I couldn't, even if I could."

Hilda leaned back in her corner with her arms extended along the back and the end of the sofa. Her hands drooped in their vigour, her knees were crossed, and her skirts draped them in long simple lines. In her symmetry and strength and the warm cloud of her hair and the soul that sat behind the shadows of her eyes Vedder might have drawn her as a tragic symbol for the poet who sang what he sometimes thought of wine and death and roses.

"I would go farther," she said, and looked as if some other thing charged with sweetness had come before her.

"And even if one gained, one would never trust one's success," Alicia faltered.

"Ah, if one gained one would hold," Hilda said; and while she smiled on her pupil in the arts of life, the tenderness grew in her eyes and came upon her lips. Her thought turned inward absently; it embraced with sweet irony, a picture of poverty, chastity, obedience. As if she knew her betrayal already complete, "I wish I had such a chance," she said.

"You wish you had such a chance!"

"I didn't mean to tell you - you have enough to do to work out your own problem; but - "

She seemed to find a joy in hesitating, to keep back the words as a miser might keep back gold. She let her secret escape through her eyes instead. She was deliberately radiant and silent. Alicia looked at her as they might have looked, across the desert, at a mirage of the Promised Land.

"Then after all he has prevailed," she said.

"Who?"

"Hamilton Bradley."

Hilda laughed - the laugh was full and light and spontaneous, as if all the training of the notes of her throat came unconsciously to make it beautiful.

"How you will hold me to my metier," she said. "Hamilton Bradley has given up trying."

"Then - "

"Then think! Be clever. Be very clever."

Alicia dropped her head in the joined length of her hands. A turquoise on one of them made them whiter, more transparent than usual. Presently she drew her face up from her clinging fingers and searched the other woman with eyes that nevertheless refused confirmation for their astonishment.

"Well?" said Hilda.

"I can think of no one - there IS no one - except - oh, it's too absurd! Not Stephen - poor dear Stephen!"

The faintest shadow drifted across Hilda's face, as if for an instant she contemplated a thing inscrutable. Then the light came back, dashed with a gravity, a gentleness.

"I admit the absurdity. Stephen - poor dear Stephen. How odd it seems," she went on, while Alicia gazed, "the announcement of it - like a thing born. But it is that - a thing born."

"I don't understand - in the least," Alicia exclaimed.

Mrs. Everard Cotes

"Neither do I. I don't indeed. Sometimes I feel like a creature with its feet in a trap. The insane, insane improbability of it!" She laughed again. It was delicious to hear her.

"But - he is a priest!"

"Much more difficult. He is a saint."

Alicia glanced at the floor. The record of another lighter moment twitched itself out of a day that was forgotten.

"Are you quite certain?" she said. "You told me once that - that there had been other times."

"They are useful, those foolish episodes. They explain to one the difference." The tone of this was very even, very usual, but Alicia was aware of a suggestion in it that accused her of aggression, that almost ranged her hostile. She hurried out of that position.

"If it were possible," she said, frowning at her embarrassment. "I see nothing - nothing REALLY against it."

"I should think not! Can't you conceive what I could do for him?"

"And what could he do for you?" Alicia asked, with a flash of curiosity.

"I don't think I can let you ask me that."

"There are such strange things to consider! Would he withdraw from the Church? Would you retire from the stage? I don't know which seems the more impossible!"

Hilda got up.

"It would be a criminal choice, wouldn't it?" she said. "I haven't made it out. And he, you know, still dreams only of Bengali souls for redemption, never of me at all."

A servant of the house with the air of a messenger brought Alicia a scrap of paper. She glanced at it, and then, with hands that trembled, began folding it together.

"He has been allowed to get up and sit in a chair," she murmured, "and he wants me to come and talk to him."

"Well," said Hilda. "Come."

She put her arm about Alicia, and drew her out of the room to the foot of the stairs. They went in silence, saying nothing even when they parted, and Alicia, of her own accord, began to ascend. Halfway up she paused and looked down. Hilda turned to meet her glance, and something of primitive puissance passed, conscious, comprehended, between the eyes of the two women.

CHAPTER XVI

For three days there had certainly been, with the invalid, no sign of anything but convalescence. An appetite to cry out upon, a chartered tendency to take small liberties, to make small demands; such indications offered themselves to the eye that looked for other betrayals. There had been opportunities - even the day nurse had gone, and Lindsay came to tea in the drawing-room - but he seemed to prefer to talk about the pattern in the carpet, or the corpulence of the khansamah, or things in the newspapers. Alicia, once, at a suggestive point, put almost a visible question into a silent glance, and Lindsay asked her for some more sugar. Surgeon-Major Livingstone, coming into his office, unexpectedly one morning, found his sister in the act of replacing a volume upon its professional shelf. It was somebody on the pathology of Indian fevers. Hilda's theory lacked so little to approve it - only technical corroboration. It might also be considered that, although Laura had expressly received the freedom of the city for intercessional or any other purpose, she did not come again. They may have heard in Crooked Lane that Duff was better. We may freely imagine that Mrs. Sand was informed; it looked as if the respite to disinterested anxiety afforded by his recovery had been taken advantage of. Lindsay was to be given time for more dignified repentance; they might now very well hand him over, Alicia thought, smiling, to the Archdeacon.

As a test, as something to reckon by, the revelation to Lindsay still in prospect, of the single visit Captain Filbert did make, was perhaps lacking in essentials. It would be an experiment of some intricacy, it might very probably work out in shades. So much would infallibly have to be put down for surprise and so much reasonably for displeasure, without any prejudice to the green hope budding underneath; the key to Hilda's theory might very well be lost in contingencies. Nevertheless, Alicia postponed her story, from day to day and from hour to hour. If her ideas about it - she kept them carefully in solution - could have been precipitated, they might have appeared in a formula favourite with her brother the Surgeon-Major, who often talked of giving nature a chance.

She told him finally on the morning of his first drive. They went together and alone, Alicia taking her brother's place in the carriage at a demand for him from the hospital. It was seven o'clock, and the morning wind swept soft and warm from over the river. There was a white light on all the stucco parapets, and their shadows slanted clear and delicately purple to the west. The dust slept on the broad roads of the Maidan, only a curling trace lifted itself here and there at the heel of a cart-bullock, and nothing had risen yet of the lazy tumult of the streets that knotted themselves in the city. From the river, curving past the statue of an Indian administrator, came a string of country people with baskets on their heads. The sun struck a vivid note with the red and the saffron they wore, turned them into an ornamentation, in the profuse Oriental taste, of the empty expanse. There was the completest freedom in the wide tree-dotted

Mrs. Everard Cotes

spaces round which the city gathered her shops and her palaces, the fullest invitation to disburden any heaviness that might oppress, to give the wings of words to any joy that might rebel in prison. The advantage of the intimacy of the landau for purposes of observation was so obvious that one imagines Alicia must have been aware of it, though as a matter of fact when she finally told Lindsay she did not look at him at all, but beyond the trees of the Eden Gardens, where the yellow dome of the post-office swelled against the morning sky; and so lost it.

He heard without exclamation, but stopped her now and then with a question. On what day precisely? And how long? And afterwards? The yellow dome was her anchor; she turned her head a little, as the road trended the other way, to keep her eyes upon it. There was an endless going round of wheels, and trees passed them in mechanical succession; a tree, and another tree; some of them had flowers on them. When he broke the silence afterwards she started as if in apprehension, but it was only to say something that anybody might have said, about the self-sacrificing energy of the organisation to which Miss Filbert belonged. Her assent was little and meagre; nothing would help her to expand it. The Salvation Army rose before her as a mammoth skeleton, without a suggestive bone.

Presently he said in a different way, as if he uttered an unguarded thought, "I had so little to make me think she cared." There was in it that phantom of speculation and concern which a sick man finds under pressure, and it penetrated Alicia that he abandoned himself to his invalid's privileges as if he valued them. He lay extended beside her among his cushions and wraps; she tried to look at him, and got as far as the hand nearest her, ungloved and sinewy, on the plaid of the rug.

"She told me it was not for your life she had been praying - only that if you died you might be saved first." Her eyes were still on his hand, and she saw the fingers close into the palm as if by an impulse. Then they relaxed again, and he said, "Oh, well," and smiled at the balancings of a crow drinking at a city conduit.

That was all. Alicia made an effort, odd and impossible enough, to postpone her impressions, even her emotions. In the meantime it was something to have got it over, and she was able at a bound to talk about the commonplaces of the roadside. In her escape from this oppression, she too gathered a freshness, a convalescent pleasure in what they saw; everything had in some way the likeness of the leafing teak-trees, tender and curative. In the broad early light that lay over the tanks there was a vague allurement, almost a presage, and the wide spaces of the Maidan made room for hope. She asked Lindsay presently if he would mind driving to the market; she wanted some flowers for that night. I think she wanted some flowers for that hour. Her thought broke so easily into the symbol of a rose.

They turned into Chowringhee, where the hibiscus bushes showed pink and crimson over the stucco walls, and at the gates of the pillared houses servants with brown and shining backs sat on their haunches in the sun and were shaved. Where the street ran into shops there was still a shuttered blankness, but here and there a doorkeeper yawned and stretched himself before an open door, and a sweeper made a cloud of dust beneath a commercial verandah. The first hoarding in a side street announced the appearance of Miss Hilda Howe for one night only as Lady Macbeth, under the kind patronage of His Excellency the Viceroy; with Jimmy Finnigan in the close proximity of professional jealousy, advertising five complete novelties for the same evening. It made a cheerful note which appealed to them both; it was a pictorial combination, Hilda and Jimmy Finnigan and the Viceroy, there was something of gay burlesque in the metropolitan posters against the crumbling plaster of the outer mosque wall where Mussulmans left their shoes. Talking of Hilda they smiled; it was a way her friends had, a testimony to the difference of her. In Alicia's smile there was a satisfaction rather subtle and in a manner superior; she knew of things.

The life of the market, the bazar, was all awake and moving. They rolled up through a crowd of inferior vehicles, empty for the moment and abandoned, where the leisurely crowd with calculation under its turbans, swayed about the market-house, and the pots of a palm-dealer ran out of bounds and made a little grove before the stall of the man who sold pith helmets. The warm air held the smell of all sorts of commodities; there was a great hum of small transactions, clink of small profits. "It makes one feel immensely practical and acquisitive," Duff said, looking at the loaded baskets on the coolies' heads; and he insisted on getting out. "I am dying to buy an enormous number of desirable things very cheap. But not combs or shirt-buttons, thank you, nor any ribbons or lace - is that good lace, Miss Livingstone? Nor even a live duck - really I am difficult. We might inquire the price of the duck though."

The sense of being contributive to his holiday

satisfaction reigned in her. She abandoned herself to it with a little smile that played steadily about her lips, as if it would tell him without her sanction, how continually she rejoiced in his regained well-being. They made their way slowly toward the flower-corner; there were so many things he wanted to stop before as they went, leaning on his stick to examine them and delighting in opportunities for making himself quite ridiculous. The country tobacco-dealer laughed too, squatting behind his basket - it was a mad sahib, but not madder than the rest; and there was no hurry. Alicia saw the pink glow of the roses beyond, where the sun struck across them over the shoulders of the crowd, and was content to reach them by degrees. They would be in their achieved sweetness a kind of climax to the hour's experience, and after that she was not entirely sure that the day would be as grey as other days.

This was the flood-time of roses, and it was exquisite in the flower-corner with the soft wind picking up their fragrance and squares of limpid sunlight standing on the wet flagstones. Some of the stall-keepers had little glass cases, and in these there was room only for the Gloire de Dijons and the La Frances and the velvety Jacks, the rest over-ran the tables and the floor in anything that would hold them. The place rioted with the joy and the passion of roses, for buying and selling. There were other flowers, nasturtiums, cornbottles, mignonette, but they had a diminished insignificant look in their tied-up bunches beside the triumph of the roses. Farther on, beyond the cage of the money-changer, the country people were hoarse with crying their vegetables, in two green rows, and beyond that where the jostling crowd divided, shone a glimpse of oranges and pomegranates. In this part there were many comers and goers, lean Mussulman table-servants, and fat Eurasian ladies who kept boarding-houses, Armenian women with embroidered shawls drawn over their heads, sailors of the port. They came to pass that way, through the sweetness of it, and this made a coign of vantage for the men with trays who were very persecuting there. Lindsay and Alicia stood together beside the roses, her hands were deep in them, he perceived with pleasure that their glow was reflected in her face. "No," she exclaimed with dainty aplomb to the man who sat cross-legged in muslin draperies on the table. "These are certainly of yesterday. There is no scent left in them - and look!" she held up the bunch and shook it, a shower of pink petals and drops of water fell upon the round of her arm above the wrist where the laces of her sleeve slipped back. Lindsay had something like a poetic appreciation of her, observing her put the bunch down tenderly as if she would not, if she could help it, find fault with any rose. The dealer drew out another, and handed it to her; a long-stemmed, wide-open, perfect thing, and it was then that her glance of delight, wandering, fell upon Laura Filbert. Lindsay looked instantly, curiously in the same direction, and Alicia was aware that he also saw. There ensued a terse moment with a burden of silence and the strangest misgivings, in which he may have imagined that he had his part alone but which was the heavier for her because of him. These two had seen the girl before only under circumstances that suggested protection, that made excuse, on a platform receiving the respect of attention, marching with her fellows under common conventions, common orders. Here, alone, slipping in and out among the crowd, she looked abandoned, the sight of her in her bare white feet and the travesty of her dress was a wound. Her humility screamed its violation, its debasement of her race; she woke the impulse to screen her and hurry her away as if she were a woman walking in her sleep. She had on her arm a sheaf of the War Cry. This was another indignity; she offered them right and left, no one had a pice for her except one man, a sailor, who refused the paper. When he rejoined his companions there was a hoarse laugh, and the others turned their heads to look after her.

The flower-dealer eyed his customers with contemptuous speculation, seeing what had claimed their eyes. There was nothing new, the "mem" passed every day at this hour. She did no harm and no good. He, too, looked at her as she came closer, offering her paper to Alladiah Khan, a man impatient in his religion, who refused it, mumbling in his beard. With a gesture of appeal she pressed it on him, saying something. Then Alladiah's green turban shook, his beard, dyed red in Mecca, waggled; he raised his arm, and Laura in white astonishment darted from under it. They seldom did that.

Alicia caught at the stall table and clung to it, as Lindsay made his stride forward. She saw him twist his hand in the beard of Mecca and fling the man into the road; she was aware of a vague thankfulness that it ended there, as if she expected bloodshed. More plainly she saw the manner of Duff's coming back to the girl and the way in which, with a look of half-frightened satisfaction, Laura gave herself up to him. He was hurrying her away without a word. Her surrender was as absolute and final as if she had been one of those desirable things he said he wanted to buy. Alicia intercepted, as it were, the indignity of being forgotten, stepping up to them. "Take her home in the carriage," she said to Duff, "and send it back for me. I shall be here a long time still - quite a long time." She stared at Captain Filbert as she spoke, but made no answer to the "Good-morning! God bless you!" with which the girl perfunctorily addressed her. When they left her she looked down at the long-stemmed rose, the perfect one, and drove a thorn of it deep into her palm, as other creatures will sometimes hurt themselves more to suffer less. It was not in the least fantastic of her, for she was not aware that she still held it, but that was the only rose she brought away.

CHAPTER XVII

Hilda left the road, with a trace of its red dust on the hem of her skirt, and struck out into the Maidan. It spread before her, green where the slanting sun searched through the short blades, brown and yellow in the distance, where the light lay on the top of the withered grass. It was like a great English park, with something of the village common, only the trees, for the most part, made avenues over it, running an arbitrary half-mile this way or that, with here and there a group dotted about in the open; and the brimming tank-pots were of India, and of nowhere else in the world. The sun was dipping behind the masts that showed where the straight border of the river ran, and the shadows of the pipals and the banyans were richly purple over the roads. The light struck on the stuccoed upper verandahs of the houses in Chowringhee which made behind their gardens the other border, and seemed to push them back, to underline their scattered insignificance, hinting that the Maidan at its pleasure might surge over them altogether. Calcutta, the teeming capital, lived in the streets and gullies behind that chaste frontage, and quarrelled over drainage schemes; but out here cattle grazed in quiet companies, and squirrels played on the boles of the trees. Calcutta the capital indeed was superimposed; one felt that always at this time, when the glow came and stood in the air among the tamarinds, and there was nothing anywhere but luminous space and indolent stillness, and the wrangling and winging of crows. What persisted then under the span of the sky, was the old India of rich tradition, and a bullock beneath the yoke, jogging through the evening to his own place where the blue haze hid the little huts on the rim of the city, the real India, and the rest was fiction and fabrication.

The grass was crisp and pleasant. Hilda deliberately sought its solace for her feet, letting their pressure linger. All day long the sun had been drawing the fragrance and the life out of it, and now the air had a sweet, warm, and grateful scent, like that of harvests. The crickets had been at it since five o'clock, and though the city rose not half a mile across the grass, it was the crickets she heard and listened to. In making private statements of things, the crickets offered a chorus of agreement, and they never interrupted. Not that she had much to consider, poor girl, which lent itself to a difference of opinion. One might have thought her, to meet a situation at any point like her own, not badly equipped. She had all the argument - which is like saying all the arms - and the most accurate understanding; but the only practical outcome of these things had been an intimate lesson in the small value of the intelligence, that flavoured her state with cynicism and made it more piquant. She did not altogether scorn her own intelligence as the result, because it had always admitted the existence of dominating facts that belonged to life and not to reason; it was only the absurd unexpectedness of coming across one herself. One might think round such a fact and talk round it - there were less exquisite satisfactions - but it was not to be cowed or abated, and in the end the things one said were only words.

Out there in the grassy spaces she let her thoughts flow through her veins with her blood, warm and free. The primitive things she saw helped her to a fulness of life; the south wind brought her profound sweet presciences. A coolie-woman, carrying a basket on her head, stopped and looked at her with full glistening eyes; they smiled at each other, and passed on. She found herself upon a narrow path, worn smooth by other barefooted coolie-folk; it made in its devious way toward the rich mists where the sun had gone down; and Hilda followed, breasting the glow and the colour and the wide, flat expanse, as if in the India of it there breathed something exquisitely sensuous and satisfying. It struck sharp on her senses; she almost consciously thanked Heaven for such a responsive set of nerves. Always and everywhere she was intensely conscious of what she saw and of how she saw it; and it was characteristic of her that she found in that saffron February evening, spreading to a purple rim, with wandering points of colour in a soldier's coat or a coachman's turban, an atmosphere and a mise en scene for her own complication. She could take a tenderly artistic view of that, more soothing a good deal than any result that came of examining it in other lights. And she did, aware, with smiling eyes, of how full of colour, how dramatic it was.

Nevertheless, she had hardly closed with it; any material outcome seemed a great way off, pursuable by conjecture when there was time for that. For the present, there on the Maidan with the south wind, she took it with her head thrown up, in her glad, free fashion, as something that came in the way of life - the delightful way of life - with which it was absurd to quarrel because of a slight inconvenience or incongruity, things which helped, after all, to make existence fascinating.

A marigold lay in the path, an orange-coloured scrap with a broken stem, dropped from some coolie's necklace. Hilda picked it up, and drew in the crude, warm pungency of its smell. She closed her eyes and drifted on the odour, forgetting her speculations, losing her feet. All India and all her passion was in that violent, penetrating fragrance; it brought her, as she gave her senses up to it, a kind of dual perception of being near the core, the throbbing centre of the world's meaning.

Her awakened glance fell upon Duff Lindsay. He hastened to meet her, in his friendly way; and she was glad of the few yards that lay between them and gave transit to her senses from that other plane. They encountered each other in full recognition of the happiness of the accident, and he turned back with her as a matter of course. It was a kind of fruition of all that light and colour and passive delight that they should meet and take a path together; she at least was aware. Hilda asked him if he was quite all right now, and he said "Absolutely" with a shade of emphasis. She charged him with having been a remarkable case, and he piled up illustrations of what he felt able to do in his convalescence. There was something in the way he insisted upon his restoration which made her hasten to take her privilege of intimacy.

"And I hear I may congratulate you," she said. "You have got what you wanted."

"Someone has told you," he retorted, "who is not friendly to it."

"On the contrary, someone who has given it the most cordial support - Alicia Livingstone."

He mused upon this for an instant, as if it presented Alicia for the first time under such an aspect.

"She has been immensely kind," he asserted. "But she wasn't at first. At first, she was hostile, like you, only that her hostility was different, just as she is different. She had to be converted," he went on hopefully, "but it was less difficult than I imagined. I think she takes a kind of pride in conquering her prejudices, and being true to the real breadth of her nature."

"I am sure she would like her nature to be broad. She might very well be content that it is charming. And what is the difference between her hostility and mine?"

"The main difference," Lindsay said, with a gay half round upon her, "is that hers has sweetly vanished, while yours" - he made a dramatic gesture - "walks between us."

"I know. I tried to stiffen her. I appealed to the worst in her on your behalf. But it wasn't any use. She succumbed, as you say, to her nobler instincts."

Hilda stabbed a great crisp fallen teak leaf with her parasol, and spent her paradox in twirling it.

"One can so easily get an affair of one's own out of all proportion," Duff said. "And I should be sorry - do you really want me to talk about this?"

"Don't be stupid. Of course."

He took her permission with plain avidity.

"Well, it grew plain to Miss Livingstone, as it will to everybody else who knows or cares," he said; "I mean chiefly Laura's tremendous desirability. Her beauty would go for something anywhere, but I don't want to insist on that. What marks her even more is the wonderful purity and transparency of her mind; one doesn't find it often now, women's souls are so clouded with knowledge. I think that sort of thing appeals especially to me because my own design isn't in the least esoteric. I'm only a man. Then she was so ludicrously out of her element. A creature like that should be surrounded by the softest refinement in her daily life. That was my chance. I could offer her her place. It's not much to counterbalance what she is, but it helps, roughly speaking, to equalise matters."

Hilda looked at him with sudden critical interest, missing an emanation from him. It was his enthusiasm. A cheerfulness had come upon him instead. Also what he said had something categorical in it, something crisp and arranged. He himself received benefit from the consideration of it, and she was aware that if this result followed, her own "conversion" was of very secondary importance.

"So!" she said meditatively, as they walked.

"After it happens, when it is an accomplished fact, it will be so plainly right that nobody will think twice about it," Duff went on in an encouraged voice. "It's odd how one's ideas materialise. I want her drawing-room to be white and gold, with big yellow silk cushions."

"When is it to happen?"

"Beginning of next cold weather - in not quite a year."

"Ah! then there will be time. Time to get the white and gold furniture. It wouldn't be my taste quite. Is it Alicia's?"

"It's our own at present, Laura's and mine. We have talked it over together. And I don't think she would ask Miss Livingstone. In matters of taste women are rather rivals, aren't they?"

"Oh Lord!" Hilda exclaimed, and bit her lip. "Where is Miss Filbert now?"

"At Number Ten, Middleton Street."

"With the Livingstones?"

"Is it so astonishing? Miss Livingstone has been most practical in her kindness. I have gone back, of course, to my perch at the club, and Laura is to stay with them until she sails."

"She sails?"

"In the Sutlej, next Wednesday. She's got three months' leave. She really hasn't been well, and her superior officer is an accommodating old sort. She resigns at home, and I'm sending her to some dear old friends of mine. She hasn't any particular people of her own. She's got a notion of taking lessons of some kind - perfectly unnecessary, but if it amuses her - during the summer. And of course she will have to get her outfit together."

"And in December," said Hilda, "she comes out and marries you?"

"Not a Calcutta wedding. I meet her in Madras and we come up together."

"Ideal," said Hilda; "and is Calcutta much scandalised?"

"Calcutta doesn't know. If I had had my way in the beginning I fancy I would have trumpeted it. But now I suppose it's wiser - why should one offer her up at their dinner-tables?"

"Especially when they would make so little of her," said Hilda absently.

The coolie track had led them into the widest part of the Maidan, where it slopes to the south, and the huts of Bowanipore. There was nothing about them but a spreading mellowness and the baked turf underfoot. The cloudy yellow twilight disclosed that a man a little way off was a man, and not a horse, but did hardly more. "I'm tired," Hilda said suddenly, "let us sit down," and sank comfortably on the fragrant grass. Lindsay dropped beside her and they sat for a moment in silence. A cricket chirped noisily a few inches from them. Hilda put out her hand in that direction and it ceased. Sounds wandered across from the encircling city, evening sounds, softened in their vagrancy, and lights came out, topaz points in the level glow.

"She is making a tremendous sacrifice," Lindsay went on; "I seem to see its proportions more clearly now."

Hilda glanced at him with infinite kindness. "You are

an awfully good sort, Duff," she said; "I wish you were out of Asia."

"Oh, a magnificent sort." The irony was contemplative, as if he examined himself to see.

"You can make her life delightful to her. The sacrifice will not endure, you know."

"One can try. It will be worth doing." He said it as if it were a maxim, and Hilda, perceiving this, had no answer ready. As they sat without speaking, the heart of the after-glow drew away across the river, and left something chill and empty in the spaces about them. Things grew hard of outline, the Maidan became an unlimited expanse of commonplace, grey and unyielding; the lines of gas-lamps on the roads came very near. "What a difference it makes!" Lindsay exclaimed, looking after the vanished light, "and how suddenly it goes!"

Hilda turned concerned eyes upon him, and then looked with keen sadness far into the changed landscape. "Ah, well, my dear," she said, with apparent irrelevance, "we must take hold of life with both hands." She made a movement to rise, and he, jumping to his feet, helped her. As if the moment had some special significance, something to be underlined, he kept her hand while he said, "you will always represent something in mine. I can depend upon you - I shall know that you are there."

"Yes," she said sincerely. "Yes indeed," and it seemed to her that he looked thin and intense as he stood beside her - unless it was only another effect of atmosphere. "After all," she said, as they turned to walk back again across the withered grass, "your fever has taken a good deal out of you."

CHAPTER XVIII

Finally the days of Laura Filbert's sojourn under the Livingstones' roof followed each other into the past that is not much pondered. Alicia at one time valued the impression that life in Calcutta disappeared entirely into this kind of history, that one's memory there was a rubbish heap of which one naturally did not trouble to stir up the dust. It gave a soothing wistfulness to discontent to think this, which a discerning glance might often have seen about her lips and eyebrows as she lay back among her carriage cushions under the flattery of the south wind in the course of her evening drive. She had ceased latterly, however, to note particularly that or any impression. Such things require range and atmosphere, and she seemed to have no more command over these; her outlook was blocked by crowding, narrowing facts. There was certainly no room for perceptions creditable to one's intellect or one's taste. Also it may be doubted whether Alicia would have tried the days of her hospitality to Captain Filbert by her general standard of worthlessness. She turned away from them more actively than from the rest, but it was because they bristled, naturally enough, with dilemmas and distresses which she made a literal effort to forget. As a matter of fact there were not very many days, and they were largely filled with millinery. Even the dilemmas and distresses, when they asserted themselves, were more or less overswept, as if for the

Mrs. Everard Cotes

sake of decency, by billows of spotted muslin, with which Celine, who felt the romance of the situation, made herself marvellously clever. Celine, indeed, was worth in this exigency many times her wages. Alicia hastened to "lend" her to the fullest extent, and she spent hours with Miss Filbert contriving and arranging, a kind of conductor of her mistress's beneficence. It became plain that Laura preferred the conductor to the source, and they stitched together while she, with careful reserves, watched for the casual sidelights upon modes and manners that came from the lips of the maid. At other times she occupied herself with her Bible - she had adopted, as will be guessed, the grateful theory of Mrs. Sand, that she had only changed the sphere of her ministrations. She had several times felt, seated beside Celine, how grateful she ought to be that her spiritual paths for the future would be paths of such pleasantness, though Celine herself seemed to stand rather far from their border, probably because she was a Catholic. Mrs. Sand came occasionally to upbuild her, and after that Laura had always a fresh remembrance of how much she had done in giving so generous a friend as Duff Lindsay to the Army in Calcutta. It was reasonable enough that there should be a falling off in Mr. Lindsay's atten- dance just now in Laura's absence, but when they were united, Mrs. Sand hoped there would be very few evening services when she, the Ensign, would miss their bright faces.

Lindsay himself came every afternoon, and Laura made tea, and pressed upon him, solicitously, everything there was to eat. He found her submissive and wishful to be pleasant. She sat up straight, and said it was much hotter than they had it this time of year up-country, but nothing at all to complain of yet. He also discovered her to be practical; she showed him the bills for the muslins, and explained one or two bargains. She seemed to wish to make it clear to him that it need not be, after all, so very expensive to take a wife. In the course of a few days one of the costumes was completed, and when he came she had it on, appearing before him for the first time in secular dress. The stays insisted a little cruelly on the lines of her figure, and the tight bodice betrayed her narrow-chested. Above its frills her throat protruded unusually, with a curve outward like that of some wading bird's, and her arms, in their unaccustomed sleeves, hung straight at her sides. She had put on the hat that matched; it was the kind of pretty disorderly hat with waving flowers that demands the shadow of short hair along the forehead, and she had not thought of that way of making it becoming. Among these accessories the significance of her face retreated to a point vague and distant, its lightly-pencilled lines seemed half erased.

She made no demand for admiration on this occasion, she seemed sufficiently satisfied with herself; but after a time when they were sitting together on the sofa, and he still pursued the lines of her garment with questioning eyes, she recalled him to the conventionalities of the situation.

"You needn't be afraid of mussing it," she said.

The ship she took her departure in sailed from its jetty in the river at six o'clock in the morning. Preparations for her comfort had been completed over night; indeed she slept on board, and Duff had only the duty and the sentiment of actual parting in the morning. He found her in a sequestered corner of the fresh swabbed quarter-deck. She wore her Army clothes - she had come on board in one of the muslins - and she was softly crying. From the jetty on the other side of the ship arose, amid tramping feet and shouted orders and the creaking of the luggage-crane, the over-ruling sound of a hymn. Ensign Sand and a company had come apparently to pay the last rites to a fellow-officer whom they should no more meet on earth, bearing her heavenly commission.

> "Farewell, faithful friend, we must now bid adieu
> To those joys and pleasures we've tasted with you,
> We've laboured together, united in heart,
> But now we must close and soon we must part."

They had said good-bye to her and God bless you, all of them, but they evidently meant to sing the ship out of port. Lindsay sat down beside the victim of the demonstration and quietly took her hand. There was a consciousness newly guilty in his discomfort, which he owed perhaps to a ghost of futility that seemed to pace up and down before him, between the ranks of the steamer-chairs. Nevertheless as she presently turned a calmed face to him with her pale apology he had the sensation of a rebound toward the ideal that had finally perished in the spotted muslin, and when a little later he watched the long backward trail of smoke as the steamer moved down the clear morning river, he reflected that it was a satisfaction to have prevailed.

The Sutlej had gone far on her tranquil course by the evening of a dinner in Middleton Street, at which the guests, it was understood, were to proceed later to a party given at Government House by his Excellency the Viceroy. Alicia, when she included Duff in her invitations, felt an assurance that the steamer must by that time have reached Aden, and rose almost with buoyancy to the illusion you can make if you like, with the geographical mile. She could hardly have left him out in any case - he could almost have demanded an explanation - since it was one of those parties which she gave every now and then, undiscouraged, with the focus of Hilda Howe. It had to be every now and then, because Calcutta society was so little adapted to appreciate meeting talented actresses - there were so many people whom Alicia had to consider as to whether they would "mind." Hilda marvelled at the sanguine persistence of Miss Livingstone's efforts in this direction, the results were so fragmentary, so dislocated and indecisive, but she also rejoiced. She took life, as may have appeared, at a broad and generous level, it quite comprehended the salient points of a Calcutta dinner-party; and it was seldom that she failed, metaphorically speaking, to carry away a bone from the feast. If you found this reprehensible she would have told you she had observed they do it in Japan, where manners are the best in the world.

Doubtless Hilda would have dwelt longer upon such a dinner-party than I, with no consolatory bone to gnaw in private, find myself inclined to do. To me it is depressing and a little cruel to be compelled to betray the inadequacy of the personal element at Alicia's banquets, especially in connection with the conspicuous excellence of the cooking. A poverty of cuisine would have provoked no contrast, and one irony the less would have been offered up to the gods that season. The limitations of her resources were, of course, arbitrary, that is plain in the fact that she asked such a person as the Head of the Department of Education, with no better reason than that he had laid almost the whole of Shelley under critical notes for the benefit of Calcutta University. There was also a civilian who had written a few years before an article in the Nineteenth Century about the aboriginal tribes of the Central Provinces, and the lady attached to him, who had been at one time the daughter of a Lieutenant-Governor. The Barberrys were there because Mrs. Barberry loved meeting anybody that was clever, admired brains beyond anything; and an A.D.C. who had to be asked because Mrs. Barberry was; and Captain Salter Symmes, who took leading male parts in Mr. Pinero's plays when they were produced in Simla and was invariably considered up there to have done them better than any professional they have at home, though he was even more successful as a contortionist when the entertainment happened to be a burlesque. Taking Hilda and Lindsay and Stephen Arnold as a basis, Alicia had built up her party, with the contortionist as it were at the apex, on his head. The Livingstones had family connection with a leading London publishing firm, and Alicia may possibly have reflected as she surveyed her completed work, how much better than capering captains she could have done in Chelsea, though it cannot be admitted likely that she would harbour, at that particular instant, so ungracious a thought. And indeed it was a creditable party, it would almost unanimously call itself, next day, a delightful one. Miss Howe made the most agreeable excitement, you might almost have heard the heart-beats of the wife of the literary civilian, as she just escaped being introduced, and so availed herself of the dinner's opportunity for intimate observation without letting herself in a particle - most clever. Mrs. Barberry, of course, rushed upon the spear, she always did, and made a gushing little speech with every eye upon her in the middle of the room, without a thought of consequences. The A.D.C. was also empresse, one would have thought that he himself was acting, the way he bowed and picked up Hilda's fan - a grace lingered in it from the minuet he had danced the week before, in ruffles and patches, with the daughter of the Commander-in-Chief. Duff got out of the way to enable the newly introduced Head of the Department of Education to inform Miss Howe that he never went to the theatre in Calcutta himself, it was much too badly ventilated; and Stephen Arnold arriving late, shot like an embarrassed arrow through the company to Alicia's side, and was still engaged there in grieved explanation when dinner was announced.

There were pink water-lilies, and Stephen said grace - those were the pictorial features. Half of the people had taken their seats when he began; there was a hasty scramble, and a decorous half-checked smile. Hilda, at the first word of the brief formula, blushed hotly; then she stood while he spoke, with bowed head and clasped hands like a reverently inclining statue. Her long lashes brushed her cheek; she drew a kind of isolation from the way her manner underlined the office. The civilian's wife, with a side-glance, settled it off-hand that she was absurdly affected; and indeed to an acuter intelligence it might have looked as if she took, with the artistry of habit, a cue that was not offered.

That was the one instant, however, in which the civilian's wife, observing the actress, was gratified; and it was so brief that she complained afterwards that Miss Howe was disappointing. She certainly went out of her way to be normal. Since it was her daily business to personate exceptional individuals, it seemed to be her pleasure that night to be like everybody else. She did it on opulent lines; there was a richness in her agreement that the going was as hard as iron on the Ellenborough course, and a soft ingenuousness in her inquiries about punkahs and the brain-fever bird that might have aroused suspicion, but after a brief struggle to respond to the unusualness she ought to have represented, Alicia's guests gratefully accepted her on their own terms instead. She expanded in the light and the glow and the circumstance; she looked with warm pleasure at the orchids the men wore and the jewelled necks of the women. The social essence of Alicia's little dinner-party passed into her, and she moved her head like the civilian's wife. She felt the champagne investing her chatter and the chatter of the Head of the Department of Education with the most satisfying qualities, which were oddly stimulated when she glanced over the brim of her glass at Stephen, sitting at the turn of the oval, giving a gravely humble but perfunctory attention to Mrs. Barberry, and drinking water. The occasion grew before her into a gorgeous flower, living, pulsating, and in the heart of its light and colour the petals closed over her secret, over him, the unconscious priest with the sloping shoulders, thinking of abstinence and listening to Mrs. Barberry.

It transpired when the men came up that there was no unanimity about going to Government House. The Livingstones craved the necessity of absence, if anyone would supply it by staying on; it would be a boon they said, and cited the advancement of the season. "One gets to bed so much earlier," Surgeon-Major Livingstone urged, at which Alicia raised her eyebrows and everybody laughed. Lindsay elected to gratify them, with the proclaimed purpose of seeing how long Livingstone could be kept up, and the civilian pair agreed, apparently from a tendency to remain seated. The A.D.C. had, of course, to go; duty called him; and he declared a sense of slighted hospitality that anybody should remain behind. "Besides," he cried, with ingenuous privilege, "who's goin' to chaperone Miss Howe?"

Hilda stood in the midst. Tall, in violet velvet, she had a flush that made her magnificent; her eyes were deep and soft. It was patent that she was out of proportion to the other women, body and soul; there was altogether too much of her; and it was only the men, when Captain Corby spoke, who looked silently responsive.

"We're coming away so early," said Mrs. Barberry, buttoning her glove. Hilda had begun to smile, and, indeed, the situation had its humour, but there was also behind her eyes an appreciation of another sort. "Don't," she said to Alicia, in the low, quick reach of her prompting tone, as if the other had mistaken her cue, but the moment hardly permitted retreat, and Alicia turned an unflinching graceful front to the lady in the Department of Education. "Then I think I must ask you," she said.

The educational husband was standing so near Hilda that she got the very dregs of the glance of consternation his little wife gave him as she replied, a trifle red and stiff, that she was sure she would be delighted.

"Nobody suggests ME!" exclaimed Captain Corby resentfully. They were gathered in the hall, the carriages were driving to the open door, the Barberry's glistening brougham whisking them off, and then the battered vehicle in Hilda's hire. It had an air of ludicrous forlornness, with its damaged paint and its tied-up harness. Hilda, when its door closed upon the purple vision of her, might have been a modern Cinderella in mid-stage of backward transformation.

"I could chaperone you all!" she cried gaily back at them, as she passed down the steps; and in the relief of the general exclamation it seemed reasonable enough that Stephen Arnold should lean into the gharry to see that she was quite comfortable. The unusual thing, which nobody else heard, was that he said to her then with shamed discomfort, "It doesn't matter - it doesn't matter," and that Hilda, driving away, found herself without a voice to answer the good-nights they chorussed after her.

Arnold begged a seat in Captain Corby's dogcart, and Hilda, with her purple train in her lap, heard the wheels following all the way. She re-encountered the lady to whom she had been entrusted, whose name it occurs to me was Winstick, in the cloakroom. They were late; there was hardly anybody else but the attendants; and Mrs. Winstick smiled freely, and said she loved the colour of Hilda's dress; also that she would give worlds for an invisible hairpin - oh, thank you! - and that it was simply ducky of her Excellency to have pink powder as well as white put out. She did hope Miss Howe would enjoy the evening - they would meet again later on; she must not forget to look at the chunam pillars in the ballroom - perfectly lovely. So she vanished; but Hilda went with certainty into the corridor to find Arnold pacing up and down the red strip of carpet, with his hands clasped behind him and his head thrust forward, waiting for her.

They dropped together into the crowd and walked among well-dressed women, men in civilian black and men in uniform, up and down the pillared spaces of the ballroom. People had not been asked to dance, and they seemed to walk about chiefly for observation. There was, of course, the opportunity of talking and of listening to the band which discoursed in a corner behind palms, but the distraction which is the social Nemesis of bureaucracy was in the air, visibly increasing in the neighbourhoods of the Viceroy and the Commander-in-Chief, and made the commonplaces people uttered to each other disjointed and fragmentary, while it was plain that few were aware whether music was being rendered or not. Anyone sensitive to pervading mental currents in gatherings of this sort would have found the relief of concentration and directness only near the buffet that ran along one side of the room, where the natural instinct played, without impediment, upon soup and sandwiches.

They did not look much at Hilda, even on the arm of her liveried priest. She was a strange vessel, sailing in from beyond their ken, and her pilot was almost as novel, yet they were incurious. Their interests were not in any way diffused, they had one straight line and it led upward, pausing at the personalities clerked above them, with an ultimate point in the head of a department. The Head of the Department was the only person unaware, when addressed, of a travelling eye in search over his shoulder of somebody with whom it would be more advantageous to converse. Yet there were a few people apparently not altogether indifferent to the presence of Miss Howe. She saw them here and there, and when Arnold said, "It must seem odd to you, but I know hardly anybody here. We attempt no social duties," she singled out this one and that, whom Alicia had asked to meet her, and mentioned them to him with a warm pleasure in implying one of the advantages of belonging to the world rather than to the cloister. Stephen knew their names and their dignities. He received what she said with suitably impressed eyebrow and nods of considerate assent. Hilda carried him along, as it were, in their direction. She was full that night of a triumphant sense of her own vitality, her success and value as a human unit. There was that in her blood which assured her of a welcome, it had logic in it, with the basis of her rarity, her force, her distinction among other women. She pressed forward to human fellowship with a smile on her lips, as a delightful matter of course, going towards the people who were not indifferent to the fact that she was there, who could not be entirely, since they had some sort of knowledge of her.

In no case did they ignore her, but they were so cheerfully engaged in conversation that they were usually quite oblivious of her. She encountered this animated absorption two or three times, then turning she found that the absorbed ones had changed their places - were no longer in her path. One lady put herself at a safe distance and then bowed, with much cordiality. It was extraordinary in a group of five how many glistening shoulders would be presented, quite without offence, to her approach. Mrs. Winstick had hidden behind the Superintendent of Stamps and Stationery, to whom she was explaining, between spoonfuls of strawberry ice, her terrible situation. And from the lips of another lady whose face she knew, she heard after she had passed, "Don't you think it's rather an omnium gatherum?"

It was like Hilda Howe to note at that moment with serious interest, how the little world about them had the same negative attitude for the missionary priest beside her, presenting it with a hardly perceptible difference. Within its limits there was plainly no room for him either. His acquaintances - he had a few - bowed with the kind of respect which implies distance, and in the wandering eyes of the others it was plain that he did not exist. She saw, too, with a very delicate pleasure, that he carried himself in his grave humility untouched and unconscious. Expecting nothing he was unaware that he received nothing. It was odd, and in its way charming, that she who saw and knew drew from their mutual grievance a sense of pitiful protection for him, the unconscious one. For herself, the tide that bore her on was too deep to let these things hurt her, she looked down and saw the soreness and humiliation of them pictorially, at the bottom, gliding smoothly over. They brought no stereotype to her smile, no dissonance to what she found to say. When at last she and Arnold sat down together her standpoint was still superior, and she herself was so aloof from it all that she could talk about it without bitterness, divorcing the personal pang from a social manifestation of some dramatic value. In offering up her egotism that way she really only made more subtle sacrifices to it, but one could hardly expect such a consideration, just then, to give her pause. She anointed his eyelids, she made him see, and he was relieved to find in her light comment that she took the typical Mrs. Winstick less seriously than he had supposed when they drove away from the Livingstones'. It could not occur to him to correct the impression he had then by the sound of his own voice uttering sympathy.

"But I know now what a wave feels like dashing against a cliff," she said. "Fancy my thinking I could impose myself! That is the wave's reflection."

"It goes back into the sea which is its own; and there,"

said the priest, whom nature had somehow cheated by the false promise of high moralities out of an inheritance of beauty, - "and there, I think, is depth and change and mystery, with joy in the obedience of the tides and a full beating upon many shores - "

"Ah, my sea! I hear it calling always, even," she said half-reflectively, "when I am talking to you. But sometimes I think I am not a wave at all, only a shell, to be stranded and left, always with the calling in my ears - " She seemed to have dropped altogether into reverie, and then looked up suddenly, laughing, because he could not understand.

"After all," she said practically, "what has that to do with it? One doesn't blame these people. They are stupid - that's all. They want the obvious. The leading lady of Mr. Llewellyn Stanhope - without the smallest diamond - who does song and dance on Saturday nights - what can you expect! If I had a great name they would be pleased enough to see me. It is one of the rewards of the fame." She was silent for a moment, and then she added, "They are very poor."

"Those rewards! I have sometimes thought," Arnold said, "that you were not devoured by thirst for them."

"When we are together, you and I," she answered simply, "I never am."

He took it at its face value. They had had some delightful conversations. If her words awakened anything in him it was the remembrance of these. The solace of her companionship presented itself to him again, and her statement gave their mutual confidence another seal; that was all. They sat where they were for half an hour, and something like antagonism and displeasure towards the secretaries' wives settled upon them, from which Hilda, interrupting a glance or two from the ladies purring past, drew suspicion. "I am going now," she said. "It - it isn't quite suitable here," and there was just enough suggestion in the point of her fan to make him think of his frock. "It is an unpardonable truth that if we stay any longer I shall make people talk about you."

He turned astonished eyes upon her, eyes in which she remembered afterwards there was absolutely nothing but a literal and pained apprehension of what she said. "You are a good woman," he exclaimed. "How could such a thing be possible!"

The faintest embarrassment, the merest suggestion of distress, came into her face and concentrated in her eyes, which she fixed upon him as if she would bring his words to the last analysis, and answer him as she would answer a tribunal.

"A good woman?" she repeated, "I don't know - isn't that a refinement of virtue? No; standing on my sex I make no claim, but as PEOPLE go I am good. Yes, I am good."

"In my eyes you are splendid," he replied, content, and gave her his arm. They went together through the reception-rooms, and the appreciation of her grew in him. If in the bright and silken distance he had not seen his Bishop it might have glowed into a cordiality of speech with his distinctive individual stamp on it. But he saw his Bishop, his ceinture tightened on him, and he uttered only the trite saying about the folly of counting on the sensibility of swine.

"Yes," she laughed into her good-night to him, "but I'm not sure that it isn't better to be the pig than the pearl."

CHAPTER XIX

"Not long ago," said Hilda, "I had a chat with him. We sat on the grass in the middle of the Maidan, and there was nothing to interfere with my impressions."

"What were your impressions? No!" Alicia cried. "No! Don't tell me. It is all so peaceful now, and simple, and straightforward. You think such extraordinary things. He comes here quite often, to talk about her. He is coming this afternoon. So I have impressions too - and they are just as good."

"All right." Hilda crossed her knees more comfortably. "WHAT did you say the Surgeon-Major paid for those Teheran tiles?"

"Something absurd - I've forgotten. He writes to her regularly, diary letters, by every mail."

"Do you tell him what to put into them?"

"Hilda, sometimes - you're positively gross."

"I daresay, my dear. You didn't come out of a cab, and you never are. I like being gross, I feel nearer to nature then, but I don't say that as an excuse. I like the smell of warm kitchens and the talk of bus-drivers, and bread and herrings for my tea - all the low satisfactions appeal to me. Beer, too, and hand-organs."

"I don't know when to believe you. He talks about her quite freely, and - and so do I. She is really interesting in her way."

"And in perspective."

"Why should you be odiously smart. He and Stephen" - her glance was tentative - "have made it up."

"Oh?"

"He admits now that Stephen was justified, from his point of view. But of course that is easy enough when you have come off best."

"Of course."

"Hilda, what do you THINK?"

"Oh, I think it's deplorable - you have always known what I think. Have you seen him lately - I mean your cousin?"

"He lunched with us yesterday. He was more enthusiastic than ever about you."

"I wish you could tell me that he hadn't mentioned my name. I don't want his enthusiasm. The pit gives one that."

"Hilda, tell me; what is your idea of - of what it ought to be? What is the principal part of it? Not enthusiasm - adoration?"

"Goodness, no! Something quite different and quite simple - too simple to explain. Besides, it is a thing that requires the completest ignorance to discuss comfortably. Do you want me to vivisect my soul? You yourself, can you talk about what most possesses you?"

"Oh," protested Alicia, "I wasn't thinking about myself," and at the same moment the door opened and Hilda said, "Ah! Mr. Lindsay."

There was a hint of the unexpected in Duff's response to Miss Howe's greeting, and a suggestion in the way he sat down that this made a difference, and that he must find other things to say. He found them with facility, while Hilda decided that she would finish her tea before she went. Alicia, busy with the urn, seemed satisfied to abandon them to each other, to take a decorative place in the conversation, interrupting it with brief inquiries about cream and sugar. Alicia waited, it was her way; she sank almost palpably into the tapestries until some reviving circumstance should bring her out again, a process which was quite compatible with her little laughs and comments. She waited, offering repose, and unconscious even of that. You know Hilda Howe as a creature of bold reflections. Looking at Alicia Livingstone behind the teapot, the conviction visited her that a sex three-quarters of this fibre explained the monastic clergy.

"It is reported that you have performed the wonderful, the impossible," Lindsay said; "that Llewellyn Stanhope goes home solvent."

"I don't know how he can help it now. But I have to be very firm. He's on his knees to me to do Ibsen. I tell him I will if he'll combine with Jimmy Finnigan and bring the Surprise Party on between the acts. The only way it would go, in this capital."

"Oh, do produce Ibsen," Alicia exclaimed; "I've never seen one of his plays - doesn't it sound terrible!"

"If people will elect to live upon a coral strand - oh, I should like to, for you and Duff here, but Ibsen is the very last man to deliver to a scratch company. He must have equal merit, or there's no meaning. You see he makes none of the vulgar appeals. It would be a tame travesty - nobody could redeem it alone. You must keep to the old situations, the reliable old dodges, when you play in any part of Asia."

"I never shall cease to regret that I didn't see you in The Offence of Galilee?" Duff said. "Everyone who knows the least bit about it said you were marvellous in that."

"Marvellous," said Alicia

Hilda gazed straight before her for an instant without speaking. The others looked at her absent eyes. "A bazar trick or two helped me," she said, and glanced with vivacity at any other subject that might be hanging on the wall, or visible out of the window.

"And are you really invincible about not putting it on again in Calcutta?" Duff asked.

"Not in Calcutta, or anywhere. The rest hate it - nobody has a chance but me," Hilda said, and got up.

"Oh, I don't know," Alicia began, but Miss Howe was

already half-way out of the discussion, in the direction of the door. There was often a brusqueness in her comings and goings, but she usually left a flavour of herself behind. One turned with facility to talk about her, this being the easiest way of applying the stimulus that came of talking to her. It was more conspicuous than either of these two realised that they accepted her retreat without a word, that there was even between them a consciousness of satisfaction that she had gone.

"This morning's mail," said Alicia, smiling brightly at Lindsay, "brought you a letter, I know." It was extraordinary how detached she could be from her vital personal concern in him. It seemed relegated to some background of her nature while she occupied herself with the immediate play of circumstance or was lost in her observation of him.

"How kind of you to think of it," Lindsay said. "This was the first by which I could possibly hear from England."

"Ah, well, now you will have no more anxiety. Letters from on board ship are always difficult to write and unsatisfactory," Alicia said. Miss Filbert's had been postcards, with a wide unoccupied margin at the bottom.

"The Sutlej seems to have arrived on the third; that's a day later, isn't it, than we made out she would be?"

Alicia consulted her memory, and found she couldn't be sure. Lindsay was vexed by a similar uncertainty, but they agreed that the date was early in the month.

"Did they get comfortably through the Canal? I

remember being tied up there for forty-eight hours once."

"I don't think she says, so I fancy it must have been all right. The voyage is bound to do her good. I've asked the Simpsons to watch particularly for any sign of malaria later, though. One can't possibly know what she may have imported from that slum in Bentinck Street."

"And what was it like after Gibraltar?" Alicia asked, with a barely perceptible glance at the envelope edges showing over his breast-pocket.

"I'll look," and he sorted one out. It was pink and glossy, with a diagonal water-stripe. Lindsay drew out the single sheet it contained, and she could see that every line was ruled and faintly pencilled. "Let me see," said he. "To begin at the beginning. 'We arrived home on the third,' - you see it was the third, - 'making very slow progress the last day on account of a fog in the Channel' - ah, a fog in the Channel! - 'which was a great disappointment to some on board who were impatient to meet their loved ones. One lady had not seen her family of five for seven years. She said she would like to get out and swim, and you could not wonder. She was my s - stable companion."

"Quaint!" said Alicia.

"She has picked up the expression on board. 'So - so she told me this.' Oh yes. 'Now that it is all over I have written the voyage down among my mercies in spite of three days' sickness, when you could keep nothing on - ' What are those two words, Miss Livingstone? I can't quite make them out."

"'Your' - cambric? - stom - 'stomach' - 'your stomach.'"

"Oh, quite so. Thanks! - 'in the Bay of Biscay.' You see it WAS rough after Gib. 'Everybody was' - yes. 'The captain read Church of England prayers on Sunday mornings, in which I had no objection to join, and we had mangoes every day for a week after leaving Ceylon.'"

"Miss Filbert was so fond of mangoes," Alicia said.

"Was she? 'The passengers got up two dances, and quite a number of gentlemen invited me, but I declined with thanks, though I would not say it is wrong in itself.'" Lindsay seemed to waver; her glance went near enough to him to show her that his face had a red tinge of embarrassment. He looked at the letter uncertainly, on the point of folding it up.

"You see she hasn't danced for so long," Alicia put in quickly; "she would naturally hesitate about beginning again with anybody but you. I shouldn't wonder," she added gently, "if she never does, with anybody else."

"I know it's an idea some women have," he replied. "I think it's rather - nice."

"And her impressions of the Simpsons - and Plymouth?"

"She goes on to that." He reconsulted the letter. "'Mr. and Mrs. Simpson met me as expected and welcomed me very affably.' She has got hold of a wrong impression there, I fancy; the Simpsons couldn't be 'affable.' 'They seem very kind and pleasant for such stylish people, and their house is lovely, with electric light in the parlour and hot and cold water throughout. They seem very earnest people and have family prayers regularly, but I have not yet been asked to lead. Four servants come in to prayers. Mr. and Mrs. Simpson are deeply interested in the work of the Army, though I think Plymouth as a whole is more taken up with the C.M.S.; but we cannot have all things.' Dear me, yes! I remember those evangelical teas and the disappointment that I could not speak more definitely about the work among the Sontalis."

"Fancy her having caught the spirit of the place already!" exclaimed Alicia. "He went on: 'Mr. and Mrs. Simpson have a beautiful garden and grow most of their own vegetables. We sit in it a great deal and I think of all that has passed. I hope ever that it has been for the best and pray for you always. Oh that your feet may be set in the right path and that we may walk hand in hand upon the way to Zion!'" Lindsay lowered his voice and read the last sentences rapidly, as if the propulsion of the first part of the letter sent him through them. Then he stopped abruptly, and Alicia looked up.

"That's all, only," he added, with an awkward smile, "the usual formula."

"'God bless you'?" she asked, and he nodded.

"It has a more genuine ring than most formulas," she observed.

"Yes, hasn't it? May I have another cup?" He restored the pink sheet to its pink envelope, and both to his breast-pocket, while she poured out the other cup, but Miss Filbert was still present with them. They went on talking about her, and entirely in the tone of congratulation - the suitability of the Simpsons, the suitability of Plymouth, the probability that she would entirely recover, in its balmy atmosphere, her divine singing voice. Plymouth certainly was in no sense a tonic, but Miss Filbert didn't need a tonic; she was too much inclined to be strung up as it was. What she wanted was the soothing, quieting influence of just Plymouth's meetings and just Plymouth's teas. The charms that so sweetly and definitely characterised her would expand there; it was a delightful flowery environment for them, and she couldn't fail to improve in health. Devonshire's visitors got tremendously well fed, with fish items of especial excellence.

CHAPTER XX

Nobody could have been more impressed with Hilda's influence upon Mr. Llewellyn Stanhope's commercial probity than Mr. Llewellyn Stanhope himself. He was a prey to all noble feelings; they ruled his life and spoiled his bargains; and gratitude, when it had a chance, which was certainly seldom in connection with leading ladies, dominated him entirely. He sat in the bar of the Great Eastern Hotel with tears in his eyes, talking about what Miss Howe had done for him, and gave unnecessary backsheesh to coolies who brought him small bills - so long, that is, as they were the small bills of this season. When they had reference to the liabilities of a former and less prosperous year he waved them away with a bitter levity which belonged to the same period. His view of his obligations was strictly chronological, and in taking it he counted, like the poet, only happy hours. The bad debt and the bad season went consistently together to oblivion; the sun of to-day's remarkable receipts could not be expected to penetrate backwards.

He had only one fault to find with Miss Howe - she had no artistic conscience - none, and he found this with the utmost leniency, basking in the consciousness that it made his own more conspicuous. She was altogether in the grand style, if you understood Mr. Stanhope, but nothing would induce her to do herself justice before Calcutta; she seemed to have taken the measure of the place and to be as indifferent! Try to ring in anything worth doing and she was off with the bit between her teeth, and you simply had to put up with it. The second lead had a great deal more ambition, and a very good little woman in her way, too, but of course not half the talent. He was obliged to confess that Miss Howe wasn't game for risks, especially after doing her Rosalind the night the circus opened to a twenty-five rupee house. It WAS monstrous. She seemed to think that nothing mattered so much as that everybody should be paid on the first of the month. There was one other grievance, which Llewellyn mentioned only in confidence with a lowered voice. That was Bradley. Hilda wasn't lifting a finger to keep Bradley. Result was, Bradley was crooking his elbow a great deal too often lately and going off every way. He, Llewellyn, had put it to her if that was the way to treat a man the Daily Telegraph had spoken about as it had spoken about Hamilton Bradley. Where was she - where was he - going to find another? No, he didn't say marry Bradley; there were difficulties, and after all that might be the very way to lose him. But a woman had an influence, and that influence could never be more fittingly exercised than in the cause of dramatic art based on Mr. Stanhope's combinations. Mr. Stanhope expressed himself with a difference, but it came to that.

Perhaps if you pursued Llewellyn, pushed him, as it were, along the track of what he had to put up with, you would have come upon the further fact that as a woman of business Miss Howe had no parallel for procrastination. Next season was imminent in his arrangements, as Christmas numbers are imminent to publishers at midsummer, and here she was shying at a contract as if they had months for consideration. It wasn't either as if she complained of anything in the terms - that would be easy enough fixed - but she said herself that it was a bigger salary than he, Llewellyn, would ever be able to pay unless she went round with the hat. Nor had she any objection to the tour - a fascinating one - including the Pacific Slope and Honolulu. It stumped him, Llewellyn, to know what she did object to, and why she couldn't bark it out at once, seeing she must understand perfectly well it was no use his going to Bradley without first settling with her.

Hilda, alone in her own apartment - it was difficult to keep Llewellyn Stanhope away from even that door in his pursuit of her signature - considered the vagary life had become for her that was so whimsical, and the mystery of her secret which was so solely hers. Alicia knew, of course; but that was as if she had written it down on a sheet of perfect notepaper and locked it up in a drawer. Alicia did not speculate about it, and the whole soul of it was tangled now in a speculation. There had been a time filled with the knowledge and the joy of this new depth in her like a buoyant sea, and she had been content to float in it, imagining desirable things. Stanhope's waiting contract made a limit to the time - a limit she brought up against without distress or shock, but with a kind of recognising thrill in contact at last with the necessity for action, decision, a climax of high heart-beats. She saw with surprise that she had lived with her passion these weeks and months half consciously expecting that a crucial moment would dissolve it, like a person aware that he dreams and will presently awake. She had not faced till now any exigency of her case. But the crucial moment had leapt upon her, pointing out the subjection of her life, and she, undefended, sought only how to accomplish her bonds.

Certainly she saw no solution that did not seem monstrous; yet every pulse in her demanded a solution; there was no questioning the imperious need. She had the fullest, clearest view of the situation, and she looked at it without flinching and without compromise. Above all she had true vision of Stephen Arnold, glorifying nowhere, extenuating nothing. It was almost cruel to be the victim of such circumstance, and be denied the soft uses of illusion; but if that note of sympathy had been offered to Hilda she would doubtless have retorted that it was precisely because she saw him that she loved him. His figure, in its poverty and austerity, was always with her; she made with the fabric of her nature a kind of shrine for it, enclosing, encompassing; and her possession of him, by her knowledge, was deep and warm and protecting. I think the very fulness of it brought her a kind of content with which, but for Llewellyn and his contract, she would have been willing to go on indefinitely. It made him hers in a primary and essential way, beside which any mere acknowledgment or vow seemed chiefly decorative, like the capital of a pillar firmly rooted. There may be an appearance that she took a good deal for granted; if there is, I fear that in the baldness of this history it has not been evident how much and how variously Arnold depended on her, in how many places her colour and her vitality patched out the monkish garment of his soul. This with her enthusiasm and her cognisance. It may be remembered, too, that there was in the very tenderness of her contemplation of the priest in her path an imperious tinge born of the way men had so invariably melted there. Certainly they had been men and not priests; but the little flickering doubt that sometimes leaped from this source through the glow of her imagination she quenched very easily with the reflection that such a superficies was after all a sophistry, and that only its rudiments were facts. She proposed, calmly and lovingly, to deal with the facts.

She told herself that she would not be greedy about the conditions under which she should prevail; but her world had always, always shaped itself answering her hand, and if she cast her eyes upon the ground now, and left the future, even to-morrow, undevisaged, it was because she would not find any concessions of her own among its features if she could help it. It was a trick she played upon her consciousness; she would not look, but she could see without looking. She saw that which explained itself to be best, fittest, most reasonable; and thus she sometimes wandered with Arnold anticipatively, on afternoons when there was no matinee, through the perfumed orange orchards of Los Angeles, on the Pacific slope.

She would not search to-morrow; but she took toward it one of those steps of vague intention, at the end of which we beckon to possibilities. She wrote to Stephen and asked him to come to see her then. She had not spoken to him since the night of the Viceroy's party, when she put her Bohemian head out of the ticca-gharry to wish him good-night, and he walked home alone under the stars, trying to remember a line of Horace, a chaste one, about woman's beauty. She sent the note by post. There was no answer; but that was as usual; there never was an answer unless something prevented him; he always came, and ten minutes before the time. When the time arrived she sat under the blue umbrellas devising what she would say, creating fifty different forms of what he would say, while the hands slipped round the clock past the moment that should have brought his step to the door. Hilda noted it, and compared her watch. A bowl of roses stood on a little table near a window; she got up and went to it, bending over and rearranging the flowers. The light fell on her and on the roses; it was a beautiful attitude, and when at a footfall she looked up expectantly it was more beautiful. But it was only another boarder - a Mr. Gonzalves, with a highly varnished complexion, who took off his hat elaborately as he passed the open door. She became conscious of her use of the roses, and abandoned them. Presently she sat down on a bentwood rocking-chair, and swayed to and fro, aware of an ebbing of confidence. Half an hour later she was still sitting there. Her face had changed, something had faded in it; her gaze at the floor was profoundly speculative, and when she glanced at the empty door it was with timidity. Arnold had not come and did not come.

The evening passed without explanation, and next morning the post brought no letter. It was simplest to suppose that her own had not reached him, and Hilda wrote again. The second letter she sent by hand, with a separate sheet of paper addressed for signature. The messenger brought back the sheet of paper with strange initials, "J. L. for S. A.," and there was no reply. There remained the possibility of absence from Calcutta, of illness. That he should have gone away was most unlikely, that he had fallen ill was only too probable. Hilda looked from her bedroom window across the varying expanse of parapeted flat roofs and mosque bubbles that lay between her and College Street, and curbed the impulse in her feet that would have resulted in the curious spectacle of Llewellyn

Stanhope's leading lady calling in person at a monastic gate to express a kind of solicitude against which precisely it was barred. A situation after all could be too pictorial, looked at from the point of view of the Order, a consideration which flashed with grateful humour across her anxiety. Alicia would have known; but both the Livingstones had gone for a short sea change to Ceylon, with Duff Lindsay and some touring people from Surrey. They were most anxious, Hilda remembered, that Arnold should accompany them. Could he in the end have gone? There was, of course, the accredited fount and source of all information, the Father Superior; but with what propriety could Hilda Howe apply for it! Llewellyn might write for her; but it was glaringly impossible that the situation should lay itself so far open to Llewellyn. Looking in vain for resources she came upon an expedient. She found a sheet of cheap notepaper, and made it a little greasy. On it she wrote with red ink, in the cramped hand of the hired scribe of the bazar: -

"SIR - Will you please to inform to me if Mr. Arnold has gone mofussil or England as I have some small business with him.

Yours obedient servant, - WUN SING."

"It can't be forgery," she reflected, "since there isn't a Wun Sing," and added an artistic postscript, "Boots and shoes verry much cheap for cash." She made up the envelope to match, and addressed it with consistent illiteracy to the head of the Mission. The son of the Chinese basketmaker, who dwelt almost next door, spoke neither English nor Hindustani, but showed an easy comprehension of her promise of backsheesh when he should return with an answer. She had a joyful anticipation, while she waited, of the terms in which she should tell Arnold how she passed disguised as a Chinese shoemaker, before the receptive and courteous consciousness of his spiritual senior; of how she penetrated, in the suggestion of a pigtail and an unpaid bill, within the last portals that might be expected to receive her in the form under which, for example, certain black and yellow posters were presenting her to the public at that moment. She saw his scruples go swiftly down before her laughter and the argument of her tender anxiety, which she was quite prepared to learn foolish and unnecessary. There was even an adventurous instant in which she reaped at actual personation of the Chinaman, and she looked in rapture at the vivid risk of the thing before she abandoned it as involving too much. She sent no receipt form this time - that was not the practice of the bazar - and when, hours after, her messenger returned with weariness and dejection written upon him, in the characters of a perfunctory Chinese smile, she could only gather from his negative head and hands that no answer had been given him, and that her expedient had failed.

Hilda stared at her dilemma. Its properties were curiously simple. His world and hers, with the same orbit, had no point of contact. Once swinging round their eastern centre they had come close enough for these two, leaning very far out, to join hands. When they loosed it seemed they lost.

The more she gazed at it the more it looked a preposterous thing that in a city vibrant with human communication by all the methods which make it easy, it should be possible for one individual thus to drop suddenly and completely from the knowledge of another - a mediaeval thing. Their isolation as Europeans of course accounted for it; there was no medium in the brown population that hummed in the city streets. Hilda could not even bribe a servant without knowing how to speak to him. She ravaged the newspapers; they never were more bare of reference to consecrated labours. The nearest approach to one was a paragraph chronicling a social evening given by the Wesleyans in Sudder Street, with an exhibition of the cinematograph. In a moment of defiance and determination she sent a telegram studiously colourless, "Unable find you wish communicate please inform. A. Cassidy." Arnold had never ignored the name she was born to, in occasional scrupulous moments he addressed her by it; he would recognise and understand. There was no reply.

The enigma pressed upon her days, she lived in the heaviness of it, waiting. His silence adding itself up, brought her a kind of shame for the exertions she had made. She turned with obstinacy from the further schemes her ingenuity presented. Out of the sum of her unsuccessful efforts grew a reproach of Arnold; every one of them increased it. His behaviour she could forgive, arbitrarily putting against it twenty explanations, but not the futility of what she had done. Her resentment of that undermined all the fairness of her logic and even triumphed over the sword of her suspense. She never quite gave up the struggle, but in effect she passed the week that intervened pinioned in her unreason - bands that vanished as she looked at them, only to tie her thrice in another place.

Life became a permanent interrogation point. Waiting

under it, with a perpetual upward gaze, perhaps she grew a little dizzy. The sun of March had been increasing, and the air of one particular Saturday afternoon had begun to melt and glow and hang in the streets with a kind of inertia, like a curtain that had to be parted to be penetrated. Hilda came into the house and faced the stairs with an inclination to leave her body on the ground-floor and mount in spirit only. When she glanced in at the drawing-room door and saw Arnold sitting under the blue umbrellas, a little paler, a thought more serene than usual, she swept into the room as if a tide carried her, and sank down upon a footstool close to him, as if it had dropped her there. He had risen at her appearance, he was all himself but rather more the priest, his face of greeting had exactly its usual asking intelligence but to her the fact that he was normal was lost in the fact that he was near. He held out his hand but she only sought his face, speechless, hugging her knees.

"You are overcome by the sun," he said. "Lie down for a moment," and again he offered her a hand to help her to rise. She shook her head but took his hand, enclosing it in both of hers with a sort of happy deliberation, and drew herself up by it, while her eyes, shining like dark surfaces of some glorious conscious-ness within, never left his face. So she stood beside him with her head bowed, still dumb. It was her supreme moment; life never again brought her anything like it. It was not that she confessed so much as that she asserted, she made a glowing thing plain, cried out to him, still standing silent, the deep-lying meaning of the tangle of their lives. She was shaken by a pure delight, as if she unclosed her hand to show him a strange jewel in her palm, hers and his for the looking. The intensity of her consciousness swept round him and enclosed him, she knew this profoundly, and had no thought of the insulation he had in his robe. The instant passed; he stood unmoved definitely enough, yet some vibration in it reached him, for there was surprise in his involuntary backward step.

"You must have thought me curiously rude," he said, as if he felt about for an explanation, "but your letters were only given to me an hour ago. We have all been in retreat, you know."

"In RETREAT!" Hilda exclaimed. "Ah, yes. How foolish I have been! In retreat," she repeated softly, flicking a trace of dust from his sleeve. "Of course."

"It was held in St. Paul's College," Stephen went on, "by Father Neede. Shall we sit down? And of course at such times no communications reach us, no letters or papers."

"No letters or papers," Hilda said, looking at him softly, as it were, through the film of the words. They sat down, he on the sofa, she on a chair very near it. There was another placed at a more usual distance, but she seemed incapable of taking the step or two toward it, away from him.

Stephen gave himself to the grateful sense of her proximity. He had come to sun himself again in the warmth of her fellowship; he was stirred by her emphasis of their separation and reunion. "And what, please," he asked, "have you been doing? Account to me for the time."

"While you have been praying and fasting? Wondering

what you were at, and waiting for you to finish. Waiting," she said, and clasped her knees with her intent look again, swaying a little to and fro in her content, as if that which she waited for had already come, full, and very desirable.

"Have you been reading? - "

"Oh, I have been reading nothing! You shall never go into retreat again," she went on, with a sudden change of expression. "It is well enough for you, but I am not good at fasting. And I have an indulgence," she added, unaware of her soft, bright audacity, "that will cover both our cases."

His face uttered aloud his reflection that she was extravagant. That it was a pity, but that what was not due to her profession might be ascribed to the simple, clear impulse of her temperament - that temperament which he had found to be a well of rare sincerity.

"I am not to go any more into retreat?" he said, in grave interrogation; but the hint of rebuke in his voice was not in his heart, and she knew it.

"No!" she cried. "You shall not be hidden away like that. You shall not go alive into the tomb and leave me at the door. Because I cannot bear it."

She leaned toward him, and her hand fell lightly on his knee. It was a claiming touch, and there was something in the unfolded sweetness of her face that was not ambiguous. Arnold received the intelligence. It came in a vague grey monitory form, a cloud, a portent, a chill menace; but it came, and he paled under it. He seemed to lean upon his hands, pressed one on each side of him to the seat of the sofa for support, and he looked in fixed silence at hers, upon his knee. His face seemed to wither, new lines came upon it as the impression grew in him; and the glamour faded out of hers as she was sharply reminded, looking at him, that he had not traversed the waste with her, that she had kept her vigils alone. Yet it was all said and done, and there was no repentance in her. She only gathered herself together, and fell back, as it were, upon her magnificent position. As she drew her hand away, he dropped his face into the cover of his own, leaning his elbow on his knee, and there was a pulsing silence. The instant prolonged itself.

"Are you praying?" Hilda asked, with much gentleness, almost a childlike note; and he shook his head. There was another, instant's pause, and she spoke again.

"Are you so grieved, then," she said, "that this has come upon us?"

Again he held his eyes away from her, clasping his hands, and looking at the thing nearest to him, while at last blood from the heart of the natural man in him came up and stained his face, his forehead under the thin ruffling of colourless hair, his neck above the white band that was his badge of difference from other men.

"I - fear - I hardly understand," he said. The words fell cramped and singly, and his lip twitched. "It - it is impossible to think - " He looked as if he dared not lift his head.

One would not say that Hilda hesitated, for there was

no failing in the wings of her high confidence, but she looked at him in a brave silence. Her glance had tender investigation in it; she stood on the brink of her words just long enough to ask whether they would hurt him. Seeing that they would, she nevertheless plunged, but with infinite compassion and consideration. She spoke like an agent of Fate, conscious and grieved.

"*I* understand," she said simply. "Sometimes, you know, we are quicker. And you in your cell, how should you find out? That is why I must tell you, because, though I am a woman, you are a priest. Partly for that reason I may speak, partly because I love you, Stephen Arnold, better and more ardently than you can ever love me, or anybody, I think, except perhaps your God. And I am tired of keeping silence."

She was so direct, so unimpassioned, that half his distress turned to astonishment, and he faced her as if a calm and reasoned hand had been laid upon the confusion in him. Meeting his gaze, she unbarred a floodgate of happy tenderness in her eyes.

"Love!" he gasped in it, "I have nothing to do with that."

"Oh," she said, "you have everything to do with it."

Something thrilled him without asking his permission, assuring him that he was a man - until then a placid theory with an unconscious basis. It was therefore a blow to his saintship, or it would have been, but he warded it off, flushed and trembling. It was as if he had been ambuscaded. He had to hold himself from the ignominy of flight; he rose to cut his way out, making an effort to strike with precision.

"Some perversity has seized you," he said. The muscles about his mouth quivered, giving him a curious aspect. "You mean nothing of what you say."

"Do you believe that?"

"I - I cannot think anything else. It is the only way I can - I can - make excuse."

"Ah, don't excuse me!" she murmured, with an astonishing little gay petulance.

"You cannot have thought - " in spite of himself he made a step towards the door.

"Oh, I did think - I do think. And you must not go." She too stood up, and stayed him. "Let us at least see clearly." There was a persuading note in her voice, one would have thought that she was dealing with a patient or a child. "Tell me," she clasped her hands behind her back and looked at him in marvellous simple candour, "do I really announce this to you? Was there not in yourself anywhere - deep down - any knowledge of it?"

"I did not guess - I did not dream!"

"And - now?" she asked.

A heavenly current drifted from her, the words rose and fell on it with the most dazing suggestion in their soft hesitancy. It must have been by an instinct of her art that her hand went up to the cross on Arnold's breast and closed over it, so that he should see only her. The familiar vision of her stood close, looking things intolerably new and different. Again came out of it that sudden liberty, that unpremeditated rush and shock in him. He paled with indignation, with the startled resentment of a woman wooed and hostile. His face at last expressed something definite, it was anger; he stepped back and caught at his hat. "I am sorry," he said, "I am sorry. I thought you infinitely above and beyond all that."

Hilda smiled and turned away. If he chose it was his opportunity to go, but he stood regarding her, twirling his hat. She sat down, clasping her knees, and looked at the floor. There was a square of sunlight on the carpet, and motes were rising in it.

"Ah well, so did I," she said meditatively, without raising her eyes. Then she leaned back in the chair and looked at him, in her level simple way.

"It was a foolish theory," she said, "and - now - I can't understand it at all. I am amazed to find that it even holds good with you."

It was so much in the tone of their usual discussions that Arnold was conscious of a lively relief. The instinct of flight died down in him; he looked at her with something like inquiry.

"It will always be to me curious," she went on, "that you could have thought your part in me so limited, so poor. That is enough to say. I find it hard to understand, anybody would, that you could take so much good from me and not - so much more." She opened her lips again, but kept back the words. "Yes," she added, "that is enough to say."

But for the colourless face and the tenseness about her

lips it might have been thought that she definitely abandoned what she had learned she could not have. There was a note of acquiescence and regret in her voice, of calm reason above all; and this sense reached him, induced him to listen, as he generally listened, for anything she might find that would explain the situation. His fingers went from habit, as a man might play with his watch chain, to the symbol of his faith; her eyes followed them, and rested mutely on the cross. There was a profundity of feeling in them, wistful, acknowledging, deeply speculative. "You could not forget that?" she said, and shook her head as if she answered herself. He looked into her upturned face and saw that her eyes were swimming.

"Never!" he said, "Never!" but he walked to the nearest chair and sat down. He seemed suddenly endowed with the courage to face this problem, and his head, as it rose in the twilight against the window, was grave and calm. Without a word a great tenderness of under-standing filled the space between them; an interpreting compassion went to and fro. Suddenly a new light dawned in Hilda's eyes, she leaned forward and met his in an absorption which caught them out of themselves into some space where souls wander, and perhaps embrace. It was a frail adventure upon a gaze, but it carried them infinitely far. The moment died away, neither of them could have measured it, and when it had finally ebbed - they were conscious of every subsiding throb - the silence remained, like a margin for the beauty of it. They sat immovable, while the light faded. After a time the woman spoke. "Once before," she began, but he put up his hand, and she stopped. Then as if she would no longer be restrained. "That is all I want," she whispered. "That is enough."

For a time they said very little, looking back upon their divine moment; the shadows gathered in the corners of the room and made quiet conversation which was almost audible in the pauses. Then Hilda began to speak, steadily, calmly. You, too, would have forgotten her folly in what she found to say, as Arnold did; you too would have drawn faith and courage from her face. One would not be irreverent, but if this woman were convicted of the unforgiveable sin, she could explain it, and obtain justification rather than pardon. Her horizon had narrowed, she sought now only that it should enfold them both. She begged that he would wipe out her insanity, that he would not send her away. He listened and melted to conviction.

"Then I may stay?" she said at the end.

"I am satisfied - if a way can be found."

"I will find a way," she replied.

After which he went back through the city streets to his disciples in new humility and profounder joy, knowing that virtue had gone out of him. She in her room where she lodged also considered the miracle, twice wonderful in that it asked no faith of her.

CHAPTER XXI

It is difficult to be precise about such a thing, but I should think that Hilda gave herself to the marvellous aspect of what had come and gone between them, for several hours after Arnold left her. It was not for some time, at all events, that she arrived at the consideration - the process was naturally downward - that the soul of the marvel lay in the exact moment of its happening. Nothing could have been more heaven-sent than her precious perception, exactly then, that before the shining gift of Arnold's spiritual sympathy, all her desire for a lesser thing from him must creep away abashed for ever. Even when the lesser thing, by infinitely gradual expansion, again became the greater, it remained permanently leavened and lifted in her by the strange and lovely incident that had taken for the moment such command of her and of him. She would not question it or reason about it, perhaps with an instinct to avert its destruction; she simply drew it deeply into her content. Only its sweet deception did not stay with her, and she let that go with open hands. She wanted, more than ever, the whole of Stephen Arnold, all that was so openly the Mission's and all that was so evidently God's. It will be seen that she felt in no way compelled to advise him of this her backsliding. I doubt whether such a perversion of her magnificent course of action ever occurred to her. It was magnificent, for it entailed a high disregarding stroke; it implied a sublime confidence of what the end would be, a capacity to wait and endure. She smiled buoyantly, in the intervals of arranging it, at the idea that Stephen Arnold stood beyond her ultimate possession.

There were difficulties, but the moment was favourable to her, more favourable than it would have been the year before, or any year but this. Before ten days had passed she was able to write to Arnold describing her plan, and she was put to it to keep the glow of success out of her letter. She kept it out, that, and everything but a calm and humble statement - any Clarke Brother might have dictated it - of what she proposed to do. Perhaps the intention was less obvious than the desire that he should approve it.

The messenger waited long by the entrance to the Mission House for an answer, exchanging, sitting on his feet, the profane talk of the bazar with the gatekeeper of the Christians. Stephen was in chapel. There was no service; he had half an hour to rest in and he rested there. He was speculating, in the grateful dimness, about the dogma - he had never quite accepted it, though Colquhoun had - of the intercessory power of the souls of saints. A converted Brahmin, an old man, had died the day before. Arnold luxuriated in the humility of thinking that he would be glad of any good word dear old Nourendra Lal could say for him. The chapel was deliciously refined. The scent of fresh cut flowers floated upon the continual presence of the incense; a lily outlined its head against the tall carved altarpiece the Brothers had brought from Damascus. The seven brass lamps that hung from the rafters above the altar rails were also Damascene, carved and pierced so that the light in them was a still thing like a prayer;

and the place breathed vague meanings which did not ask understanding. It was a refuge from the riot and squalor of the whitewashed streets with a double value and a treble charm - I.H.S. among plaster gods, a sanctuary in the bazar. Stephen sat in it motionless, with his lean limbs crossed in front of him, until the half-hour was up; then he bent his knee before the altar and went out to meet a servant at the door with Hilda's letter. The chapel opened upon an upper verandah, he crossed it to get a better light and stood to read with his back half turned upon the comers and goers.

It was her first communication since they parted, and in spite of its colourlessness it seemed to lay strong eager hands upon him, turning his shoulder that way, upon the world, bending his head over the page. He had not dwelt much upon their strange experience, in the days that followed. It had retreated, for him, behind the veil of tender mystery with which he shrouded, even from his own eyes, the things that lay between his soul and God. The space from that day to this had been more than usually full of ministry; its pure uses had fallen like snow, blotting and deadening the sudden wonder that blossomed then. Latterly he had hardly thought of it.

So far was he removed, so deeply drawn again within his familiar activities, that he regarded Hilda's letter for an instant with a lip of censure, as if, for some reason, it should not have been admitted. It was, in a manner, her physical presence, the words expanded into her, through it she walked back into his life, with an interrogation. Standing there by the pillar he became gradually aware of the weight of the interrogation.

A passing Brother cast at him the sweet smile of the

cloister. Arnold stopped him and transferred an immediate duty, which the other accepted with a slightly exaggerated happiness. They might have been girls together, with their apologies and protestations. The other Brother went on in a little glow of pleasure, Arnold turned back into the chapel, carrying, it seemed to him, a woman's life in his hand.

He took his seat and folded his arms almost eagerly; there was a light of concentration in his eye and a line of compression about his lips which had not marked his meditation upon Nourendra Lal. The vigour in his face suggested that he found a kind of athletic luxury in what he had to think about. Brother Colquhoun, with his flat hat clasped before his breast, passed down the aisle. Stephen looked up with a trace of impatience. Presently he rose hurriedly as if he remembered something, and went and knelt before one of several paintings that hung upon the chapel walls. They were old copies of great works, discoloured and damaged. They had sailed round the Cape to India when the century was young, and a lady friend of the Mission had bought them at the sale of the effects of a ruined Begum. Arnold was one of those who could separate them from their incongruous history and consecrate them over again. He often found them helpful when he sought to lift his spirit, and in any special matter a special comfort. He bent for ten minutes before a Crucifixion, and then hastened back to his place. Only one reflection corrected the vigorous satisfaction with which he thought out Hilda's proposition. That disturbed him in the middle of it, and took the somewhat irrelevant form of a speculation as to whether the events of their last meeting should have had any place in his Thursday confession. He was able to find almost at once a conscientious negative for it, and it did not recur again.

He got up reluctantly when the Mission bell sounded, and indeed he had come to the end of a very absorbing interest. His decision was final against Hilda's scheme. His worn experience cried out at the sacrifice in it without the illumination - which it would certainly lack - of religious faith. She confessed to the lack, and that was all she had to say about her motive, which, of course, placed him at an immense disadvantage in considering it. But the question then descended to another plane, became merely a doubt as to the most useful employment of energy, and that doubt nobody could entertain long, nobody of reasonable breadth of view, who had ever seen her expressing the ideals of the stage. Arnold did his best to ward off all consideration which he could suspect of a personal origin, but his inveterate self-sacrifice slipped in and counted, naturally enough, under another guise, against her staying.

He went to his room and wrote to Hilda at once, the kindest, simplest of letters, but conveying a definitely negative note. He would have been perhaps more guarded, but it was so plainly his last word to her; Llewellyn Stanhope was proclaiming the departure of his people in ten days' time upon every blank wall. So he gave himself a little latitude, he let in an undercurrent of gentle reminiscence, of serious assurance as to the difference she had made. And when he had finally bade her begone to the light and fulness of her own life, and fastened up his letter, he deliberately lifted it to his lips and placed a trembling, awkward kiss upon it, like the kiss of an old man, perfunctory yet bearing a tender intention.

The Livingstones and Duff Lindsay had come back, the people from Surrey having been sped upon their way to the Far East. Stephen remembered with more than his usual relish an engagement to dine that evening in Middleton Street. He involuntarily glanced at his watch. It was half-past one. The afternoon looked arid, stretching between. Consulting his tablets he found that he had nothing that was really of any consequence to do. There were items, but they were unimportant, transferable. He had dismissed Hilda Howe, but a glow from the world she helped to illumine showed seductively at the end of his day. He made an errand involving a long walk, and came back at an hour which left nothing but evensong between him and eight o'clock.

He was suddenly aware as he talked to her later, of a keener edge to his appreciation of the charm of Alicia Livingstone. Her voyage, he assured her, had done her all the good in the world. Her delicate bloom had certainly been enhanced by it, and the graceful spring of her neck and her waist seemed to have its counterpart in a freshened poise of the agreeable things she found to say. It was delightful the way she declared herself quite a different being, and the pleasure with which she moved, dragging fascinating skirts behind her, about the room. She made more of an impression upon him on the aesthetic side than she had ever done before; she seemed more highly vitalised, her fineness had greater relief, and her charm more freedom. Lindsay was there, and Arnold glanced from one to the other of them, first with a start then with a smile, at the recollection of Hilda's conception of their relations. If this were a type and instance of hopeless love he had certainly misread all the songs and sayings. He kept the idea in his mind and went on regarding her in the light of it with a pondering smile, turning it over and finding a lively pleasure in his curious acumen in such an unwonted direction. It was a very flower of emotional naivete, though a moment later he cast it from him as a weed, grown in idleness; and indeed it might have abashed him to say what concern it had in the mind of the Order of St. Barnabas. It was gratifying, nevertheless, to have his observation confirmed by the way in which Alicia leaned across him toward Lindsay with occasional references to Laura Filbert, apparently full of light-heartedness, references which Duff received in the square-shouldered matter-of-course fashion of his countrymen approaching their nuptials in any quarter of the globe. It was gratifying, and yet it enhanced in Stephen this evening the indrawing of his under-lip, a plaintive twist of expression which spoke upon the faces of quite half the Order, of patience under privation.

The atmosphere was one of congratulation, the week's Gazette had transformed Surgeon-Major Livingstone into Surgeon-Lieutenant-Colonel. The officer thus promoted, in a particularly lustrous shirt bosom, made a serious social effort to correspond, and succeeded in producing more than one story of the Principal Medical Officer with her Majesty's forces in India, which none of them had heard before. They were all delighted at Herbert's step, he was just the kind of person to get a step, and to get it rather early; a sense of the propriety of it mingled with the general gratification. There was a feeling of ease among them, too, of the indefeasibly won, which the event is apt to bring even when the surgeon-lieutenant-colonelcy is most strikingly deserved. With no strain imaginable one could see the relaxation.

"We can't do much in celebration," Lindsay was saying, "but I've got a box at the theatre, if you'll come. Our people had some pomfret and oysters over on ice from Bombay this morning, and I've sent my share to Bonsard to see what he can do with it for supper. Jack Cummins and Lady Dolly are coming. By the way, what do you think the totalizator paid Lady Dolly on Saturday - six thousand!"

"Rippin'," Herbert agreed. "We'll all come - at least - I don't know. What do you say, Arnold?"

"Of course Stephen will come," Alicia urged. "Why not?" It was putting him and his gown at once beyond the operation of vulgar prejudice, intimating that they quite knew him for what he was.

"What's the piece?" Herbert inquired.

"Oh, the piece isn't up to much, I'm afraid, only that Hilda Howe is worth seeing in almost anything."

"Thanks," Stephen put in, "but I think, thanks very much, I would rather not."

"I remember," Alicia said, "you were with us the night she played in The Offence of Galilee. I don't wonder that you do not wish to disturb that impression."

Stephen fixed his eyes upon a small pyramid of crystallised cherries immediately in front of him, and appeared to consider, austerely, what form his reply should take. There was an instant's perceptible pause, and then he merely bowed toward Alicia as if vaguely to acknowledge the kindness of her recollection. "I think," he said again, "that I will not accompany you to-night, if you will be good enough to excuse me."

"You must excuse us both," Alicia said definitely, "I should much rather stay at home and talk to Stephen."

At this they all cried out, but Miss Livingstone would not change her mind. "I haven't seen him for three weeks," she said, with gentle effrontery, making nothing of his presence, "and he's much more improving than either of you. I also shall choose the better part."

"How you can call it that, with Hilda in the balance - " Duff protested.

"But then you've invited Lady Dolly. After winning six thousand there will be no holding Lady Dolly. She'll be capable of cat-calls! How I should love," Alicia went on, "to have Hilda meet her. She would be a mine to Hilda."

"For pity's sake," cried her brother, "stop asking Hilda and people who are a mine to Hilda! It's too perceptible, the way she digs in them."

"You dear old thing, you're quite clever to-night! What difference does it make? They never know - they never dream! I wish I could dig." Alicia looked pensively at the olive between her finger and thumb.

"Thank Heaven you can't," Duff said warmly. It was a little odd, the personal note. Alicia's eyes remained upon the olive.

"It's all she lives for."

"Well," Duff declared, "I can imagine higher ends."

"You're not abusing Hilda!" Alicia said, addressing the olive.

"Not at all. Only vindicating you."

It did single them out, this fencing. Herbert and Arnold sat as spectators, pushed, in a manner, aside.

"I suppose she will be off soon," Livingstone said.

"Oh, dreadfully soon. On the fifteenth. I had a note from her to-day."

"Did she say she was going?" Stephen asked quickly.

"She mentioned the Company - she is the Company surely."

"Oh, undoubtedly. May I - might I ask for a little more soda-water, Alicia?" He made the request so formally that she glanced at him with surprise.

"Please do - but isn't it very odious, by itself, that way? I suppose we shouldn't leave out Hamilton Bradley - he certainly counts."

"For how much?" inquired her brother. "He's going to pieces."

"Hilda can pull him together again," Lindsay said incautiously.

"Has she an influence for good - over him?" Stephen inquired, and cleared his throat. He caught a glance

Mrs. Everard Cotes

exchanged, and frowned.

"Oh yes," Duff said, "I fancy it is for good. For good, certainly. The odd part of it is that he began by having an influence over her which she declares improved her acting. So that was for good, too, as it turned out. I think she makes too much of him. To my mind he speaks like a bit of consecrated stage tradition and looks like a bit of consecrated stage furniture - he, and his thin nose, and his thin lips, and his thin eyebrows. Personally, I'm sick of his eyebrows."

"They'll end by marrying," said Surgeon-Lieut.-Colonel Livingstone.

"HERBERT! How little you know her!"

"It's possible enough," Duff said, "especially if she finds him in any way necessary to her production of herself. Hilda has knocked about too much to have many illusions. One is pretty sure she would place that first."

"You are saying a thing which is monstrous!" cried Alicia.

Unperturbed, her brother supported his conviction. "She'll have to marry him to get rid of him," he said. "Fancy the opportunities of worrying her the brute will have in those endless ocean voyages!"

"Oh, if you think Hilda could be WORRIED into anything!" Miss Livingstone exclaimed derisively. "If the man were irritating, do you suppose she wouldn't arrange - wouldn't find means? - "

"She would have him put in irons, no doubt," Herbert retorted, "or locked up with the other sad dogs, in charge of the ship's butcher."

The three laughed immoderately, and Stephen, looking up, came in at the end with a smile. Alicia pronounced her brother too absurd, and unfitted by nature to know anything about creatures like Hilda Howe. "A mere man to begin with," she said. "You haven't the ghost of a temperament, Herbert; you know you haven't."

"He got's a lovely bedside manner," Lindsay remarked, "and that's the next thing to it."

"Rubbish! I don't want to hurry you," Alicia glanced at the watch on her wrist, "but unless you and Herbert want to miss half the first act you had better be off. Stephen and I will have our coffee comfortably in the drawing-room and find what excuses we can for you."

But Stephen put out his hand with a movement of slightly rigid deprecation.

"If it is not too vacillating of me," he said, "and I may be forgiven, I think I will change my mind, and go. I have no business to break up your party, and besides, I shall probably not have another opportunity - I should rather like to go. To the theatre, of course, that is. Not to Bonsard's, thanks very much."

"Oh, do come on to Bonsard's," Lindsay said, and Alicia protested that he would miss the best of Lady Dolly, but Stephen was firm. Bonsard's was beyond the limit of his indulgence.

CHAPTER XXII

Only the Sphinx confronted them after all when they arrived at the theatre, the Sphinx and Lady Dolly. The older feminine presentment sent her belittling gaze over their heads and beyond them from the curtain; Lady Dolly turned a modish head to greet them from the front of the box. Lady Dolly raised her eyes but not her elbows, which were assisting her a good deal with the house in exploring and being explored, enabling Colonel John Cummins, who sat by her side, to observe how very perfect and adorable the cut of her bodice was. Since Colonel Cummins was accustomed to say in moments when his humour escaped his discretion, things highly appreciative of bodices, the role of Lady Dolly's elbows could hardly be dismissed as unimportant. Moreover, the husband attached to the elbows belonged to the Department of which Colonel John was the head, so that they rested, one may say, upon a very special plane.

Alicia disturbed it with the necessity of taking Colonel Cummins place, which Lady Dolly accepted with admirable spirit; assuring the usurper, with the most engaging candour, that she simply ought never to be seen without turquoises. "Believe it or not as you like, but I love you better every time I see you in that necklace." Lady Dolly clasped her hands, with her fan in them, in the abandonment of her affection, and "love you better" floated back and dispersed itself among the men. Alicia smiled the necessary acknowledgment. All the women she knew made compliments to her; it was a kind of cult among them. The men had sometimes an air of envying their freedom of tongue. "Don't say that," she returned lightly, "or Herbert will never give me any diamonds." She too looked her approval of Lady Dolly's bodice, but said nothing. It was doubtless precisely because she disdained certain forms of feminine barter that she got so much for nothing.

"And where," demanded Lady Dolly, in an electric whisper, "did you find that dear sweet little priest? Do introduce him to me - at least by and by, when I've thought of something to say. Let me see, wasn't it Good Friday last week? I'll ask him if he had hot-cross buns - or do people eat those on Boxing Day? Pancakes come in somewhere, if one could only be sure!"

Stephen clung persistently to the back of the box. His senses were filled for the moment by its other occupants, the men in the fresh correctness of their evening dress, whose least gesture seemed to spring from an indefinite fulness of life, the two women in front, a kind of lustrous tableau of what it was possible to choose and to enjoy. They were grouped and shut off in a high light which seemed to proceed partly from the usual sources and partly from their own personalities; he saw them in a way which underlined their significance at every point. It seemed to Stephen that in a manner he profaned this temple of what he held to be poorest and cheapest in life, a paradox of which he was but dimly aware in his dejection. A sharp impression of his physical inferiority to the other men assailed him; his appreciation of their muscular shoulders had a rasp in it. For once the poverty of spirit to which he held failed to offer him a refuge, his eye wandered restlessly as if attempting futile reconciliations, and the thing most present with him was the worn-all-day feeling about the neck of his cassock. He fixed his attention presently in a climax of passive discomfort on the curtain, where unconsciously, his gaze crept with a subtle interrogation in it to the wide eyeballs of the Sphinx.

The stalls gradually filled, although it was a second production, in the middle of the week, and although the gallery and the rupee seats under it were nearly empty. The piece accounted for both. When Duff Lindsay said at dinner that it wasn't "up to much," he spoke, I fancy, from the nearest point of view he could take to that of the Order of St. Barnabas. As a matter of fact, The Victim of Virtue was up to a very great deal, but its points were so delicate that one must have been educated rather broadly to grasp them, which is again perhaps a foolish contrariety of terms. At all events they carried no appeal to the theatre-goers from the sailing ships in the river or the regiments in the fort, who turned as one than that night to Jimmy Finnigan.

Stephen was aware, in the abstract, of what he might expect. He savoured the enterprises of the London theatres weekly in the Saturday Review; he had cast a remotely observing eye upon the productions of this particular playwright through that medium for a long time. They formed a manifestation of the outer world fit enough to draw a glance of speculation from the inner; their author was an acrobat of ideas. Doubtless we are all clowns in the eyes of the angels, yet we have the habit of supposing that they sometimes look down upon us. It was thus, if the parallel is not exaggerated, that Arnold regarded the author of The Victim of Virtue. His attitude was quite taken before the orchestra ceased playing; it was made of negation rather than criticism, on the basis that he had no concern with, and no knowledge of, such things. Deliberately he gave his mind a surface which should shed promiscuous invitation, and folded his lips as it were, against the rising of the curtain. He thought of Hilda separately, and he looked for her upon the boards with the simplicity of a desire to see the woman he knew.

When finally he did see her she made before him a picture that was to remain with him always as his last impression of an art from which in all its manifestations on that night he definitely turned. From the aigrette in her hair to the paste buckle on her shoe she was mondaine. Her dress, of some indefinite, slight white material, clasped at the waist with a belt that gave the beam of turquoises and the gleam of silver, ministered as much to the capricious ideal of the moment as to the lines and curves of the person it adorned. The set was the inevitable modern drawing-room, and she sat well out on a sofa, with her hands, in long black gloves, resting stiffly, palm downward on each side of her. It was as if she pushed her body forward in an impulse to rise, her rigid arms thrust her shoulders up a little and accentuated the swell of her bosom. It was a vivid, a staccato attitude; it expressed a temperament, a character, fifty other things; but especially it epitomised the restraints and the licenses of a world of drawing- rooms. In that first brief mute instant of disclosure she was all that she presently, by voice and movement, proclaimed herself to be - so dazzling and complete that Stephen literally blinked at the revelation. He made an effort, for a moment or two, to pursue and detect the woman who had been his friend; then the purpose of his coming gradually faded from his mind, and he stood with folded arms and absorbed eyes watching the other, the Mrs. Halliday, on the sofa, setting about the fulfilment of a purple destiny.

The play proceeded and Stephen did not move - did not wince. When Mrs. Halliday, whose mate was exacting, exclaimed, "The greatest apostle of expediency was St. Paul. He preached 'wives love your husbands,'" he even permitted himself the ghost of a smile. At one point he wished himself familiar with the plot; it was when Hamilton Bradley came jauntily on as Lord Ingleton, assuring Mrs. Halliday that immorality was really only shortsightedness. Lady Dolly in front, repeated Lord Ingleton's phrase with ingenuous wonder. "I know it's clever," she insisted, "but what does it mean? Now that other thing - what was it? - 'Subtract vice, and virtue is what is left' - that's an easy one. Write it down on your cuff for me, will you, Colonel Cummins? I SHALL be so sick if I forget it."

Stephen was perhaps the only person in the box quite oblivious of Lady Dolly. He looked steadily over her animated shoulders at the play, wholly involved in an effort to keep its current and direction through the floating debris of constrained sayings with which it was encumbered; to know in advance whither it was carrying its Mrs. Halliday, and how far Lord Ingleton would accompany. When Lord Ingleton paused as it were to beg four people to "have nothing to do with sentiment - it so often leads to conviction," and the house murmured its amusement, Arnold shifted his shoulders impatiently. "How inconsistent," Lord

Ingleton reproached Mrs. Halliday a moment later, "to wear gloves on your hands and let your thoughts go candid." Arnold turned to Duff. "There's no excuse for that," he said, but Lindsay was hanging upon Hilda's rejoinder and did not hear him.

At the end of the first act, where, after introducing Mrs. Halliday to her husband's divorced first wife, Lord Ingleton is left rubbing his hands with gratification at having made two such clever women "aware of each other," Stephen found himself absolutely unwilling to discuss the piece with the rest of the party. As he left the box to walk up and down the corridor outside where it was cooler, he heard the voice of Colonel Cummins lifted in further quotation, "'To be good AND charming - what a sinful superfluity!' I'm sure nobody ever called you superfluous, Lady Dolly," and was vividly aware of the advisability of taking himself and his Order out of the theatre. He had not been gratified, or even from any point appealed to. Hilda's production of Mrs. Halliday was so perfect that it failed absolutely to touch him, almost to interest him. He had no means of measuring or of valuing that kind of woman, the restless brilliant type that lives upon its emotions and tilts at the problems of its sex with a curious comfort in the joust. He was too far from the circle of her modern influence to consider her with anything but impatience if he had met her original person, and her reflection, her reproduction seemed to him frivolous and meaningless. If he went then, however, he would go as he came, in so far as the play was concerned; the first act, relying altogether upon the jugglery of its dialogue, gave no clue to anything. He owed it to Hilda after all to see the piece out. It was only fair to give her a chance to make the best of it. He decided that it was worth a personal sacrifice to give it her, and went back.

He was sufficiently indignant with the leading idea of
the play, and sufficiently absorbed in its progress, at
the end of the second act, to permit Lady Dolly to
capture him before it occurred to him that he had the
use of his legs. Her enthusiasm was so great that it
reduced him to something like equivocation. She
wanted to know if anything could be more splendid
than Mr. Bradley as Lord Ingleton; she confided to
Stephen that that was what she called REAL wicked-
ness, the kind that did the most harm, and invited him
by inference, to a liberal judgment of stupid sinners.
He sat emitting short unsmiling sentences with eyes
nervously fugitive from Lady Dolly's too proximate
opulence until the third act began. Then he gave place
with embarrassed alacrity to Colonel Cummins, and
folded his arms again at the back of the box.

Before it was finished he had the gratification of
recognising at least one Hilda that he knew. The
newspapers found in her interpretation the development of a soul, and one remembered, reading them,
that a cliche is a valuable thing in a hurry. A phrase
which spoke of a soul bruised out of life and rushing to
annihilation would have been more precise. The
demand upon her increased steadily as the act went on,
and as she met it there slipped into her acting some of
her own potentialities of motive and of passion. She
offered to the shaping circumstance rich material and
abundant plasticity, and when the persecution of her
destiny required her to throw herself irretrievably away
she did it with a splendid appreciation of large and
definite movement that was essentially of herself.

The moment of it had a bold gruesomeness that caught

the breath - a disinterment on the stage in search of letters that would prove the charge against the second year of Mrs. Halliday's married life, her letters buried with the poet. It was an advantage which only the husband of Mrs. Halliday would have claimed to bring so helpless a respondent before even the informal court at the graveyard; but it gave Hilda a magnificent opportunity of wild, mad apostrophe to the skull, holding it tenderly with both hands, while Lord Ingleton smiled appreciatively in advance of the practical benevolence which was to sustain the lady through the divorce court, and in the final scene offer to her and to the prejudices of the British public the respectability of his name.

It was over with a rush at the end, leaving the audience uncertain whether after all enough attention had been paid to that tradition of the footlights which insists on so nice a sense of opprobrium and compensation, but convinced of its desire to applaud. Duff Lindsay turned as the wave of clapping spent itself, to say to Stephen that he had never respected Hamilton Bradley's acting so much. He said it to Herbert Livingstone instead; the priest had disappeared.

The outgoers looked at Arnold curiously as he made his way among them in a direction which was not that of the exit. He went with hurried purpose in the face of them all toward the region, badly lighted and imperfectly closed, which led to the rear of the stage. He opened doors into dark closets, and one which gave upon the road, retraced his unfamiliar steps and asked a question, to which - it was so unusual from one in his habit - he received a hesitating but correct reply. A moment later he passed Mr. Llewellyn Stanhope, who stood in his path with a hostile stare, and got out of it with a deferential bow, and knocked at a door upon which was pasted the name, in large red letters cut from a poster, of Miss Hilda Howe. It was a little ajar, so he entered, when she cried "Come in!" with the less hesitation. Hilda sat on the single chair the place contained, in the dress and make-up of the last scene. A servant, who looked up incuriously, was unlacing her shoes. Various garments hung about on nails driven into the unpainted walls, others overflowed from a packing-box in one corner. A common teakwood dressing-table held make up saucers and powder-puffs and some remnants of cold fowl which had not been partaken of, apparently, with the assistance of a knife and fork. A candle stood in an empty soda-water bottle on each side of the looking-glass, and there was no other light. On the floor a pair of stays, old and soiled, sprawled with unconcern. The place looked sordid and miserable, and Hilda sitting in the middle of it, still in the yellow wig and painted face of Mrs. Halliday, all wrong at that range, gave it a note of false artifice, violent and grievous. Stephen stood in the doorway grasping the handle, saying nothing, and an instant passed before she knew with certainty, in the wretched light, that it was he. Then she sprang up and made a step toward him as if toward victory and reward, but checked herself in time. "Is it possible!" she exclaimed. "I did not know you were in the theatre."

"Yes," he said, with moderation, "I have seen this - this damnable play."

"Damnable? Oh! - "

"It has caused me," he went on, "to regret the substance of my letter this morning. I failed to realise that this was the kind of work you devote your life to. I now see that you could not escape its malign influence - that no women could. I now think that the alternative that has been revealed to you, of remaining in Calcutta, is a chance of escape offered you by God Himself. Take it. I withdraw my foolish, ignorant opposition."

"Oh," she cried, "do you really think - "

"Take it," he repeated, and closed the door.

Hilda sat still for some time after the servant had finished unlacing her shoes. A little tender smile played oddly about her carmined lips. "Dear heart," she said aloud, "I was going to."

CHAPTER XXIII

"I would simply give anything to be there," Miss Livingstone said, with a look of sincere desire.

"I should love to have you, but it isn't possible. You might meet men you knew who had been invited by particular lady friends among the company."

"Oh, well, that of course would be odious."

"Very, I should think," Hilda agreed. "You must be satisfied with a faithful report of it. I promise you that."

"You have asked Mr. Lindsay," Alicia complained.

"That's quite a different thing. And if I hadn't, Llewellyn Stanhope would; Stanhope cherishes Duff as he cherishes the critic of the Chronicle. He refers to him as a pillar of the legitimate. Whenever he begs me to turn the Norwegian crank, he says, 'I'm sure Mr. Lindsay would come.'"

Miss Howe was at the top of the staircase in Middleton Street, on the point of departure. It was to be the night of her last appearance for the season and her benefit, followed by a supper in her honour, at which Mr. Stanhope and his company would take leave of those whose acquaintance, as he expressed it, business and pleasure had given them during the months that were past. It was this function that Alicia, at the top of the staircase, so ardently desired to attend.

"No, I won't kiss you," Hilda said, as the other put her cool cheek forward; "I'm so divinely happy - some of it might escape."

Alicia's voice pursued her as she ran downstairs. "Remember," she said, "I don't approve. I don't at all agree either with my reverend cousin or with you. I think you ought to find some other way, or let it go. Go home instead; go straight to London and insist on your chance. After six weeks you will have forgotten the name of his Order."

Hilda looked back with a smile. Her face was splendid with the dawn and the promise of success. "Don't say that," she cried.

Alicia, leaning down, was visited by a flash of quotation. "Well," she said, "nothing in this life becomes you like the leaving of it," and went back to her room to write to Laura Filbert in Plymouth. She wrote often to Miss Filbert, at Duff's request. It gratified her that she was able, without a pang, to address four pages of pleasantly colourless communication to Mr. Lindsay's fiancee. Her letters stood for a medicine surprisingly easy to take, aimed at the convalescence which she already anticipated in the future immediately beyond Duff's miserable marriage. If that event had promised felicitously she would have faced it, one fancies, with less sanguine anticipations for herself: but the black disaster that rode on with it brought her certain aids to the spirit, certain hopes of herself. Laura's prompt replies, with their terrible margins and painstaking solecisms, came to be things Miss Livingstone looked forward to. She read them with a beating heart, however, in the unconscious apprehension of some revelation of improvement. She was quite unaware of it, but she entertained towards the Simpsons an attitude of misgiving in this regard.

Hilda went on about her business. As usual her business was important and imperative; nothing was lightened for her this last day. She drove about from place to place in the hot, slatternly city, putting more than her usual vigour and directness into all she did. It seemed to her that the sunlight burning on the tiles, pouring through the crowded streets, had more than ever a vivid note; and so much spoke to her, came to her, from the profuse and ingenuous life which streamed about her, that she leaned a little forward to meet it with happy eyes and tender lips that said, "I know. I see." She was living for the moment which should exhale itself somewhere about midnight after the lights had gone out on her last appearance - living for it as a Carmelite might live for the climax of her veil and her vows if it were conceivable that beyond the cell and the grating she saw the movement and the colour and the passion of a wider life. All Hilda's splendid vitality went into her intention, of which she was altogether mistress, riding it and reining it in a straight course through the encumbered hours. It keyed her to a finer and more eager susceptibility; and the things she saw stayed with her, passing into a composite day which the years were hardly to dim for her.

She could live like that, for the purposes of a period, wrought up to immense keenness of sense and brilliancy of energy, making steadily for some point of feeling or achievement flashing gloriously on the horizon. It is already plain, perhaps, that she rejoiced in such strokes, and that life as she found it worth living was marked by a succession of them.

She had kept, even from Lindsay, what she meant to do. When she stepped from his brougham, flushed after the indubitable triumph of the evening, with her arms full of real bouquets from Chatterjee's - no eight-anna bazar confections edged with silver tinsel - it occurred to her that this reticence was not altogether fair to so constant a friend. He was there, keen and eager as ever in all that concerned her, foremost with his congratulations on the smiling fringe of the party assembled to do her honour. It was a party of some brilliance in its way, though its way was diverse; there was no steady glow. Fillimore said of the company that it comprised all the talent, and Fillimore, Editor of the Indian Sportsman and Racing Gazelle, was a judge. He said it to Hagge, of the Bank of Hindostan, who could hardly have been an owner on three hundred rupees a month without conspicuous ability disconnected with his ledgers; and Hagge looked gratified. Though so promising, he was young. Lord Bobby was there from Government House. Lord Bobby always accompanied the talent, who were very kind to him. He was talking when Hilda arrived to the Editor of the Indian Empire, who wanted to find out the date of her Excellency's fancy dress party for children, in order that he might make a leaderette of it; but Lord Bobby couldn't remember - had to promise to drop him a line. Gianacchi was there, trying to treat Fillimore with coldness because the Sportsman had discovered too many virtues in his Musquito, exalted her indeed into a favourite for Saturday's hurdle race, a notability for which Gianacchi felt himself too modest. "They say,"

Fillimore had written, "that Musquito has been seen jumping by moonlight" - the sort of thing to spoil any book. Fillimore was an acute and weary-looking little man, with a peculiarly sweet smile and an air of cynicism which gave to his lightest word a dangerous and suspicious air. It was rumoured in official circles that he had narrowly escaped beheading for pointing out too ironically the disabilities of a Viceroy who insisted on reviewing the troops from a cushioned carriage with the horses taken out. Fillimore seemed to think that if nature had not made such a nobleman a horseman, the Queen-Empress should not have made him Governor-General of India. Fillimore was full of prejudices. Gianacchi, however, found it impossible to treat him coldly. His smoothness of temperament stood in the way. Instead, he imparted the melodious information that Musquito had pecked badly twice at Tollygunge that morning, and smiled with pathetic philosophy. "Always let 'em use their noses," said Fillimore, and there seemed to be satire in it. Fillimore certainly had a flair, and when Beryl Stace presently demanded of him, "What's the dead bird going to be on Saturday, Filly?" he put it generously at her service. Among the friends of Mr. Stanhope and his company were also several gentlemen, content, for their personal effect, with the lustre they shed upon the Stock Exchange - gentlemen of high finance, who wrote their names at the end of directors' reports, but never in the visitors' book at Government House, who were little more to the Calcutta world than published receipts for so many lakhs, except when they were seen now and then driving, in fleet dogcarts across the Maidan toward comfortable suburban residences where ladies were not entertained. They were extremely, curiously, devoted to business; but if they allowed themselves any amusement other than company promoting, it was the theatre, of which their appreciation had sometimes an odd relation to the merits of performance. This supper, on the part of Miss Beryl Stace and one or two others of Mr. Stanhope's artistes, might have been considered a return of hospitality to these gentlemen, since the suburban residences stood lavishly open to the profession.

Altogether, perhaps, there were fifty people, and an eye that looked for the sentiment, the pity of things, would have distinguished at once on about half the faces, especially those of the women, the used, underlined look that spoke of the continual play of muscle and forcing of feeling. It gave them a shabbily complicated air, contrasting in a strained and sorry way even, with the countenances of the brokers and bankers, where nature had laid on a smooth wash and experience had not interfered. They were all gay and enthusiastic as Miss Howe entered, they loafed forward, broad shirt-fronts lustrous, fat hands in financial pockets, with their admiration, and Fillimore put out his cigarette. Hilda came down among them from the summit of her achievement, clasping their various hands. They were all personally responsible for her success, she made them feel that, and they expanded in the conviction. She moved in a kind of tide of infectious vitality, subtly drawing from every human flavour in the room the power to hold and show something akin to it in herself, a fugitive assimilation floating in the lamplight with the odour of the flowers and the soup, to be extinguished with the occasion. They looked at her up and down the table with an odd smiling attraction, they told each other that she was in great form. Mr. Fillimore was of the opinion that she couldn't be outclassed at the Lyceum, and Mr. Hagge responded with vivacity that there were few places where she wouldn't stretch the winner's neck. The feast was not after all one of great bounty, Mr. Stanhope justly holding that the opportunity, the little gathering, was the thing, and it was not long before the moment of celebration arrived for which the gentlemen of the Stock Exchange, to judge from their undrained glasses, seemed to be reserving themselves. There certainly had been one tin of pate, and it circulated at that end; on the other hand the ladies had all the fondants. So that when Mr. Llewellyn Stanhope rose with the sentiment of the evening he found satisfaction, if not repletion, in the regards turned upon him.

Llewellyn got up with modest importance, and ran a hand through his yellow hair, not dramatically, but with the effect of collecting his ideas. He leaned a little forward, he was extremely, happily conspicuous. The attention of the two lines of faces seemed to overcome him, for an instant, with dizzy pleasure; Hilda's beside him was bent a little, waiting.

"Ladies and gentlemen," said Mr. Stanhope, looking with precision up and down the table to be still more inclusive, "we have met together to-night in honour of a lady who has given this city more pleasure in the exercise of her profession than can be said of any single performer during the last twenty years. Cast your eye back over the theatrical record of Calcutta for that space of time, and you yourselves will admit that there has been nobody that could be said to have come within a mile of her shadow, if I may use the language of metaphor." (Applause, led by Mr. Fillimore.) "I would ask you to remember, at the same time, that this pleasure has been of a superior class. I freely admit that this is a great satisfaction to me personally. Far be it from me to put myself forward on this auspicious occasion, but, ladies and gentlemen, if I have one ambition more than another, it is to promote the noble cause of the unfettered drama. To this I may say I have been vowed from the cradle, by a sire who was well-known in the early days of the metropolis of Sydney as a pioneer of the great movement which has made the dramatic talent of Australia what it is. To-day a magnificent theatre rises on the site forever consecrated to me by those paternal labours, but - but I can never forget it. In Miss Hilda Howe I have found a great coadjutor, and one who is willing to consecrate her royal abilities in the same line as myself, so that we have been able to maintain a high standard of production among you, prices remaining as usual. I have to thank you, as representing the public of the Indian capital, for the kind support which has been so encouraging to Miss Howe, the Company, and myself personally, during the past season. Many a time ladies and gentlemen of my profession have said to me, 'Mr. Stahhope, why do you go to Calcutta? That city is a death-trap for professionals,' and now the past season proves that I was right and they were wrong; and the magnificent houses, the enthusiasm, and the appreciation that have greeted our efforts, especially on the Saturday evening performances, show plainly enough that when a good thing is available the citizens of Calcutta won't be happy till they get it. Ladies and gentlemen, I invite you to join me in drinking the health, happiness, and prosperity of Miss Hilda Howe!"

"Miss Howe!" "Miss Howe!" "Miss Hilda Howe!" In the midst of a pushing back of chairs and a movement of feet, the response was quick and universal. Hilda accepted their nods and becks and waving glasses with a slow movement of her beautiful eyes and a quiet smile, in the subsidence of sound Mr. Stanhope's voice was heard again, "We can hardly expect a speech from Miss Howe, but perhaps Mr. Hamilton Bradley, whose international reputation need hardly be referred to, will kindly say a few words on her behalf."

Then with deliberate grace, Hilda rose from her chair, a tall figure among them, looking down with a hint of compassionateness on the little man at her left. She stood for an instant without speaking, as if the flushed silence, the expectation, the warm magnetism that drew all their eyes to her were enough. Then out of something like reverie she came to the matter, she threw up her beautiful face with one of the supreme gestures which belonged to her. "I think," she said, with a little smiling bow in his direction, "that I will not trouble my friend Mr. Bradley. He has rendered me so many kind services already that I am sure I might count upon him again, but this is a thing I should like to do for myself. I would not have my thanks chilled by even the passage from my heart to his." There was something like bravado in the glance that rested lightly on Bradley with this. One would have said that parley of hearts between them was not a thing that as a rule she courted. "I can only offer you my thanks, poor things to which we can give neither life nor substance, yet I beg that you will somehow take them and remember them. It is to me, and will always be, a kind of crowning satisfaction that you were pleased to come together to-night to tell me I had done well. You know yourselves, and I know, how much too flattering your kindness is, but perhaps it will hurt nobody if to-night I take it as it is generously offered, and let it make me as happy as you intend me to be. At all events, no one could disturb me in believing that in obtaining your praise and your good wishes I have done well enough."

For a few seconds she stopped speaking, but she held them with her eyes from the mistake of supposing she had done. Lindsay, who was watching her closely and hanging with keen pleasure on the sweetness and precision of what she found to say, noted a swift constriction pass upon her face. There was a half-tone of difference, too, in her voice, when she raised it again, a firmer vibration, as if she passed, deliberate and aware, out of one phase into another.

"No," she went on, "I am not shy on this occasion; indeed, I feel that I should like to keep your eyes upon me for a long time to-night, and go on talking far past your patience or my wit. For I cannot think it likely that our ways will cross again." Here her words grew suddenly low and hurried. "If I may trespass upon your interest so much further, I have to tell you that my connection with the stage closes with this evening's performance. To-morrow I join the Anglican Order of the Sisters of St. Paul - the Baker Institution - in Calcutta, as a novice. They have taken me without much question because - because the plague hospitals of this cheerful country" - she contrived a smile - "have made a great demand upon their body. That is all. I have nothing more to say."

It was, after all, ineffective, the denouement, or perhaps it was too effective. In any case it was received in silence, the applause that was ready falling back on itself, inconsistent and absurd. The incredulity of Llewellyn Stanhope might have been electric had it found words, but that gentleman's protests were made in violent whispers, to which Hilda, who sat playing with a faded rose, seemed to pay no attention whatever. One might have thought her more overcome than anyone. She seemed to make one or two unsuccessful efforts to raise her head. There was a moment of waiting for someone to reply; eyes were turned towards Mr. Bradley, and when it became plain that no one would, broken murmurs of talk began with a note of deprecation and many shakes of the head. The women, especially, looked tragically at their neighbours with very wide-open eyes. Presently a chair was drawn back, and then another, and people began to filter, in slow embarrassment, towards the door. Lindsay came with Hilda's cloak. "You won't mind my coming with you," he said, "I should like to hear the details." Beryl Stace made as if to embrace her, pouring out abusive disbelief, but Hilda waved her away with a gesture almost of irritation. Some of the others said a perfunctory word or two, and went away with lingering backward looks. In a quarter of an hour, Mr. Lindsay's brougham had followed the other vehicles into the lamp-lit ways of Calcutta, and only the native table-servants remained in somewhat resentful possession of what was left.

CHAPTER XXIV

If Duff Lindsay had apprehended that the reception of Miss Filbert by the Simpsons would involve any strain upon the affection his friends bore him, the event must have relieved him in no small degree. He was soon made aware of its happy character, and constantly kept assured; indeed, it seemed that whenever Mrs. Simpson had nothing else to do she laid her pen to the task of telling him once again how cherished a satisfaction they found in Laura, and how reluctant they would be to lose it. She wrote in that strain of facile sympathy which seems part of an English-woman's education, and often begged him to believe that the more she knew of their sweet and heavenly-minded guest the more keenly she realised how dreary for him must have been the pang of parting and how arid the months of separation. Mrs. Simpson herself was well acquainted with these trials of the spirit. She and her husband had been divided by those wretched thousands of miles of ocean for three years one week and five days all told during their married life: she knew what it meant. But if Duff could only see how well and blooming his beloved one was - she had gained twelve pounds already - Mrs. Simpson was sure the time of waiting would pass less heavily. For herself, it was cruel but she smiled upon the deferred reunion of hearts, she would keep Laura till the very last day, and hoped to establish a permanent claim on her. She was just the daughter Mrs. Simpson would have liked, so unspotted, so pure, so wrapped in high ideals; and then the page would reflect something of the adoring awe in which Mrs. Simpson would have held such a daughter. It will be seen that Mrs. Simpson knew how to express herself, but there was a fine sincerity behind the mask of words; Miss Filbert had entered very completely into possession.

It had its abnormal side, the way she entered into possession. Everything about Laura Filbert had its abnormal side, none the less obvious because it was inward, and invisible. Nature, of course, worked with her, one might say that nature really did it all, since in the end she was practically unconscious, except for the hope that certain souls had been saved, that anything of the sort had happened. She conquered the Simpsons and their friends chiefly by the simple impossibility that they should conquer her, walking immobile among them even while she admired Mr. Simpson's cauli-flowers and approved the quality of Mrs. Simpson's house linen. It must be confessed that nothing in her surroundings spoke to her more loudly or more subtly than these things. In view of what happened, poor dear Alicia Livingstone's anticipation that the Simpsons and their circle would have a radical personal effect upon Laura Filbert became ludicrous. They had no effect at all. She took no tint, no curve. She appeared not to see that these precious things were to be had for the assimilation. Her grace remained exclusively that of holiness, and continued to fail to have any relation to the common little things she did and said.

The Simpsons were more plastic. Laura had been with them hardly a week before Mrs. Simpson, with touching humility, was trying to remodel her spiritual nature upon the form so fortuitously, if the word is admissible, presented. The dear lady had never before realised, by her own statement, how terribly her religious feelings were mingled with domestic and social considerations, how firmly her spiritual edifice was based upon the things of this world. She felt that her soul was honeycombed - that was her word - with conventionality and false standards, and she made confessions like these to Laura, sitting in the girl's bedroom in the twilight. They were very soothing, these confessions. Laura would take Mrs. Simpson's thin, veined, middle-aged hand in hers and seem to charge herself for the moment with the responsibility of the elder lady's case. She did not attempt to conceal her pity or even her contempt for Mrs. Simpson's state of grace, she made short work of special services and ladies' Bible classes. The world was white with harvest, and Mrs. Simpson's chief activity was a recreation society for shop girls. But it was something, it was everything, to be uneasy, to be unsatisfied, and they would uplift themselves in prayer, and Laura would find words of such touching supplication in which to represent the matter that the burden of her friend and hostess would at once be lessened by the weight of tears. Mrs. Simpson had never wept so much without perceived cause for grief as since Laura arrived, and this alone would testify, such was the gentle paradox of her temperament, how much she enjoyed Miss Filbert's presence.

Laura's room was a temple, for which the gardener daily gave up his choicest blooms, the tenderest interest watched upon her comings and goings, and it was the joy of both the Simpsons to make little sacrifices for her, to desert their beloved vicar on a Sunday evening, for instance, and accompany her to the firemen's halls and skating rinks lent to the publishing of the Word in the only manner from which their guest seemed to derive benefit. With all this, the Simpsons were sometimes troubled by the impression that they could not claim to be making their angel in the house completely happy. The air, the garden, the victoria, the turbot and the whitebait, these were all that has been vaunted, and even to the modesty of the Simpsons it was evident that the intimacy they offered their guest should count for something. There were other friends too, young friends who tried to teach her to play tennis, robust and silent young persons who threw shy flushed glances at her in the pauses of the games, and wished supremely, without daring to hint it, that she would let fall some word about her wonderful romance - a hope ever renewed, ever to be disappointed. And physically Laura expanded before their eyes. The colour that came into her cheek gave her the look of a person painted by Bouguereau; that artist would have found in her a model whom he could have represented with sincerity. Yet something was missing to her, her friends were dimly aware. Her desirable surroundings kindled her to but a perfunctory interest in life - the electric spark was absent. Mrs. Simpson relied strategically upon the wedding preparations and hurried them on, announcing in May that it was quite time to think about various garments of which the fashion is permanent, but the issue was blank. No ripple stirred the placid waters, unless indeed we take that way of describing Laura's calm demand, when the decision lay between Valenciennes and Torchon lace for under-bodies, to hear whether Mrs. Simpson had ever known Duff Lindsay to be anxious about his eternal future. The girl continued to give forth a mere pale reflection of her circumstances, and Mrs. Simpson was forced into the deprecation that perhaps one would hardly call her a joyous Christian.

But for the Zenana Light Society this impression of Miss Filbert might have deepened. The committee of that body was almost entirely composed of Mrs. Simpson's friends, and naturally came to learn much about her guest. The matter was vastly considered, but finally Miss Filbert was asked to speak at one of the monthly meetings the ladies held among themselves to keep the society "in touch" with the cause. Laura brought them, as one would imagine, surprisingly in touch. She made pictures for them, letting her own eyelashes close deliberately while they stared. She moved these ladies, inspired them, carried them away, and the fact that none of them found themselves able afterward to quote the most pathetic passages seemed rather to add to the enthusiasm with which they described the address. The first result was a shower of invitations to tea, occasions when Laura was easily led into monologue. Miss Filbert became a cult of evangelistic drawing- rooms, and the same kind of forbearance was extended to her little traces of earlier social experiences as is offered, in salons of another sort, to the eccentricities of persons of genius. Very soon other applications had to be met and considered, and Mrs. Simpson freely admitted that Laura would not be justified in refusing to the Methodists and Baptists what she had given elsewhere. She reasserted her platform influence over audiences that grew constantly larger, and her world began to revolve again in that great relation to the infinities which it was her life to perceive and point out. Mrs. Simpson charged her genially with having been miserable in Plymouth until she was allowed to do good in her own way, and saw that she had beef-tea after every occasion of doing it. She became in a way a public character, and a lady journalist sent an account of her, with a photograph, to a well-known London fashion paper. Perhaps the strongest effect she made was as the voice of the Purity Association, when she delivered an address, in the picturesque costume she had abandoned, attacking measures contemplated by Government for the protection of the health of the Army in India. This was reported in full in the local paper, and Mr. Simpson sent a copy to Duff Lindsay, who received it, I regret to say, with an unmistakable imprecation. But Laura rejoiced. Deprived of her tambourine she nevertheless rejoiced exceedingly.

CHAPTER XXV

The Mother Superior had a long upper lip, which she was in the habit of drawing still further down; it gave her an air of great diplomatic caution, almost of casuistry. Her face was pale and narrow; she had eyes that desired to be very penetrating, and a flat little stooping figure within her voluminous draperies. She carried about with her all the virtues of a monastic order, patience was written upon her, and repression, discipline, and the love of administration, written and underlined, so that the Anglican Sister whom no Pope blessed was more priestly in her personal effect than any Jesuit. It was difficult to remember that she had begun as a woman; she was now a somewhat anaemic formula making for righteousness. Sister Ann Frances, who in her turn suggested the fat capons of an age of friars more indulgent to the flesh, and whose speech was of the crispest in this world where there was so much to do, thought poorly of the executive ability of the Mother Superior, and resented the imposition, as it were, of the long upper lip. Out of this arose the only irritations that vexed the energetic flow of duty at the Baker Institution, slight official raspings which the Mother Superior immediately laid before Heaven at great length. She did it with publicity, too, kneeling on the chunam floor of the chapel for an hour at a time obviously explaining matters. The bureaucracy of the country was reflected in the Baker Institution; it

Mrs. Everard Cotes

seemed to Sister Ann Frances that her superior officer took undue advantage of her privilege of direct communication with the Supreme Authority, giving any colour she liked to the incident. And when the Mother Superior's lumbago came on in direct consequence of the cold chunam, the annoyance of Sister Ann Frances was naturally not lessened.

There were twenty or thirty of them, with their little white caps tied close under their chins, their long veils and their girdled black robes. They were the most self-sacrificing women in Asia, the most devout, the most useful. Government gave hospitals and doctors into their hands; they took the whole charge of certain schools. They differed in complexion, some of the newly arrived being delightfully fresh and pink under their starched bandeaux; but they were all official, they all walked discreetly and directly about their business, with a jangle of keys in the folds of their robes, immensely organised, immensely under orders. Hilda, when she had time, had the keenest satisfaction in contemplating them. She took the edge off the fact that she was not quite one, in aim and method, with these dear women as they supposed her to be, with the reflection that after all it might be worth while to work out a solution of life in those terms, standing aside from the world - the world was troublesome - and keeping an unfaltering eye upon the pity of things, an unfaltering hand at its assuagement. It was simple and fine and indisputable, this work of throwing the clear shadow of the Cross upon the muddy sunlight of the world; it carried the boon of finality in itself. One might be stopped and put away at any moment, and nothing would be spoiled, broken, unfinished; and it absolutely barred out such considerations as were presented by Hamilton Bradley. There was a time early in her probation when she thought seriously that if it were not Stephen Arnold it should be this.

She begged to be put on hospital work, and was sent for her indiscretion to teach in the Orphanage for Female Children of British Troops. The first duty of a novice was to be free of preference, to obey without a sigh of choice. On the third day, however, Sister Ann Frances, supervising, stopped at the open schoolroom door to hear the junior female orphans repeating in happy chorus after their instructress the statement that seven times nine were fifty-six. I think Hilda saw Sister Ann Frances in the door. That couldn't go on, even in the name of discipline, and Miss Howe was placed at the disposal of the Chief Nursing Sister at the General Hospital next day. Sister Ann Frances was inclined to defend Hilda's imperfect acquaintance with primary arithmetic.

"We all have our gifts," she said. "Miss Howe's is not the multiplication table; but neither is mine stage-acting." At which, the upper lip lengthened further into an upward curving smile, and the Mother Superior remarked cautiously that she hoped Miss Howe would develop one for making bandages, otherwise - And there for the time being the matter rested.

The depth of what was unusual in Hilda's relation with Alicia Livingstone - perhaps it has been plain that they were not quite the ordinary feminine liens - seems to me to be sounded in the tacit acceptance of Hilda's novitiate on its merits that fell between the two women. The full understanding of it was an abyss between them, across which they joined hands, looking elsewhere. Even in the surprise of Hilda's announce- ment Alicia had the instinct to glance away, lest her

Mrs. Everard Cotes

eyes should betray too many facts that bore upon the situation. It had never been discussed, but it had to be accepted, and occasionally referred to; and the terms of acceptance and reference made no implication of Stephen Arnold. In her inmost privacy Alicia gazed breathless at the conception as a whole; she leaped at it, and caught it and held it to look, with a feverish comparison of possibilities. It was not strange, perhaps, that she took a vivid personal interest in the essentials that enabled one to execute a flank movement like Hilda's, not that she should conceive the first of them to be that one must come out of a cab. She dismissed that impression with indignation as ungenerously cynical, but it always came back for redismissal. It did not interfere in the least, however, with her deliberate invitations to Stephen to come to Ten, Middleton Street, on afternoons or evenings when Hilda was there. She was like one standing denied in the Street of Abundance; she had an avidity of the eye for even love's reflection.

That was a little later. At first there was the transformation to lament, the loss, the break.

"You look," cried Miss Livingstone, the first time Hilda arrived in the dress of the novice, a kind of under-study of the Sisters' black and white, "you look like a person in a book, full of salient points, and yet made so simple to the reader. If you go on wearing those things I shall end by understanding you perfectly."

"If you don't understand me," Hilda said, dropping into the corner of a sofa, "Cela que je m'en doute, it's because you look for too much elaboration. I am a simple creature, done with rather a broad brush -

voila tout!"

Nevertheless, Miss Livingstone's was a happy impression. The neutrality of her hospital dress left Hilda in a manner exposed: one saw in a special way the significance of lines and curves; it was an astonishingly vigorous human expression.

Alicia leaned forward, her elbow on the arm of her chair, her chin tucked into her palm, and looked at it. The elbow bent itself in light blue muslin of extreme elegance, trimmed with lace. The colour found a wistful echo in the eyes that regarded Miss Howe, who was accustomed to the look, and met it with impenetrable commonplace, being made impatient by nothing in this world so much as by futility, however charming.

"Just now," Alicia said, "the shadows under your eyes are brushed too deep."

"I don't believe I sleep well in a dormitory."

"Horrible! All the little comforts of life - don't you miss them?"

"I never had them, my dear - I never had them. Life has never given me very many luxuries - I don't miss them. An occasional hour to one's self - and that we get even at the Institution. The conventions are strictly conserved, believe me."

"One imagines that kind of place is always clean."

"When I have time I think of Number Three, Lal Behari's Lane, and believe myself in Paradise. The repose is there, the angels also - dear commanding things - and a perpetual incense of cheap soap. And there is some good in sleeping in a row. It reminds one that after all one is very like other women."

"It wouldn't convince me if I were you. And how did the sisters receive you - with the harp and the psaltery?"

"That was rather," said Hilda gravely, "what I expected. On the contrary. They snubbed me - they really did. There were two of them. I said, 'Reverend ladies, please be a little kind. Convents are strange to me; I shall probably commit horrible sins without knowing it. Give me your absolution in advance - at least your blessing.'"

"Hilda, you didn't!"

"It is delightful to observe the Mother Abbess, or whatever she is, disguising the fact that she takes any interest in me. Such diplomacy - funny old thing."

"They must be devoured with curiosity!"

"Well, they ask no questions. One sees an everlasting finger on the lip. It's a little boring. One feels inclined to speak up and say, 'Mesdames, entendez - it isn't so bad as you think.' But then their fingers would go into their ears."

"And the rules, Hilda? I can't imagine you, somehow, under rules."

"I am attached to the rules; I think about them all day long. They make the thing simple and - possible. It is a little like living for the first time in a house all right angles after - after a lifelong voyage in a small boat."

"Isn't the house rather empty?"

"Oh, well!"

Alicia put out her hand and tucked an irrelevant bit of lace into Hilda's bosom. "I can tell you who is interested," she cried. "The Archdeacon - the Archdeacon and Mrs. Barberry. They both dined here last night; and you lasted from the fish to the pudding. I got so bored with you, my dear, in your new capacity."

A new ray of happiness came into the smile of the novice. "What did they say? Do tell me what they said."

"There was a difference of opinion. The Archdeacon held that with God all things were possible. He used an expression more suitable to a dinner-party; but I think that is what he meant. Mrs. Barberry thought it wouldn't last. Mrs. Barberry was very cynical. She said anyone could see that you were as emotional as ever you could be."

The eyes of the two women met, and they laughed frankly. A sense of expansion came between them, in which for an instant they were silent.

"Tell me about the hospital," Alicia said presently. "Ah, the hospital!" Hilda's face changed; there came into her eyes the moved look that always waked a thrill in Alicia Livingstone, as if she were suddenly aware that she had stepped upon ground where feet like hers passed seldom.

"There is nothing to tell you that is not - sad. Such odds and ends, of life, thrown together!"

"Have you had any experiences yet?"

Hilda stared for a moment absently in front of her, and then turned her head aside to answer as if she closed her eyes on something.

"Experiences? Delightful Alicia, speaking your language, no. You are thinking of the resident surgeon, the medical student, the interesting patient. My resident surgeon is fifty years old; the medical student is a Bengali in white cotton and patent leather shoes. I am occupied in a ward full of deck hands. For these I hold the bandage and the bottle; they are hardly aware of me."

"You are sure to have them," Alicia said. "They crop up wherever you go in this world, either before you or behind you."

Hilda fixed her eyes attentively upon her companion. "Sometimes," she said, "you say things that are extremely true in their general bearing. A fortuneteller with cards gives one the same shock of surprise. Well, let me tell you, I have been promoted to temperatures. I took thirty-five to-day. Next week I am to make poultices; the week after, baths and fomentations."

"What are the others like - the other novices?"

"Nearly all Eurasians, one native, a Hindu widow - the Sisters are almost demonstrative to her - and one or two local European girls: the commissariat sergeant class, I should think."

"They don't sound attractive, and I am glad. You will depend the more upon me."

Hilda looked thoughtfully at Miss Livingstone. "I will depend," she said, "a good deal upon you."

It was Alicia's fate to meet the Archdeacon again that evening at dinner. "And is she really throwing her heart into the work?" asked that dignitary, referring to Miss Howe.

"Oh, I think so," Alicia said. "Yes."

CHAPTER XXVI

The labours of the Baker Institution and of the Clarke Mission were very different in scope, so much so that if they had been secular bodies working for profit, there would have been hardly a point of contact between them. As it was they made one, drawing together in affiliation for the comfort of mutual support in a heathen country where all the other Englishmen wrote reports, drilled troops, or played polo, with all the other Englishwomen in the corresponding female parts. Doubtless the little communities prayed for each other. One may imagine, not profanely, their petitions rising on either side of the heedless, multitudinous, idolatrous city, and meeting at some point in the purer air above the yellow dust-haze. I am not aware that they held any other mutual duty or privilege, but this bond was known, and enabled people whose conscience pricked them in that direction to give little garden teas to which they invited Clarke Brothers and Baker Sisters, secure in doing a benevolent thing and at the same time embarrassing nobody except, possibly, the Archdeacon, who was officially exposed to being asked as well and had no right to complain. The affiliation was thus a social convenience, since it is unlikely that without it anybody would have hit upon so ingenious a way of killing, as it were, a Baker Sister and a Clarke Brother with one stone. It is not surprising that this degree of intelligence should fail to see the profound official difference between Baker Sisters and Baker novices. As the Mother Superior said, it did not seem to occur to people that there could be in connection with a religious body, such words as discipline and subordination, which were certainly made ridiculous for the time being, when she and Sister Ann Frances were asked to eat ices on the same terms as Miss Hilda Howe. It must have been more than ever painful to these ladies, regarded from the official point of view, when it became plain, as it usually did, that the interest of the afternoon centred in Miss Howe, whether or not the Archdeacon happened to be present. Their displeasure was so clear, after the first occasion, that Hilda felt obliged when the next one came, to fall back on her original talent, and ate her ice abashed and silent speaking only when she was spoken to, and then in short words and long hesitations. Thereupon the Sisters were of opinion that after all poor Miss Howe could not help her unenviable lot, she was perhaps more to be pitied on account of it than - anything else. It came to this, that Sister Ann Frances even had an exhibitor's pride in her, and Hilda knew the sensations of a barbarian female captive in the bonds of the Christians. But she could not afford to risk being cut off from those little garden teas. All told, they were few; ladies disturbed by ideas of social duties toward missionaries being so uncommon.

She told Stephen so, frankly, one afternoon when he charged her with being so unlike herself, and he heard her explanation with a gravity which contained an element of satisfaction. "It is, of course, a pleasure to us to meet," he said, "a pleasure to us both." That was part of the satisfaction, that he could meet her candour with the same openness. He was not even afraid to mention to her the stimulus she gave him always and his difficulty in defining it, and once he told her how, after a talk with her, he had lain awake until the small hours unable to stop his excited rush of thought. He added that he was now personally and selfishly glad she had chosen as she did three months before; it made a difference to him, her being in Calcutta, a sensible and material difference. He had better hope and heart in his work. It was the last luxury he would ever have dreamed of allowing himself, a woman friend; but since life had brought it in the oddest way the boon should be met with no grudging of gratitude. A kind of sedate cheerfulness crept into his manner which was new to him; he went about his duties with the look of a man to whom life had dictated its terms and who found them acceptable. His blood might have received some mysterious chemical complement, so much was his eye clearer, his voice firmer, and the things he found to say more decisive. Nor did any consideration of their relations disturb him. He never thought of the oxygen in the air he breathed, and he seldom thought of Hilda.

They were walking toward the Institution together the day he explained to her his gratification that she had elected to remain. Sister Ann Frances and Sister Margaret led; Arnold and Hilda came behind. He had an errand to the Mother Superior - he would go all the way. It was late in May and late in the afternoon; all the treetops on the Maidan were bent under the sweep of the south wind, blowing a caressing coolness from the sea. It spread fragrances about and shook down blossoms from the gold-mohur trees. One could see nothing anywhere, so red and yellow as they were, except the long coat of a Government messenger, a point of scarlet moving in the perspective of a dusty road. The spreading acres of turf were baked to every earth-colour; wherever a pine dropped needles and an old woman swept them up, a trail of dust ran curling along the ground like smoke. The little party was unusual in walking; glances of uncomprehending pity were cast at them from victorias and landaus that rolled past. Even the convalescent British soldiers facing each other in the clumsy drab cart drawn by humped bullocks, and marked Garrison Dispensary, stared at the black-skirts so near the powder of the road. The Sisters in front walked with their heads slightly bent toward one another; they seemed to be consulting. Hilda reflected, looking at them, that they always seemed to be consulting; it was the normal attitude of that long black veil that flowed behind.

Arnold walked beside his companion, his hands loosely clasped behind him, with the air of semi-detachment that young clergymen sometimes have with their wives. Whether it was that, or the trace of custom his satisfaction carried, the casual glance might easily have taken them for a married pair.

"There is a kind of folly and stupidity in saying it," he said, "but you have done - you do - a great deal for me."

She turned toward him with a wistful, measuring look. It searched his face for an instant and came back baffled. Arnold spoke with so much kindness, so much appreciation.

"Very little," she said mechanically, looking at the fresh footprints of Sister Ann Frances and Sister Margaret.

"But I know. And can't you tell me - it would make me so very happy - that I have done something for you too

- something that you value?"

Hilda's eyes lightened curiously, reverie came into them, and a smile. She answered as if she spoke to herself, "I should not know how to tell you."

Then scenting wonder in him she added, "You were thinking of something - in particular?"

"You have sometimes made me believe," Stephen returned, "that I may account myself, under God, the accident which induced you to take up your blessed work. I was thinking of that."

"Oh," she said, "of that!" and seemed to take refuge in silence.

"Yes," Arnold said, with infinite gentleness.

"But you were profoundly the cause! I might say you are, for without you I doubt whether I should have the - courage - "

"Oh no! Oh no! He who inspired you in the beginning will sustain you to the end. Think that. Believe that."

"Will He?" Her voice was neutral, as if it would not betray too much, but there was a listlessness that spoke louder in the bend of her head, the droop of her shoulder.

"For you perhaps," Arnold said thoughtfully, "there is only one assurance of it - the satisfaction your vocation brings you now. That will broaden and increase," he went on, almost with buoyancy, "growing more and more your supreme good as the years go on."

"How much you give me credit for!"

"Not nearly enough - not nearly. Who is there like you?" he demanded simply.

His words seemed a baptism. She lifted up her face after them, and the trace of them was on her eyes and lips. "I have passed two examinations, at all events," she informed him, with sudden gaiety, "and Sister Ann Frances says that in two or three months I shall probably get through the others. Sister Ann Frances thinks me more intelligent than might be expected. And if I do pass those examinations I shall be what they call a quick-time probationer. I shall have got it over in six months. Do you think," she asked, as if to please herself; "that six months will be long enough?"

"It depends. There is so much to consider."

"Yes - it depends. Sometimes I think it will be, but oftener I think it will take longer."

"I should be inclined to leave it entirely with the Sisters."

"I am so undisciplined," murmured Hilda, "I fear I shall cling to my own opinion. Now we must overtake the others and you must walk the rest of the way with Sister Ann - no, Sister Margaret, she is senior."

"I don't at all see the necessity," Stephen protested. He was wilful and wayward; he adopted a privileged air, and she scolded him. In their dispute they laughed so imprudently that Sister Ann Frances turned her draped head to look back at them. Then they quickened their steps and joined the elder ladies, and Stephen walked with Sister Margaret to the door of the Institution. She mentioned to the Mother Superior afterwards that young Mr. Arnold was really a delightful conversationalist.

CHAPTER XXVII

They talked a great deal in Plymouth about the way the time was passing in Calcutta during those last three months before Laura should return, the months of the rains. "Now," said Mrs. Simpson, early in July, "it will be pouring every day, with great patches of the Maidan under water, and rivers, my dear, RIVERS, in the back streets"; and Laura had a reminiscence about how, exactly at that time, a green mould used to spread itself fresh every morning on the matting under her bed in Bentinck Street. Later on they would agree that perhaps by this time there was a "break in the rains," and that nothing in the world was so trying as a break in the rains, the sun grilling down and drawing up steam from every puddle. In September, things, they remembered, would be at their very worst and most depressing; one had hardly the energy to lift a finger in September. Mrs. Simpson looked back upon the discomfort she had endured in Bengal at this time of year with a kind of regret that it was irretrievably over; she lingered upon a severe illness which had been part of the experience. She seemed to think that with a little judicious management she might have spent more time in that climate, and less in England. There was in her tone a suggestion of gentle envy of Laura, going forth to these dismal conditions with her young life in her hands all tricked out for the sacrifice, which left Duff Lindsay and his white and gold drawing-room entirely

Mrs. Everard Cotes

out of consideration. Any sacrifice to Mrs. Simpson was alluring, she would be killed all day long, in a manner, for its own sake.

The victim had taken her passage early in October, and during the first week of that month Plymouth gathered itself into meetings to bid her farewell. A curiously sacred character had fastened itself upon her; it was not in the least realised that she was going out to be married to an altogether secular young broker moving in fashionable circles in one of the gayest cities in the world. Ones or two reverend persons in the course of commending their young sister to the protection of the Almighty in her approaching separation from the dear friends who surrounded her in Plymouth, made references implying that her labours would continue to the glory of God, taking it as a matter of course. Miss Filbert was by this time very much impregnated with the idea that they would, she did not know precisely how, but that would open itself out. Duff had long been assimilated as part of the programme. All that money and humility could contribute should be forthcoming from him; she had a familiar dream of him as her standard-bearer, undistinguished but for ever safe.

Yet it was with qualified approval that Mrs. Simpson, amid the confusion of the Coromandel's preparations for departure at London Docks, heard the inevitable strains of the Salvation Army rising aft. Laura immediately cried, "I shall have friends among the passengers," and Mrs. Simpson so far forgot herself as to say, "Yes, if they are nice." The ladies were sitting on deck beside the pile of Laura's very superior cabin luggage. Mrs. Simpson glanced at it as if it offered a kind of corroboration of the necessity of their being nice. "There are always a few delightful Christian people, if one takes the trouble to find them out, at this end of the ship," she said defensively. "I have never failed to find it so."

"I don't think much of Christians who are so hard to discover," Laura said with decision; and Mrs. Simpson, rebuked, thought of the mischievous nature of class prejudices. Laura herself - had she not been drawn from what one might call distinctly the other end of the ship? - and who, among those who vaunted themselves ladies and gentlemen, could compare with Laura! The idea that she had shown a want of sympathy with those dear people who were so strenuously calling down a blessing on the Coromandel somewhere behind the smoke stacks, embittered poor Mrs. Simpson's remaining tears of farewell, and when the bell rang the signal for the last good-bye, she embraced her young friend with the fervent request, "Do make friends with them, dear one - make friends with them at once"; and Laura said, "If they will make friends with me."

By the time the ship had well got her nose down the coast of Spain, Miss Filbert had created her atmosphere, and moved about in it from end to end of the quarter-deck. It was a recognisable thing, her atmosphere, one never knew when it would discharge a question relating to the gravest matters; and persons unprepared to give satisfaction upon this point - one fears there are some on a ship bound east of Suez - found it blighting. They moved their long chairs out of the way, they turned pointedly indifferent backs, the lady who shared Miss Filbert's cabin - she belonged to a smart cavalry regiment at Mhow - went about saying things with a distinct edge. Miss Filbert exhausted all the means. She attempted to hold a meeting forward of

Mrs. Everard Cotes

the smoking cabin, standing for elevation on one of the ship's quoit buckets to preach, but with this the captain was reluctantly compelled to interfere on behalf of the whist-players inside. In the evening, after dinner, she established herself in a sheltered corner and sang. Her recovered voice lifted itself with infinite pathetic sweetness in songs about the poverty of the world and the riches of heaven; the notes mingled with the churning of the screw, and fell in the darkness beyond the ship's lights abroad upon the sea. The other passengers listened aloof; the Coromandel was crowded, but you could have drawn a wide circle round her chair. On the morning of the fourth day out - she had not felt quite well enough for adventures before - she found her way to the second-class saloon, being no doubt fully justified of her conscience in abandoning the first to the flippancies of its preference.

In the second-class end the tone was certainly more like that of Plymouth. Laura had a grateful sense of this in coming, almost at once, upon a little group gathered together for praise and prayer, of which four or five persons of both sexes, labelled "S. A.," naturally formed the centre. They were not only praying and praising without discouragement, they had attracted several other people who had brought their chairs into near and friendly relation, and even joined sometimes in the chorus of the hymns. There was a woman in mourning who cried a good deal - her tears seemed to refresh the Salvationists and inspire them to louder and more cheerful efforts. There was a man in a wide, soft felt hat with the malaria of the Terai in the hollows under his eyes; there was a Church Missionary with an air of charity and forbearance, and the bushy-eyed colonel of a native regiment looking vigilant against ridicule, with his wife, whose round red little face continually waxed and waned in a smile of true contentment. It was not till later that Laura came to know them all so very well, but her eye rested on them one after another, with approval, as she drew near. Without pausing in his chant - it happened to be one of triumph - without even looking at her, the leader indicated an empty chair. It was his own chair. "Colonel Markin, S. A." was printed in black letters on its striped canvas back; Laura noticed that.

After it was over, the little gathering, Colonel Markin specially distinguished her. He did it delicately. "I hope you won't mind my expressin' my thanks for the help you gave us in the singin'," he said. "Such a voice I've seldom had the pleasure to join with. May I ask where you got it trained?"

He was a narrow-chested man with longish sandy hair and thin features. His eyes were large, blue, and protruding, his forehead very high and white. There was a pinkness about the root of his nose, and a scanty yellow moustache upon his upper lip, while his chin was partly hidden by a beard equally scanty and even more yellow. He had extremely long white hands; one could not help observing them as they clasped his book of devotion.

Laura looked at him with profound appreciation of these details. She knew Colonel Markin by reputation, he had done a great work among the Cingalese. "It was trained," she said, casting down her eyes, "on the battlefields of our Army."

Colonel Markin attempted to straighten his shoulders and to stiffen his chin. He seemed vaguely aware of a military tradition which might make it necessary for him, as a very senior officer indeed, to say something. But the impression was transitory. Instead of using any rigour he held out his hand. Laura took it reverently, and the bones shut up, like the sticks of a fan, in her grasp. "Welcome, comrade!" he said, and there was a pause, as there should be after such an apostrophe.

"When you came among us this afternoon," Colonel Markin resumed, "I noticed you. There was something about the way you put your hand over your eyes when I addressed our Heavenly Father that spoke to me. It spoke to me and said, 'Here we have a soul that knows what salvation means - there's no doubt about that.' Then when you raised a Hallelujah I said to myself, 'That's got the right ring to it.' And so you're a sister in arms!"

"I was," Laura murmured.

"You was - you were. Well, well - I want to hear all about it. It is now," continued Colonel Markin, as two bells struck and a steward passed them with a bugle, "the hour for our dinner, and I suppose that you too," he bent his head respectfully towards the other half of the ship, "partake of some meal at this time. But if you will seek us out again at the meeting between four and five I shall be at your service afterwards, and pleased," he took her hand again, "PLEASED to see you."

Laura went back to the evening meeting, and after that missed none of these privileges. In due course she was asked to address it, and then her position became enviable from all points of view, for people who did not draw up their chairs and admire her inspirations sat at a distance and admired her clothes. Very soon, at her special request, she was allowed to resign her original place at table and take a revolving chair at the nine o'clock breakfast, one o'clock dinner, and six o'clock tea which sustained the second saloon. Daily, ascending the companion ladder to the main deck aft she gradually faded from cognisance forward. There they lay back in their long chairs and sipped their long drinks, and with neutral eyes and lips they let the blessing go.

In the intervals between the exercises Miss Filbert came and went in the cabin of three young Salvationists of her own sex. They could always make room for her, difficult as it may appear; she held for them an indefinite store of fascination. Laura would extend herself on a top berth beside the round-eyed Norwegian to whom it belonged, with the cropped head of the owner pillowed on her sisterly arm, and thus they passed hours, discussing conversions as medical students might discuss cases, relating, comparing. They talked a great deal about Colonel Markin. They said it was a beautiful life. More beautiful if possible had been the life of Mrs. Markin, who was his second wife, and who had been "promoted to glory" six months before. She had gained promotion through jungle fever, which had carried her off in three days. The first Mrs. Markin had died of drink - that was what had sent the Colonel into the Army, she, the first Mrs. Markin, having willed her property away from him. Colonel Markin had often rejoiced publicly that the lady had been of this disposition, the results to him had been so blessed. Apparently he spoke without reserve of his domestic affairs in connection with his spiritual experiences, using both the Mrs. Markins when it was desirable as "illustrations."

The five had reached this degree of intimacy by the time the Coromandel was nearing Port Said, and every day the hemispheres of sea and sky they watched through the porthole above the Norwegian girl's berth grew bluer.

From the first Colonel Markin had urged Miss Filbert's immediate return to the Army. He found her sympathetic to the idea, willing indeed to embrace it with open arms, but there were difficulties. Mr. Lindsay, as a difficulty, was almost insuperable to anything like a prompt step in that direction. Colonel Markin admitted it himself. He was bound to admit it he said, but nothing, since he joined the Army, had ever been so painful to him. "I wish I could deny it," he said with frankness; "but there is no doubt that for the present your first duty is towards your gentleman, towards him who placed that ring upon your finger." There was no sarcasm in his describing Lindsay as a gentleman; he used the term in a kind of extra special sense where a person less accustomed to polite usages might have spoken of Laura's young man. "But remember, my child," he continued, "it is only your poor vile body that is yours to dispose of, your soul belongs to God Almighty, and no earthly husband, especially as you say he is still in his sins, is going to have the right to interfere." This may seem vague, as the statement of a position, but Laura found it immensely fortifying. That and similar arguments built her up in her determination to take up what Colonel Markin called her life-work again at the earliest opportunity. She had forfeited her rank, that she accepted humbly as a proper punishment, ardently hoping it would be found sufficient. She would go back as a private, take her place in the ranks, and nothing in her married life should interfere with the things that cried out to be done in Bentinck Street. Somehow she had less hope of securing Lindsay as a spiritual companion in arms since she had confided the affair to Colonel Markin. As he said, they must hope for the best, but he could not help admitting that he took a gloomy view of Lindsay.

"Once he has secured you," the Colonel said, with an appreciative glance at Laura's complexion, "what will he care about his soul? Nothing."

Their enthusiasm had ample opportunity to strengthen, their mutual satisfactions to expand, in the close confines of life on board ship, and as if to seal and sanctify the voyage permanently a conversion took place in the second saloon, owning Laura's agency. It was the maid of the lady in the cavalry regiment, a hardened heart, as two stewards and a bandmaster on board could testify. When this occurred the time that was to elapse between Laura's marriage and her return to the ranks was shortened to one week. "And quite long enough," Colonel Markin said, "considering how much more we need you than your gentleman does, my dear sister."

It was plain to them all that Colonel Markin had very special views about his dear sister. The other dear sisters looked on with pleasurable interest, admitting the propriety of it, as Colonel Markin walked up and down the deck with Laura, examining her lovely nature, "drawing her out" on the subject of her faith and her assurance. It was natural, as he told her, that in her peculiar situation she should have doubts and difficulties. He urged her to lay bare her heart, and she laid it bare. One evening - it was heavenly moonlight on the Indian Ocean, and they were two days past

Aden on the long south-east run to Ceylon - she came and stood before him with a small packet in her hand. She was all in white, and more like an angel than Markin expected ever to see anything in this world, though as to the next his anticipations may have been extravagant.

"Now I wonder," said he, "where you are going to sit down?"

A youngster in the Police got up and pushed his chair forward, but Laura shook her head.

"I am going out there," she said, pointing to the farther-most stern where passengers were not encouraged to sit, "and I want to consult you."

Markin got up. "If there's anything pressin' on your mind," he said, "you can't do better."

Laura said nothing until they were alone with the rushing of the screw, two Lascars, some coils of rope, and the hand-steering gear. Then she opened the packet. "These," she said, "these are pressing on my mind."

She held out a string of pearls, a necklace of pearls and turquoises, a heavy band bracelet studded, Delhi fashion, with gems, one or two lesser fantasies.

"Jewellery!" said Markin. "Real or imitation?"

"So far as that goes they are good. Mr. Lindsay gave them to me. But what have I to do with jewels, the very emblem of the folly of the world, the desire that itches in palms that know no good works, the price of sin!" She leaned against the masthead as she spoke, the wind blew her hair and her skirt out toward the following seas. With that look in her eyes she seemed a creature who had alighted on the ship but who could not stay.

Colonel Markin held the pearls up in the moonlight.

"They must have cost something to buy," he said.

Laura was silent.

"And so they're a trouble to you. Have you taken them to the Lord in prayer?"

"Oh, many times."

"Couldn't seem to hear any answer?"

"The only answer I could hear was. 'So long as you have them I will not speak with you.'"

"That seems pretty plain and clear. And yet?" said the Colonel, fondling the turquoises, "nobody can say there's any harm in such things, especially if you don't wear them."

"Colonel, they are my great temptation. I don't know that I wouldn't wear them. And when I wear them I can think of nothing sacred, nothing holy. When they were given to me I used - I used to get up in the night to look at them."

"Shall I lay it before the Almighty? That bracelet's got a remarkably good clasp."

"Oh no - no! I must part with them. To-night I can do it, to-night - "

"There's nobody on this ship that will give you any price for them."

"I would not think of selling them. It would be sending them from my hands to do harm to some other poor creature, weaker than I!"

"You can't return them to-night."

"I wouldn't return them. That would be the same as keeping them."

"Then what - oh, I see!" exclaimed Markin. "You want to give them to the Army. Well, in my capacity, on behalf of General Booth - "

"No," cried Laura with sudden excitement, "not that either. I will give them to nobody. But this is what I will do!" She seized the bracelet and flung it far out into the opaline track of the vessel, and the smaller objects, before her companion could stop her, followed it. Then he caught her wrist.

"Stop!" he cried. "You've gone off your head - you've got fever. You're acting wicked with that jewellery. Stop and let us reason it out together."

She already had the turquoises, and with a jerk of her left hand, she freed it and threw them after the rest. The necklace caught the handrail as it fell, and Markin made a vain spring to save it. He turned and stared at Laura, who stood fighting the greatest puissance of feeling she had known, looking at the pearls. As he stared she kissed them twice, and then, leaning over the ship's side, let them slowly slide out of her fingers and fall into the waves below. The moonlight gave them a divine gleam as they fell. She turned to Markin with tears in her eyes. "Now," she faltered, "I can be happy again. But not to-night."

CHAPTER XXVIII

While the Coromandel was throbbing out her regulation number of knots towards Colombo, October was passing over Bengal. It went with lethargy, the rains were too close on its heels; but at the end of the long hot days, when the resplendent sun struck down on the glossy trees and the over-lush Maidan, there often stole through Calcutta a breath of the coming respite of December. The blue smoke of the people's cooking fires began to hang again in the streets, the pungent smell of it was pleasant in the still air. The south wind turned back at the Sunderbunds; instead of it, one met round corners a sudden crispness that stayed just long enough to be recognised and melted damply away. A week might have two or three of such promises and foretastes.

Hilda Howe, approaching the end of her probation at the Baker Institution, threw the dormitory window wide to them, went out to seek them. They gave her a new stirring of vitality, something deep within her leaped up responding to the voucher the evenings brought that presently they would bring something new and different. She vibrated to an irrepressible pulse of accord with that; it made her hand strong and her brain clear for the unimportant matters that remained within the scope of the monotonous moment. There had come upon her a stimulating assurance that it would be only a moment - now. She did not consider this, she could hardly be said to be intelligently aware of it, but it underlay all that she said and did. Her spirits gained an enviable lightness, she began again to see beautiful, touching things in the life that carried her on with it. She explained to Stephen Arnold that she was immensely happy at having passed the last of her nursing examinations.

"I hardly dare ask you," he said, "what you are going to do now."

He looked furtive and anxious; she saw that he did, and the perception irritated her. She had to tell herself that she had given him the right to look in any way he pleased - indeed yes.

"I hardly dare ask myself," she answered, and was immediately conscious that for the first time in the history of their relations she had spoken to him that which was expedient.

"I hope the Sisters are not trying to influence you," he said firmly.

"Fancy!" she cried irrelevantly. "I heard the other day that Sister Ann Frances had described me as the pride of the Baker Institution!" She laughed with delight at the humour of it, and he smiled too. When she laughed, he had nearly always now confidence enough to smile too.

"You might ask for another six months."

"Heavens, no! No - I shall make up my mind."

"Then you may go away," Arnold said. They were standing at the crossing of the wide red road from which they would go in different directions. She saw that the question was momentous to him. She also saw how curiously the sun sallowed him, and how many more hollows he had in his face than most people. She had a pathetic impression of the figure he made in his coarse gown and shoes. "God's wayfarer," she murmured. There was pity in her mind, infinite pity. Her thought had no other tinge. It was a curiously simple feeling, and seemed to bring her an inconsistent lightness of heart.

"Come too," she said aloud, "come and be a Clarke Brother where the climatic conditions suit you better. The world wants Clarke Brothers everywhere."

He looked at her and tried to smile, but his lips quivered. He opened them in an effort to speak, gave it up, and turned away silently, lifting his hat. Hilda watched him for an instant as he went. His figure took strange proportions through the tears that sprang to her eyes, and she marvelled at the gaiety with which she had touched, had almost revealed, her heart's desire.

CHAPTER XXIX

"I knew it would happen in the end," Hilda said, "and it has happened. The Archdeacon has asked me to tea."

She was speaking to Alicia Livingstone in the dormitory, changing at the same time for a "turn" at the hospital. It was six o'clock in the afternoon. Alicia's landau stood at the door of the Baker Institution. She had come to find that Miss Howe was just going on duty and could not be taken for a drive.

"When?" asked Alicia, staring out of the window at the crows in a tamarind tree.

"Last Saturday. He said he had promised some friends of his the pleasure of meeting me. They had besieged him, he said, and they were his best friends, on all his committees."

"Only ladies?" The crows, with a shriek of defiance at nothing in particular, having flown away, Miss Livingstone transferred her attention.

"Bless me, yes. What Archdeacon has dear men friends! And lesquelles pense-tu, mon Dieu!"

"Lesquelles?"

Mrs. Everard Cotes

"Mrs. Jack Forrester, Mrs. Fitz - what you may call him up on the frontier, the Brigadier gentleman - Lady Dolly!"

"You were well chaperoned."

"And - my dear - he didn't ask a single Sister!" Hilda turned upon her a face which appeared still to glow with the stimulus of the archidiaconal function. "And - it was wicked considering the occasion - I dropped the character. I let myself out!"

"You didn't shock the Archdeacon?"

"Not in the least. But, my dear love, did you ever permit yourself the reflection that the Venerable Gambell is a bachelor?"

"Hilda, you shall not! We all love him - you shall not lead him astray!"

"You would not think of - the altar?"

Miss Livingstone's pale small smile fell like a snowflake upon Hilda's mood, and was swallowed up. "You are very preposterous," she said. "Go on. You always amuse one." Then, as if Hilda's going on were precisely the thing she could not quite endure, she said quickly, "The Coromandel is telegraphed from Colombo to-day."

"Ah!" said Hilda.

"He leaves for Madras to-morrow. The thing is to take place there, you know."

"Then nothing but shipwreck can save him."

"Nothing but - what a horrible idea! Don't you think they may be happy? I really think they may."

"There is not one of the elements that give people, when they commit the paramount stupidity of marrying, reason to hope that they may not be miserable. Not one. If he were a strong man I should pity him less. But he's not. He's immensely dependent on his tastes, his friends, his circumstances."

Alicia looked at Hilda; her glance betrayed an attention caught upon an accidental phrase. "The paramount stupidity." She did not repeat it aloud, she turned it over in her mind.

"You are thinking," Hilda said accusingly. "What are you thinking about?"

"Oh, nothing. I saw Stephen yesterday. I thought him looking rather wretched."

A shadow of grave consideration winged itself across Hilda's eyes.

"He works so much too hard," she said. "It is an appalling waste. But he will offer himself up."

Alicia looked unsatisfied. She had hoped for something that would throw more light upon the paramount stupidity. "He brought Mr. Lappe to tea," she said.

The shadow went. "Should you think Brother Lappe," Miss Howe demanded, "specially fitted for the cure of souls? Never, never, could I allow the process of my regeneration to come through Brother Lappe. He has such a little nose, and such wide pink cheeks, and such fat sloping shoulders. Dear succulent Brother Lappe!"

A Sister passed through the dormitory on a visit of inspection. Alicia bowed sweetly, and the Sister inclined herself briefly with a cloistered smile. As she disappeared Hilda threw a black skirt over her head, making a veil of it flowing backward, and rendered the visit, the noiseless measured step, the little deprecating movements of inquiry, the benevolent recognition of a visitor from a world where people carried parasols and wore spotted muslins. She even effaced herself at the door on the track of the other to make it perfect, and came back in the happy expansion of an artistic effort to find Alicia's regard penetrated with the light of a new conviction.

"Hilda," she said, "I should like to know what this last year has really been to you."

"It has been very valuable," Miss Howe replied. Then she turned quickly away to hang up the black petticoat, and stood like that, shaking out its folds, so that Alicia might not see anything curious in her face as she heard her own words and understood what they meant. Very valuable! She did understand, suddenly, completely. Very valuable! A year of the oddest experiences, a pictorial year, which she would look back upon, with its core in a dusty priest. . . .

A probationer came rapidly along the dormitory to where Hilda stood. She had the olive cheeks and the liquid eyes of the country; her lips were parted in a smile.

"Miss Howe," she said, in the quick clicking syllables of her race, "Sister Margaret wishes you to come immediately to the surgical ward. A case has come in, and Miss Gonsalvez is there, but Sister Margaret will not be bothered with Miss Gonsalvez. She says you are due by right in five minutes," - the messenger's smile broadened irresponsibly, and she put a fondling touch upon Hilda's apron string, - "so will you please to make haste!"

"What's the case?" asked Hilda; "I hope it isn't another ship's hold accident." But Alicia, a shade paler than before, put up her hand. "Wait till I'm gone," she said, and went quickly. The girl had opened her lips, however, but to say that she didn't know, she had only been seized to take the message, though it must be something serious since they had sent for both the resident surgeons.

CHAPTER XXX

Dr. Livingstone's concern was personal, that was plain in the way he stood looking at the floor of the corridor with his hands in his pockets, before Hilda reached him. Regret was written all over the lines of his pausing figure with the compressed irritation which saved that feeling in the Englishman's way from being too obvious.

"This is a bad business, Miss Howe."

"I've just come over - I haven't heard. Who is it?"

"It's my cousin, poor chap - Arnold, the padre. He's been badly knifed in the bazar."

The news passed over her and left her looking with a curious face at chance. It was lifted a little, with composed lips, and eyes which refused to be taken by surprise. There was inquiry in them, also a defence. Chance, looking back, saw an invincible silent readiness, and a pallor which might be that of any woman. But the doctor was also looking, so she said, "That is very sad," and moved near enough to the wall to put her hand against it. She was not faint, but the wall was a fact on which one could, for the moment, rely.

"They've got the man - one of those Cabuli money-lenders. The police had no trouble with him. He said it was the order of Allah - the brute! Stray case of fanaticism, I suppose. It seems Arnold was walking along as usual, without a notion, and the fellow sprang on him, and in two seconds the thing was done. Hadn't a chance, poor beggar."

"Where is it?"

"Root of the left lung. About five inches deep. The artery pretty well cut through, I fancy."

"Then - "

"Oh no - we can't do anything. The haemorrhage must be tremendous. But he may live through the night. Are you going to Sister Margaret?"

His nod took it for granted, and he went on. Hilda walked slowly forward, her head bent, with absorbed uncertain steps. A bar of evening sunlight came before her, she looked up and stepped outside the open door. She was handling this thing that had happened, taking possession of it. It lay in her mind in the midst of a suddenly stricken and tenderly saddened consciousness. It lay there passively; it did not rise and grapple with her, it was a thing that had happened - in Burra Bazar. The pity of it assailed her. Tears came into her eyes, and an infinite grieved solicitude gathered about her heart. "So?" she said to herself, thinking that he was young and loved his work, and that now his hand would be stayed from the use it had found. One of the ugly outrages of life, leaving nothing on the mouth but that brief acceptance. It came to hers with a note of the profound and of the supreme. She turned resolutely from searching her heart for any wild despair. She would not for an instant consider what she ought to feel. "So," she said, and pressed her lips till they stopped trembling, and went into the hospital.

She asked a question or two, in search of Sister Margaret and the new case. It was "located," an assistant surgeon told her, in Private Ward Number Two. She went more and more slowly toward Private Ward Number Two.

The door was open; she stood in it for an instant with eyes nerved to receive the tragedy. The room seemed curiously empty of any such thing, a door opposite was also open, with an arched verandah outside; the low sun streamed through this upon the floor with its usual tranquillity. Beyond the arches, netted to keep the crows away, it made pictures with the tops of the trees. There was the small iron bed with the confused outline under the bedclothes, very quiet, and the Sister - the whitewashed wall rose sharp behind her black draperies - sitting with a book in her hands. Some scraps of lint on the floor beside the bed, and hardly anything else except the silence which had almost a presence, and a faint smell of carbolic acid, and a certain feeling of impotence and abandonment and waiting which seemed to be in the air. Arnold moved on the pillow and saw her standing in the door. The bars of the bed's foot were in the way, he tried to lift his head to surmount the obstruction, and the Sister perceived her too.

"I think absolutely still was our order, wasn't it, Mr. Arnold?" she said, with her little pink smile. "And I'm afraid Miss Howe isn't in time to be of much use to us, is she?" It was the bedside pleasantry that expected no reply, that indeed forbade one.

"I'm sorry," Hilda said. As she moved into the room she detached her eyes from Arnold's, feeling as she did so that it was like tearing something.

"There was so little to do," Sister Margaret said; "Surgeon-Major Wills saw at once where the mischief lay. Nothing disagreeable was necessary, was it, Mr. Arnold? Perfect quiet, perfect rest - that's an easy prescription to take." She had rather prominent very blue eyes, and an aquiline nose, and a small firm mouth, and her pink cheeks were beginning to be a little pendulous with age. Hilda gazed at her silently, noting about her authority and her flowing draperies something classical. Was she like one of the Fates? She approached the bed to do something to the pillow - Hilda had an impulse to push her away with the cry, "It is not time yet - Atropos!"

"I must go now for an hour or so," the Sister went on. "That poor creature in Number Six needs me; they daren't give her any more morphia. You don't need it - happy boy!" she said to Stephen, and at the look he sent her for answer she turned rather quickly to the door. Dear Sister, she was none of the Fates, she was obliged to give directions to Hilda standing in the door with her back turned. Happily for a deserved reputation for self-command they were few. It was chief and absolute that no one should be admitted. A bulletin had been put up at the hospital door for the information of inquiries; later on when the doctor came again there would be another.

She went away and they were left alone. The sun on the floor had vanished; a yellowness stood in its place with a grey background, the background gaining, coming on. Always his eyes were upon her, she had given hers back to him and he seemed satisfied. She moved closer to the bed and stood beside him. Since there was nothing to do there was nothing to say. Stephen put out his hand and touched a fold of her dress.

The room filled itself with something that had not been there before, his impotent love. Hilda knelt down beside the bed and pressed her forehead against the hand upon the covering, the hand that had so little more to do. Then Arnold spoke.

"You dear woman!" he said. "You dear woman!" She kept her head bowed like that and did not answer. It was his happiest moment. One might say he had lived for this. Her tears fell upon his hand, a kind of baptism for his heart. He spoke again.

"We must bear this," he panted. "It is - less cruel - than it seems. You don't know how much it is for the best."

She lifted her wet face. "You mustn't talk," she faltered.

"What difference - " he did not finish the sentence. His words were too few to waste. He paused and made another effort.

"If this had not happened I would have been - counted - among the unfaithful," he said. "I know now. I would have abandoned - my post. And gladly - without a regret - for you."

"Ah!" Hilda cried, with a vivid note of pain. "Would

you? I am sorry for that! I am sorry!"

She gazed with a face of real tragedy at the form of her captive delivered to her in the bonds of death. A fresh pang visited her with the thought that in the mystery of the ordering of things she might have had to do with the forging of those shackles - the price of the year that had been very valuable.

"My God is a jealous God," Arnold said. "He has delivered me - into His own hands - for the honour of His name. I acknowledge - I am content."

"No, indeed no! It was a wicked, horrible chance! Don't charge your God with it."

His smile was very sweet, but it paid the least possible attention. "You did love me," he said. He spoke as if he were already dead.

"I did indeed," Hilda replied, and bent her shamed head upon her hands again in the confession. It is not strange that he heard only the affirmation in it.

He stroked her hair. "It is good to know that," he said, "very, good. I should have married you." He went on with sudden boldness and a new note of strength in his voice, "Think of that! You would have been mine - to protect and work for. We should have gone together to England - where I could easily have got a curacy - easily."

Hilda looked up. "Would you like to marry me now?" she asked eagerly, but he shook his head.

"You don't understand," he said. "It is the dear sin God

has turned my back upon."

Then it came to her that he had asked for no caress. He was going unassoiled to his God, with the divine indifference of the dying. Only his imagination looked backward and forward. And she thought, "It is a little light flame that I have lit with my own taper that has gone out - that has gone out - and presently the grave will extinguish that." She sat quiet and sombre in the growing darkness, and presently Arnold slept.

He slept through the bringing of a lamp, the arrival of flowers, subdued knocks of inquirers who would not be stayed by the bulletin - the visit of Surgeon-Major Wills, who felt his pulse without wakening him. "Holding out wonderfully," the doctor said. "Don't rouse him for the soup. He'll go out in about six hours without any pain. May not wake at all."

The door opened again to admit the probationer come to relieve Miss Howe. Hilda beckoned her into the corridor. "You can go back," she said, "I will take your turn."

"But the Mother Superior - you know how particular about the rules - "

"Say nothing about it. Go to bed. I am not coming."

"Then, Miss Howe, I shall be obliged to report it."

"Report and be - report if you like. There is nothing for you to do here to-night," and Hilda softly closed the door. There was a whispered expostulation when Sister Margaret came back, but Miss Howe said, "It is arranged," and with a little silent nod of appreciation the Sister settled into her chair, her finger marking a place in the Church Service. Hilda sat nearer to the bed, her elbow on the table, shading her eyes from the lamp, and watched.

"Is it not odd," whispered Sister Margaret, as the night wore on, "he has refused to be confessed before he goes? He will not see the Brother Superior - or any of them. Strange, is it not?"

Together they watched the quick short breathing. It seemed strangely impossible to sleep against such odds. They saw the lines of the face grow sharper and whiter, the dark eye-sockets sink to a curious round-ness, a greyness gather about the mouth. There were times when they looked at each other in the last surmise. Yet the feeble pulse persisted - persisted.

"I believe now," said Sister Margaret, "that he may go on like this until the morning. I am going to take half an hour's nap. Rouse me at once if he wakes," and she took an attitude of casual repose, turning the Prayer-book open on her knee for readier use, open at "Prayers for the Dying."

The jackals had wailed themselves out, and there was a long, dark period when nothing but the sudden cry of a night bird in the hospital garden came between Hilda and the very vivid perception she had at that hour of the value and significance of the earthly lot. She lifted her head and listened to that, it seemed a comment. Suddenly, then, a harsh quarrelling of dogs - Christian dogs - arose in the distance and died away, and again there was night and silence. Night for hours. Time for reflection, alone with death and the lamp, upon the year that had been very valuable. "I would have married you," she whispered. "Yes, I would." Later her lips moved again. "I would have taken the consequence;" and again, "I would have paid any penalty." There he lay, a burden that she would never bear, a burden that would be gone in the morning. There were moments when she cried out on Fate for doing her this kindness.

The long singing drone of a steamer's signal came across the city from the river, once, twice, thrice; and presently the sparrows began their twittering in the bushes near the verandah, an unexpected unanimous bird talk that died as suddenly and as irrelevantly away. A conservancy cart lumbered past creaking; the far shrill whistle of an awakening factory cut the air from Howrah; the first solitary foot smote through the dawn upon the pavement. The light showed grey beyond the scanty curtains. A noise of something being moved reverberated in the hospital below, and Arnold opened his eyes. They made him in a manner himself again, and he fixed them upon Hilda as if they could never alter. She leaned nearer him and made a sign of inquiry toward the sleeping Sister, with the farewells, the commendations of poor mortality speeding itself forth, lying upon her lap. Arnold comprehended, and she was amazed to see the mask of his face charge itself with a faint smile as he shook his head. He made a little movement; she saw what he wanted and took his hand in hers. The smile was still in his eyes as he looked at her, and then at the cheated Sister. "I would have married you," she whispered passionately as if that could stay him. "Yes, I would."

So in the end he trusted the new wings of his mortal love to bear his soul to its immortality. They carried their burden buoyantly, it was such a little way. The lamp was still holding its own against the paleness from the windows when the meaning finally went out of his clasp of Hilda's hand, without a struggle to stay, and she saw that in an instant when she was not looking, he had closed his eyes upon the world. She sat on beside him for a long time after that, watching tenderly, and would not withdraw her hand - it seemed an abandonment.

Three hours later Miss Howe, passing out of the hospital gate, was overtaken by Duff Lindsay, riding, with a look of singular animation and vigour. He flung himself off his horse to speak to her, and as he approached he drew from his inner coat pocket the brown envelope of a telegram.

"Good-morning," he said. "You do look fagged. I have a - curious - piece of news."

"Alicia told me that you were starting early this morning for Madras!"

"I should have been, but for this."

"Read it to me," Hilda said, "I'm tired."

"Oh, do you very much mind? I would rather - "

She took the missive; it was dated the day before, Colombo, and read -

"Do not expect me was married this morning to Colonel Markin S A we may not be unequally yoked together with unbelievers glory be to God Laura Markin"

She raised her eyes to his with the gravest, saddest irony.

"Then you - you also are delivered," she said; but he said "What?" without special heed; and I doubt whether he ever took the trouble to understand her reference to their joint indebtedness.

"One hopes he isn't a brute," Lindsay went on with most impersonal solicitude, "and can support her. I suppose there isn't any way one could do anything for her. I heard a story only yesterday about a girl changing her mind on the way out. By Jove, I didn't suppose it would happen to me!"

"If you are hurt anywhere," Hilda said absently, "it is only your vanity, I fancy."

"Ah, my vanity is very sore!" He paused for an instant, wondering to find so little expansion in her. "I came to ask after Arnold," he said. "How is he?"

"He is dead. He died at half-past five this morning."

She left him with even less than her usual circumstance, and turned in at the gate of the Baker Institution. It happened to be the last day of her probation.

There has never been any difficulty in explaining Lindsay's marriage with Alicia Livingstone even to himself; the reasons for it, indeed, were so many and so obvious that he wondered often why they had not struck him earlier. But it is worth noting, perhaps, that the immediate precipitating cause arose in one evening service at the Cathedral, where it had its birth in the very individual charm of the nape of Alicia's neck, as she knelt upon her hassock in the fitting and graceful act of the responses. His instincts in these matters seem to have had a generous range, considering the tenets he was born to, but it was to him then a delightful reflection, often since repeated, that in the sheltered garden of delicate perfumes where this sweet person took her spiritual pleasure there was no rank vegetation.

It is much to Miss Hilda Howe's credit that amid the distractions of her most successful London season she never quite abandons these two to the social joys that circle round the Ochterlony Monument and the arid scenic consolations of the Maidan. Her own experience there is one of the things, I fancy, that make her fond of saying that the stage is the merest cardboard presentation, and that one day she means to leave it, to coax back to her bosom the life which is her heritage in the wider, simpler ways of the world. She never mentions that experience more directly or less ardently. But I fear the promise I have quoted is one that she makes too often.

Mrs. Everard Cotes

www.ingramcontent.com/pod-product-compliance
Lightning Source LLC
Chambersburg PA
CBHW032137270626
47172CB00008B/133